The DreamVerse

Written by Keith Starblue

The DreamVerse
Copyright 2017 by Keith Starblue

ISBN-13: 978-0692985083 (Keith Starblue)

ISBN-10: 0692985085

Contact me at keithstarblue@twc.com

(From The Back Cover)

The DreamVerse is a tale of Barry Goldrum who discovers he can leave his mortal shell behind when he goes to sleep. His dream self steps out into The DreamVerse where millions of dreamers are constantly there in a dream state, including the dread of nightmares.

These dreamers are only part of the story, the extra in fact. In the center of this story is the realization to Barry Goldrum that The DreamVerse is also inhabited by a race of beings that were never born. The DreamVerse is their domain, it's where they're allowed to exist. These beings that were never born have a need for substance, this substance which they refer to as dream food, slates their hunger and sustains their lives.

How can one that was never born have a life? If so, is this life an afterlife? Is this race of unborn beings, dubbed 'The Gemini Dream Legion', good or evil? Are they predators or are they prey? Where does Barry Goldrum's ability fit inside this tale of universal mental proportions? Lastly, is Barry Goldrum's part in this story by his own design? Or was it simply his fate? Get ready to take a wild, sometimes light, sometimes dark, mental trip to find out these answers.

The DreamVerse

The We In My Sleep

Chapter One:

2040, 7:00 PM, "Barry you look so tired."

"I'm dragging myself to grab this cup of coffee."

"Why don't you go back to bed and get some more sleep, you look like you could use some more."

"That my sweet Tina is my problem, when I sleep, my dreams feel like they are draining my mind and my creativity. I had a hell of a time getting started last night, focusing was not easy as well, I only wrote around eight pages worth keeping. The rest was, hate to say it, was all drivel. If I only I could not dream for a night or two, I think I would feel a lot more rested instead of so tired. Besides there is the best reason to stay awake."

" And what is this reason?"

"Why being with you of course."

"Barry do not try to turn me on yet, that is for in a little while, right now I want you to listen to me. You need to make an appointment with your doctor."

"I don't know Tina, there is something else. When I sleep my dreams are becoming so intense. I swear they are in color."

"That's impossible."

"I know but at the same time I tell you they are in color, I also tell you I can smell, taste and feel in my dreams."

"Barry I love you and you are scaring me. I don't know where all this crazy talk is coming from, but I don't like it.

Please go see your doctor as soon as possible and maybe as well you might want to talk to someone that understands dreams more. That way everything can go back to nice and normal. Believe me Barry, it probably is just some small chemical imbalance or an allergy to something."

"Okay I will go see my doctor or talk to somebody. Come here and give me a hug and a kiss."

"Is that all you want?"

"Well maybe to start off with."

Five days later. Barry is sitting in the waiting room of his doctor's office, wondering one more time, before it is too late to take it back, if he should tell his doctor something else that is going on. This something else is an extension of his vivid dreams.

In the early afternoon of the following day after his talk with Tina, Barry went to sleep as usual, however this sleep cycle brought forth new, freakish events, not during sleep, but in the few moments before Barry fully woke up. Barry awoke sitting up in his bed. At first his eyes were out of focus, then like a step back within his awareness he sees another that looks exactly like him and a stranger talking to each other.

As he watched the stranger pointed towards him and his dreaming double turned around and looked at him then, poof, they were both gone. Barry wonders even more deeply to himself, making his skin crawl to a frightening point, that the reason he does not know who this stranger is, is because he is not meant to to be known.

For the fact that maybe this stranger is from another reality, perhaps one that can only be attained while a sleeper is dreaming and their dreaming mental waves are free to float or soar to other dimensions that cannot be obtained

5

while the sleeper is fully awake?

This deeper thought is making Barry start to shake from some internal coldness that seems to want to come to Barry like a beacon of no hope.

One time waking up like Barry did was intense, thinking about it happening again makes Barry say to himself, "I gotta get out of here."

Barry is about to get up and walk away very fast when his name is called out. In his paranoid mind Barry hears. "Mr. Doom of the Mind, you are next. Let's see just how mentally sick you are today, shall we? That's it, take off your clothes and put this on, the doctor will be right with you."

Barry starts to feel like just a number upon millions and says to himself, "Forget it, this has come to me and now I am different." Barry wants to find out just how different he is, for being paranoid makes Barry pissed off. Which makes him calm down and realize what is truly happening and not what's going on in his confused mind.

In moments of thick thought, Barry knows now how to start his journey to another side of life, he must make his mind stronger, strong enough to take his waking mind into a dream state that he will have total control over. Barry then thinks to himself, that this should not be so difficult to achieve. Yeah right. Barry laughs slightly out loud.

Barry tells his doctor about his vivid dreams but now the words he speaks has a poise to them which makes the doctor think that Barry is just going through something that does not seem very serious but he will run some tests on Barry just to make sure. Barry gives up his blood and urine to be tested then goes home to work on his plan.

That night Barry does not write on his novel instead he looks online for anything and everything he can find on dreams. Almost all is useless or too basic, then he finds something that is similar to what he is going through. There are cases where people have said that in their dreams they have seen a stranger and a double of themselves. The stranger takes off flying and their double follows him or her.

Then somehow in their dreams these people claim that they follow them both, as these two enter what seems to be another person's dream. Everyone that this has happened to has said the same thing happens next to them. They enter this person's dream, they have time to look around then they are discovered by the stranger and their dreaming twin and just like that they wake up, desperately wanting to experience more of this dream state that is like ecstasy to their dreaming minds.

Three days later, Barry is told by his doctor's office that nothing abnormal came from his tests. That by the looks of his results that Barry is just fine and normal. Barry thanked the voice on the phone and hung up. Barry feels relieved and now happily turned on and in the mood to take Tina to their bedroom for a relaxing of his body. A relaxing he's been craving since the special moment he had when he woke up, his sixth time now this phenomenon has happened to him.

Barry laid in silence, not moving, listening to the conversation his dream twin and the stranger were having. They are friends that trust each other and best of all they can interact with one another.

Barry cannot wait for the next time that he is aware and awake while his dream twin and the stranger have no clue at all of his plans. Hopefully Barry thinks to himself that this will happen the next time he wakes up.

'This is it, somehow I have to make myself learn how to follow them into other people's dreams and not be discovered.'

7

One month later, waking up seeing his dream twin and the stranger doesn't happen all the time, it is a few times here, then skip a few days there. Barry knows 'the We in my Sleep' (which is how he referrers to his dreaming twin and the stranger) are there every time he falls asleep, for Barry has become more aware while sleeping, seeing them appear when he begins to start dreaming. He tries his best to follow them but swoosh he is swept away to dreamland.

Barry knows that when he is almost awake and has his chance to listen to his We, they are at the end of their journey for that sleep cycle. Barry's confidence in succeeding with his plan was at an all time high until yesterday. Yesterday when Barry stopped himself for the first time from drifting away to dreamland, there was his We talking. What he heard this time froze Barry's soul.

(Let's join Barry while his mind provides us with this exciting flashback.)

Barry is staring at his dreaming twin and the Stranger, listening as they talk out their plans for the night. Barry is focusing hard on trying to keep himself from slipping into dreamland and readying himself to fly away with 'The We in his Sleep' so he can experience for himself another person's dreams.

The We are just talking like they always seem to do when his dreaming twin looks at him and says to him. "Go to sleep and have horrible nightmares one that killed me before I was born, one that I hate so much. I cannot wait until I grow stronger, as your precious living body finally dies and I will finally be able to escape your dreaming mind and fly away with my friend, forever becoming a member of 'The Gemini Dream Legion'."

"There I will discover what it is like to be a member of a family of the same as myself.

8

Friend I wish my night was tonight, I hate this constant waiting. Can we not enter Barry's dreams tonight and destroy his mind? I feel strong enough right now to make my journey to the other side."

The Stranger replies, "Not now my friend, be patient. Barry's human life, no matter how many years, is still nothing to the eternity of years you will live with us."

"I will try but I hate him so much. I mean, why him? Why not me?"

"Be glad that you never lived my friend or it would be Barry that I would have been training all these years to become one of us."

"You are right my friend. Sometimes I forget Barry is the nothing with a real life, I am the unborn that exists forever after his death."

The Stranger says, "Let's make sure Barry is dreaming before we take off for the night."

Barry quickly thinks up a hot looking naked lady that he is having sex with. Barry does not know if the We can see what he has created for himself to dream or not, but he's got to give himself credit for creating such beauty at his first attempt in creating his own dreams for himself to dream.

Barry is getting it on trying his best not to be discovered when he feels the presence of 'The We in his Sleep' enter his dream and start watching what he is dreaming about.

Barry's dream twin snorts out, "Figures that is all this dreaming horny fool dreams of."

The Stranger replies, "Good enough for me. How about you Larry?"

"Yeah but first let's turn his dreaming beauty into a monster that will try to eat him all up." 'Larry, his name is Larry?' The stranger agrees to do what Larry wants him to do.

The stranger says some words that Barry cannot understand and waves his hands around, then he says to Larry, "It is done. Let's leave and enjoy ourselves on some delicious 'Dream Food'."

Barry feels that We has left his dream, he turns around to make sure for himself. They are gone, Barry is relieved, when he turns back around and looks into the face of the sexy lady that he created, his beauty's face has now turned into an ugly monster with the same sexy body going for her.

Barry very, very quickly jumps off the monster faced woman he is having sex with. When his feet hit the floor he is moving way too fast which makes him trip and fall. The sexy bodied, monster faced woman in his dream hisses and leaps off the bed and onto the floor landing on top of Barry.

Monster lady begins to hit Barry in his face causing Barry's face to bleed. Monster lady hisses again and this time she grabs a hold of Barry's swinging around right arm and bites it, pulling out with her monster teeth a chuck of his flesh, making his blood squirt out in thick gushing spurts, some of it even landing on his face. Barry is freaking out, afraid for his life.

Barry to himself, 'The We did this to me. Somehow they found out and all that talk of waiting was for show. Along with this moment of terror my mind is also filling with the knowledge that I have been played with, like a weak minded dreaming fool that is way out of my league...

No I have come too far, I am different, this is but a dream, I am awake in my dream, I am in control. This is still my dream, I am in control.'

Barry snaps out of his thoughts seeing that his legs have already been eaten up almost to his waist. Where his legs were there are now thick red/black pools of blood on the floor.

'Focus, man focus.' Barry looks at the monster woman that is eating him, grabs her by the face and slaps it real hard, making the monster stop chewing on Barry's left stump and look at Barry with a confused look of 'What? This cannot be, I am the monster you are to be my meal.'

The monster watches in horror as Barry makes his already eaten legs reappear like they were never eaten and for that little extra, Barry even wipes all the blood away, using only one swipe from his dreaming eraser that looks a lot like a smiling face with lots of teeth.

Barry thinks to himself that this monster would look good stuffed and roasting to slow perfection on an open fire. All he has to do first, If he wants to eat monster later, is to rip its heart out of its chest. Barry laughs as he makes the monster heartless. It falls to the floor dead and Barry throws its heart over his shoulder.

With no real intention of eating monster meat, Barry walks away feeling powerful once again. Barry steps out of this dream into stillness and darkness and suddenly realizes to himself that he better hurry up and create another dream for himself to dream, for there is no more pulling at him to take him to dreamland. If there is to be any dreams for Barry to escape to they must apparently come from his imagination now. Barry creates nice and safe dreams for the rest of his sleep cycle until the We comes back to him and he makes himself wake up.

Barry gets up and does his normal nightly routine with Tina until she goes to bed for the night. Barry thinks to himself that he should get some writing done when a forgotten memory comes to his mind.

(This memory is of when Barry was young.)

One morning way back then, Barry was trying to wake up and the We that he follows into other people's dreams now, was there even back then. His young dreaming twin was all upset at Barry for being the one that got to live, the stranger, the very same stranger, tried his best to calm Larry down.

Larry full of rage, jumped on top of Barry trying his best to end Barry's mortal life. The stranger as quickly as he could, pulled Larry off of Barry. Larry still in a rage and fighting back pushed the stranger onto Barry causing a bad side effect from their connection.

Barry being a small child thought this was a nightmare and he got so scared that he woke himself up before the stranger could change things back to normal. When Barry woke up that morning half of his young conscious mind was still asleep.

For one whole day Barry was in a half dream like state, that made him believe that he could do anything that he could do while he was dreaming. He went to school this way and could not follow along with what he thought was a dream going on without getting bored. Right in the middle of class he got out of desk and walked to the door to leave this boring classroom behind.

His teacher yelled at him to to sit back down but Barry ignored her and walked out of the classroom and down the hall. Shortly after that, by force, his dream became a nightmare when his teacher and another teacher grabbed hold of him and dragged him to the principal's office.

There he was forced by his nightmare to stay seated until his mom was called to come pick him up from school for being such a very bad boy.

His mother talked to him but he ignored her too hoping to himself that this strange nightmare would finally be over with and he could dream something a whole lot more fun. But this dream would not end, Barry went home and was told that he was on restriction.

His mom made him go to his room and wait until his father came home that night. His father did the same thing his mother tried to do but Barry would not listen to him either, for just as his mother and everything else his father said was nothing but another part of this never ending nightmare.

Barry was offered food but he would not eat one bite of it. Finally his parents had enough of him and made him go to bed. Barry thought to himself 'how strange of a dream this is to be made to go to bed and sleep when he is already asleep.'

Barry closed his eyes in his dream and tried to go asleep. He laid there not moving for about an hour until he could not stand it anymore and he reopened his eyes to see, his young sleeping self and the stranger standing above him in his dream.

The stranger said a few words Barry could not understand then waved his hands around. Barry dreamed, and then the next morning when he woke up, he was fully awake. That day haunted Barry for months until his mother said enough and took him to see a psychiatrist.

For the next few months, so sad for Barry, he had to endure talking about his nightmare that happened that one day over and over again to this psychiatrist.

This psychiatrist told Barry's parents that talking was not getting through to Barry and more invasive measures had to be taken. The next time Barry went to his psychiatrist's office he put Barry under hypnosis.

There in young Barry's mind the psychiatrist dug in deep until he discovered the root of Barry's confusion. Then there like a skilled surgeon he made Barry forget that day ever happened and Barry forgot all about it until today.

For the next two months Barry follows We into other people's dreams. Every dream that Barry enters he feels himself becoming stronger, like he is feeding off these people's dreams just like the monstrous We does.

Together the We can enter anyone's dream on Earth they choose. Together the We are a sadistic entity that messes with and taunts with the horror scenes in the sleeping minds of people that they pick out on a whim. The We hardly ever go back for a second helping of dream food that they feast on and live off of.

At first Barry thought that maybe there were many others on Earth who had a dream twin. Now that has changed, he believes that he might be a singular or one of a very few, because Barry has not seen another like himself in another dream or floating in between dreams on dreaming mental waves.

Barry has become very skillful when it comes to inserting himself inside a dreamer's dream. He follows the We slowly, letting them stay far head of him. By experience Barry has discovered that timing is the key for penetrating a dream without being noticed.

When Barry inserts himself into a dream too quickly the We sense him entering and then the stranger with a few words and hand motions sends Barry out of the dream, making his conscious self fall asleep and instantly dream a dream of his own.

Barry gets only one chance every sleep cycle for his mind to stay conscious when his body falls asleep. It took a few times but Barry knows that he has to wait until the color spectrum disappears around the dream and turns into darkness.

Right then is Barry's moment to enter a dream. Barry can roam this dream as far away or as close to 'The We in his Sleep' as he wants to. For some reason that Barry does not completely understand, Barry is invisible to We and the dreamer of the dream, when he enters a dream this way.

What's even more exciting to Barry's fully conscious mind is that while he wonders around in a dream of another he has found doors, all different kinds in different colors. Some of these doors, unless you can fly while you're in another person's dream, are impossible to access without that dream power.

Barry not knowing what was going to happen decided to open one of these doors. Barry walked in, looked around and figured that what he was seeing was just another dream. How wrong Barry was. He finally realized that what he was seeing was not a dream but the dreamer's memory. A memory that was so bad that the dreamer locked it away behind a door so nobody not even in their sleep could gain access to it.

Without much effort on Barry's part, he quickly found out what this dreamer's name was and more importantly when he woke up, he went on to find out how much money this person was made of in real life. Day by day Barry grows stronger by entering dreams that he follows his We into. Every day after Barry wakes up he writes down at his leisure how much a person is worth and what this person has hidden away behind a memory dream door.

In the back of his mind Barry wants to make 'The We in his Sleep' pay for their crimes against him. Barry thinks back to the days after he was made to forget the We. Those days are not too clear to his mind. Barry thinks back again, this time he thinks about a month or so after that.

Thundering pain in Barry's head makes him stop thinking about that time in his life. Barry is starting to freak for as soon as the pain subsides in his head his memory becomes clearer.

Barry starts remembering placing himself a step or two behind himself watching himself live out his life. He has no control of the past, it happened, it cannot be changed.

With anger Barry yells out Fuck! 'The We in his Sleep' did their mojo on him, well the stranger did while his sleeping self watched on. The We messed up. The nameless stranger did not fully wake up Barry that morning. That is why Barry could not forget them, they were there with him.

They were so high, they were like junkies feeding off Barry's dreaming waves, their mind food every second of his awake life until the day that psychiatrist suppressed the we, way down deep in a dark pit in the back of his tormented mind.

The psychiatrist, that Barry cannot remember the name of, believed that through Barry's mind he could get a mental eye view of the other side.

Helping Barry was a second thought as the psychiatrist put Barry under hypnosis. With all his might the psychiatrist pushed his mind forward, trying his mightiest to insert his mind into Barry's mind. The stranger took over Barry's body. Unknown to Barry, but what I will share with you, is that the stranger cannot enter Barry's body.

However, since Barry was under hypnosis there was an opening made for him to enter and take over. The stranger enjoyed making nightmares enter the psychiatrist's awake mind. These nightmares were so intense that they drove this very sound minded psychiatrist into a raving madman. After the incident the psychiatrist pulled himself together and made Barry forget. He walked Barry out to his mother and told her he was cured, no need to bring him back.

16

Day by day the psychiatrist's mind started to unravel into insanity. His dreams were so real that one morning after he woke up his nightmare would not go away. When he looked over at his sleeping wife she was not there, instead laying beside him was a Demon with fangs. The psychiatrist walked his home looking into his children's bedrooms.

Fear and anger filled his mind as his children were also replaced with Demons with fangs. The psychiatrist walked out of his front door without waking any of the Demons. There he stood in his front yard with tears in his eyes, praying to God to help him. A murder of crows flew over his head, he watched as one of the crows change into a beautiful dove.

The dove paused a moment in flight to let all the crows fly by him. The magical and heavenly looking dove flew down to the psychiatrist and landed on his shoulder. The dove told Morgan that there was only one way to save his family. That there was only one way to send a Demon back to Hell and save his family and send their souls to Heaven and that was by the cleansing of fire.

Morgan sat on his front porch as his home burned around him. The fire department came just in time to save Morgan from burning to death but that was all, the rest of the family burned to their deaths while sleeping and dreaming in their burning home.

Morgan was found guilty by insanity for the murder of his family. During his incompetence trial Morgan did not make a move, he did not make a sound. He sat there in his own nightmare world wearing an adult diaper, being forced fed by an IV. One month later Morgan was found dead in his room in the asylum. Morgan choked to death during the night on his own tongue. Morgan's body was cremated a few days later.

'Greed, have I turned into someone that gains wealth by exposing someone's dirty deeds? I don't know? Because some of these dreamers have done some fucked up shit while they were awake. Including murder...'

'Come to think of it, I haven't entered one dreamer's dream and not found a door, there is a least a few here and there every time...'

'I got it. The We in my sleep, they like dreamers that have a bad or an evil side to their conscious self. We are a couple of A'Holes that is a fact. Even more so now that I have remembered what We did to me, how they fed off me, the nasty bastards.'

'The We in my sleep has gotten a lot darker and more relentless. Seeing blood and bruises is nothing new to experience as I have watched We destroy some dreamer's dream by adding pain and agony to it. So much so to even make these dreamers run through fire to get away from the horrifying monsters that are chasing them so they can eat them.'

'However the last few times I have traveled with them into dreams, when I fall asleep and stay awake at the same time, We have gone blood thirsty, they have become a let's kill them all in their dreams type of entity. I hate them more now, they have made over twenty dreamers die in their dreams the last two times I have slept/awake.'

'I hate myself, I do not even try to stop them. Could I even stop them? In a dreamer's dream, I open doors, I scratch my ass, I've been known to take out a monster or two in someone's dream that was all by itself out in the distance. Usually these monsters wondering around are close to a memory dream door. Makes sense to me that dreamers would invent monsters to guard their memory dream doors.'

18

'What to do? I have to become stronger. I have to slow down on entering memory dream doors and destroy some dream monsters that We are creating for these defenseless dreamers to confront.'

'Damn me, but sometimes it is funny as Hell, watching a dreamer discover a monster and when they start running without looking first and they run into a wall or right off a cliff.'

'I'm only human, a human that is in a position to get revenge and wealth at the same time. I guess I have to save the sinners so I can take away a great big chunk of their wealth. People that die in their dreams cannot pay me so I have to play the role of the hero of their nightmares.'

'In a month Tina is going to visit her mother for a week. That is when I, the hero that will be named...'

'Damn all the good ones are used already.' (Laughing.)

'I'll call myself "The Long Dong Dream Hero".'

'Will every dreamer that I save and tell my name to, will they look at my crotch? I guess I'll be "The Great Dream Hero" from the dream plane known simply as XES-96.'

Chapter Two:

(Three months have gone by now it is, 8:00 AM) "Barry are you sure you don't want to go with me to mother's house, it will be a lot of fun," Tina says jokingly.

"No babe I just want to stay around here and get some work done."

"I don't know Barry maybe you should take a break from writing, you seem so exhausted lately, have you been getting enough sleep?"

"More than enough babe, I'm fine maybe a little tired."

"So no more nightmares or whatever they were called that you were having?"

"No Tina, I am not having any more trouble with my dreams. They are just fine, in fact so fine, I feel like I have become the master of my dreams."

"Okay then and that sounds great. I guess? Are you sure you are okay Barry?"

"I'm just fine babe. You better get going daylight is burning away and before you know it, it will be dark and I want you at your mother's before that happens so that way I will know that you are there and safe." Kiss, kiss. "Goodbye."

"Goodbye."

Barry decides to get some writing done on his novel, he is very happy the way his writing has changed. His writing is more vivid with a cruel, nice twist to it, that makes it seem to Barry it is almost like someone else is writing it. 2:00 PM, Tina calls to tell Barry that she made it to her mother's house. After they hang up Barry writes a few more pages of his novel to leave himself at a good stopping point.

3:00 PM, While Barry is drinking a glass of water, he is thinking about drinking this glass of water which makes him have to take a piss. Barry downs his water, and goes to the bathroom, moments later he feels like he pisses out more then he has drank, and holds on to the wall for support from its intensity and length.

Barry's exact words after it was all over with was, "What The Fuck Was That!"

Barry is suddenly thirsty. Again his exact words, "Fuck that you fool, that was the hardest piss you've ever taken in your life, you do not want a repeat. Wait a minute, Damn, I have to take another piss, my pecker kinda hurts, I hope this is a nice normal piss."

For some reason that is not very important to the story, Barry almost pissed his pecker off the next hour. He took turns pissing and drinking from the faucet. So let's give Barry his peace for this hour.

4:15 PM, 'This sucks. I think that it's over with. Too damn tired to take anymore, I have to lay down. I hope this doesn't mess up my chance? Hero first then I have to know more secrets. The more secrets the more fortune I will be able to obtain.'

Barry falls asleep and for the first time in many days Barry reaches REM's and dreams normally undisturbed for six hours. Then the phone rings. "Hello? No, I do not want to win a free trip. I know it is free, thanks but no thanks. Goodbye."

'Damn I fell asleep without following We into dreams. I feel pretty good, almost refreshed. The way I feel now tells me that I need this, I need to sleep normally a few days a week, but not today. I'll take a piss then go back to sleep and this time We I will follow you.'

"He's back," the stranger tells Larry.

"Good just look at him all happy sleeping like nothing in the universe can bother him. Are you sure you're blocking him from hearing us this time?"

"Yes Larry, Barry is under my control, he hears and sees nothing."

Larry to stranger, "I cannot believe you let Barry follow us into our target's dreams."

"You should be glad Larry, since Barry has obtained this power all by himself he now has made The Elders take notice. And when The Elders take a notice in somebody that somebody's time of living is close to the end."

"Tomorrow Larry you get what you have wanted so very badly for so very long."

"What is that?"

"Tomorrow we together will create a monster that is so monstrous that it will make Barry die in his sleep, then my friend you are free. You Larry will finally be able to follow me home instead of seeping back into the back of Barry's mind. How does that sound to you Larry?"

"Fantastic, I cannot wait to watch Barry die, let's make his death as slow and as painful as we can."

The stranger walks up to Barry and looks down through his mortal shell right into his consciousness and inserts these words into it. "Barry you have become something special. Tomorrow, us your We in your sleep are coming to end your life. Are you going to fight us? Are you going to enter the safety of all those closed doors that you enter every time you follow us? Never mind, don't tell me I want to be surprised."

"Closed doors stranger? I have this thought, tell me if I am wrong stranger?

These doors that I enter, as you say for my safety, are they unlocked to me any time I want to go through them?"

"Yes."

"For you, and all others like yourself, are these doors locked to you? With all your power you still have no idea what's on the other side of these doors, do you?"

Silence from the stranger, "Come on stranger, ask me nicely and maybe just maybe I'll enlighten you as to the mysteries behind these doors."

"Mortal, you mock me? Not very wise. I'm going to enjoy telling you this. Barry your bargaining chip that you are trying to hold over my head is for nothing. Yes Barry, I know, everyone that is like me knows about what's behind theses doors. So very typical mortal that you think you are unique. With no thought that there has been others like yourself before who tried the very same thing, that you are trying to do right now with me..."

"Yes mortal we cannot enter these doors they are locked to us and furthermore we could care less. These doors hold no power for us so they are useless. Tomorrow Barry you will die in your sleep, now wake up I am tired of you."

Barry shakes his head. "No? You will not wake up, then enjoy this nightmare that I am about to create for you. Relax Barry this dream will seem like play time compared to the one that you will have to face tomorrow."

When the stranger leaves Barry's consciousness he says some words and waves his hands around and then walks away from Barry laughing out loud. Barry with no nightmare coming at him watches and listens to the stranger tell Larry that he created a nightmare for him not to enjoy.

Barry lays there for a moment then says Hell with it and takes his conscious out of his mortal shell and follows We into another unsuspecting dreamer's dream.

Barry waits outside the dream We has just entered until the color spectrum disappears around the dream and turns into darkness. Barry looks at We, Larry is not paying attention to him as usual. Barry watches as the stranger turns his head to look at him. The stranger gives Barry a smile with a snarl added to it. Barry stands still watching as the stranger creates a monster, with two heads, two tails and two huge peckers. The stranger looks back over at Barry and this time with that same smile he also gives Barry the middle finger.

Barry looks over at the dreamer who is a great looking lady. She's looking at this monster and screaming "No, no, no."

This monster is nasty and horny. It grabs both of his huge peckers, one with each hand and says, "Hey baby which of these do you want to be fucked by first?"

Great looking lady looks down at his huge peckers and again says, "No, no, no." Great looking lady begins to look like the world is spinning around her then 1-2-3 she faints, knocked out cold in fear of the monster's huge pair of peckers.

We laughs out loud sounding like jackals. Then the stranger gives Barry another middle finger and says to him in his mind, "Well Mr. Limp Hero do something to save this woman from being sexed to death by a monster with two huge nasty peckers."

"Oh yeah Barry, unlike every other dreamer's dreams that I usually enter, this hot looking lady is an innocent."

Barry looks away from the stranger and around the dream that he is in and notices that there are no memory dream

24

doors to be found. Barry looks back over at the great looking lady, the nasty and horny monster is walking up to her and now he is only about ten feet away from her.

Barry looks back over at the stranger and gives him both middle fingers. The stranger smiles and nods his head. With his right hand he points towards the lady and the monster and says, "Go for it hero."

Barry is pissed about everything that is going on in his life. 'Tomorrow I die. My ass, I will. Today for the first time I will save the day, tomorrow I will save my life.'

Barry concentrates hard, gathering his strength. Moment by moment Barry starts to feel stronger. Barry concentrates even harder making wings appear on his back. Slowly Barry's unconscious body changes into a body that looks like a hero's body out of a comic book. Barry laughs out loud, loving his new and improved unconscious body.

Barry says out loud, "You, monster, get away from that lady."

The monster turns towards Barry and looks at him like he just appeared there. The monster roars as Barry spreads his wings, 'I'm doing it, I'm flying.'

Barry flies towards the monster and when he reaches it he grabs it by his head and lifts it off the ground. With monster in hand Barry flies up higher into the top of the dream. When Barry reaches the top he lets go of the struggling monster.

Monster screams out in fear as it watches the bottom of the dream coming at him very fast, then with a smash it crashes down hard and bloody. The monster is hurt but it is not dead. Barry roars out a battle cry and flies like a missile towards the monster.

This time Barry does not pick up the monster, no this time Barry tries his best to fly straight through it. With a loud sick sounding splat Barry slices through the monster making the monster turn into nothing but little bloody pieces of monster flesh.

Barry lands on the bottom of the dream six feet away from his victory. Barry feels like a rock encased within a steel wrapper. Barry is also freaking out a little bit, dream be damned for what he has just done is just as monstrous as the monster he made go splat.

Barry to himself, 'That monster was not real, it was created to infect this dream with blood and terror. Great looking lady is real, she has a mortal shell. She dies in this dream, she dies in real life. I'm her savior, this feels great. Would I be cheating on my wife if I have sex with a woman while being part of her dream?'

'Figures, look at her, she is still out cold, she will probably never know that I saved her life. Hero 101, always make sure the victim you're saving is awake and watching you save them.'

'What the Hell did I just get myself into? One down two to go. Tomorrow I will not die, I will save my life by claiming victory over the We in my sleep. I am...'

Larry screams out, "No, this cannot be happening."

Barry snaps out of his thoughts. Barry looks at Larry, roars out "Victory." Barry laughs out a non-caring laugh and says to Larry, "It's your turn to die. Stranger, you I will save for last."

Larry looks at the stranger for reassurance, the look in Larry's eyes says in volumes, I'm alone, I have been betrayed. The stranger moves so fast away from Larry it makes Barry stop his motion towards them.

Larry turns away from where the stranger was just standing to look at Barry. Barry has blood on his wings, Barry is a monster. Larry in his mind, 'Barry killed me before I was born, by consuming my essence. Now he gets to kill me again. This is not fair, I hate him so much, I should be the one that gets a final afterlife.'

Larry in a rage cannot take any more of the thoughts that are going on in his mind and screams out in a crying rage to Barry, "I hate you, I will kill you, you killer of I."

Larry runs at Barry with his mouth open wide babbling out words that Barry cannot understand. Larry is six feet away from Barry when Barry flies away from his attack. Larry stops running and tells himself that it is not fair that he has no wings to fly with.

Barry, not like a missile but like a bullet descends down to Larry. The strike is fast, the strike is hard enough to knock Larry on his ass and make him bleed. Larry has never felt pain before it is so alien to him that all he can tell himself to do is to runaway from this horrible monster.

Barry looks over and away to where the stranger is standing and watching how this fight to the death will unfold. Larry out loud, "Save me Sam. Why are you not helping me? Please Sam help me, you told me I was going to become part of your family."

Sam says, "Yes that is correct but circumstances has put that on hold. You want to reach the other side? Then fight, kill Barry on your own. Fear is all in your mind, you are as strong as he is. Use the power that is inside you and change yourself into the same kind of powerhouse that Barry is."

Barry says to the stranger, "I am not a fool that will wait for this metamorphosis to happen so the chances of my survival diminishes..."

"No, I am the hero. You and my dream twin are my enemies, you We are nothing but monsters that need to be destroyed. Watch Sam, watch very closely see what will happen to you next."

Larry in confusion is trying to change himself and not paying attention to Barry. Barry's hit to Larry's face with a right hook causes teeth to become crushed inside his mouth. Larry on the ground, opens up his mouth in pain as blood and tooth dust flow out of it.

Larry looks up at the monster that wants to kill him and screams, "No, no, no, please no more, I'm sorry."

Barry knows to keep his mind on track and not to pay attention to what Larry is saying to him. For any word he spits out has no worth for Larry is a monster.

Barry is stomping on Larry, as Larry cries and begs no more. A shadow is coming from behind Barry. Barry sees this shadow out the corner of his eye but too late. Barry is hit from behind hard, hard enough to knock him on to the ground ten feet away.

Pain, no stranger to Barry, sends its torment of sensations to his mind. This stranger whose name he just found out is Sam, is strong perhaps even stronger than Barry. Barry soaked in his pain tells himself that he is bleeding but he is not down, he can still win this war.

Barry jumps up and attacks the stranger known as Sam. Barry punches and punches Sam in his face. Sam takes every punch with a step backwards. Ten, twenty punches later Sam is still on his feet but he is bleeding. Barry yells out, "If you can bleed you can die."

Sam takes ten more punches to his face then grabs Barry's right fist before it can make another contact. Barry looks into Sam's eyes as Sam says to him, "Yes I can die but sadly for you, you are too weak to kill me."

28

Barry tries his best but he can only block three punches coming from Sam. The fourth punch connects with his nose. Barry's nose is broken, his eyes are starting to swell up fast. 1-2-3 more punches to his face and Barry is out on his feet.

Sam laughs and punches Barry even harder for it to become his knock out blow. Sam's punch catches Barry under his chin and sends him off his feet. Barry floats for a second in the air, then he falls to the ground like his bones are made of gelatin.

"Kill him Sam, kill that fucking monster," Larry yells out with happiness and confidence in his voice now.

"No!"

"No?"

"Yes, no Larry, I will not kill Barry, if you want him dead you have to do it yourself. No more help will I give to you."

"Okay that's okay, but can you at least hold him still for me."

"Alright Larry, pick him up off the ground and hand him to me. But hurry up and kill him fast, I need to feed on some dream food quickly, it feels like I am starving for it."

"You too Sam? I thought it was just me, now I don't feel bad for feeling so hungry since you are hungry as well."

"Larry?"

"Yes Sam?"

"Shut the fuck up and pick Barry up off the ground."

"Okay Sam you don't have to be mean to me."

"Mean? I'll give you mean," Sam walks over to Larry and kicks him in his ass really hard.

"Ow, Sam that hurt. Why did you kick me so hard?"

"Shut up Larry or I'll do it again. Now pick up Barry."

In Barry's mind as Sam and Larry are having their back and forth banter, 'Fuck I'm going to die. Goodbye Tina, I love you so much. I am so sorry for that snowy and icy night I slid off the road and made us crash. Tina I am so sorry, you were three months pregnant, that crash caused us the life of our unborn child. It's all my fault, still you stayed with me, still you love me...'

Barry feels Larry start punching him in his face, 'I want to live, I want to live, God help me I want to live. I will cease this day, your love for me will be my strength. Tina I'm coming back to you alive and breathing. Tina my love, I love you with all my heart."

Barry is almost ready to snap out of it as Larry is still punching him in his face.

Sam is getting angry, "Larry will you stop punching Barry, all you are doing is hurting him, at this rate we will be here until tomorrow's dream before you kill him."

"What do you want me to do Sam, hit him harder?"

"No dumb ass, make a sword or an axe appear and take off his fucking head."

"I can't do that, can I?"

"Yes you can do that, you're just too stupid to do it."

"Fuck you Sam, I'm tired of all this, I'm leaving, you kill Barry all by yourself."

Larry walks away, "Get your ass back over here Larry."
Larry acts like he cannot hear Sam as he keeps on walking
away.

"Okay Larry, you dumb ass, where the Hell are you going
to go? In my hands is the unconscious mind of your host,
his mortal body is useless to you without it."

Larry turns back around, trying to play it cool, "Well Sam
why don't you stop wasting time and create an axe for me
to take Barry's head off with."

"You lazy shit, get your ass back over here and hold him,
while I do just that."

Larry's look of being pissed off changes to fright as Barry
wakes up in Sam's arms. In Barry's mind, 'I feel no pain. I
am hurting and bleeding but I feel no pain. Both of these
two are souls that were never born. They hate that I live a
life they never had the chance to live. It's not my fault, all I
did was be born. I'm not the monster of the story...'

'I'm the prey. The kind of prey that does not wait until I'm
cornered to finally strike back out of fear of dying. I'm the
prey that's strong enough to strike first and deadly. The
look in Larry's eyes makes my blood boil with rage. It is
not my fault that I have to fight nastier than the two
monsters of the story to survive.'

"Sam watch out Barry is..." Too late. Sam is holding Barry
from behind by both of his arms but his grip has become
lax. Barry, like a speed demon, jerks his arms loose.

Sam gasps and blinks twice as Barry turns around to face
him. With the strength of victory, Barry attacks Sam.
Hit-hit-hit, face then body over and over again. Sam does
not have the time to be shocked as Barry's attack beats
him down and almost out but only for a moment.

31

Barry's instincts tell him to turn around and protect himself as Larry is about to strike from behind. Barry is unstoppable as he strikes Larry first knocking him down with one punch. Larry feels this pain instantly and it is too much for his mind to take.

Larry's mind is lost in a tunnel as something else takes over him. Sam is tired of this game and strikes Barry from behind. Barry does not fall, he turns around and strikes back, knocking Sam away from him twenty feet. Barry spreads his wings and flies towards Sam. Sam watches as Barry's feathery wings instantly turn into wings of razor sharp steel.

Barry uses his new steel wings to slice into Sam the stranger's torso as he flies by him. Barry flies up higher so he can turn himself for another strike, his eyes look down upon Sam who is bleeding from belly to neck. Sam, in shock is touching his bleeding wounds and is too slow of thought to protect himself as Barry flies by for another strike.

Sam is down with wounds that are squirting out blood as Barry turns back around to face Sam and pauses his flight to a hover. From behind him he hears a roar of anger, Barry turns to see Larry standing there looking very similar to his own viciousness.

Barry roars out attack as Larry's steel wings take flight. Two winged warriors race towards each other to slice the other apart to shreds. Two winged warriors make contact with each other so deadly that blood falls to the ground like rain. Moments later two winged warriors hit the ground like two wet sacks.

Barry and Larry stare at each other, they both stand up at the same time to show no fear of the other. Silence is all both hear as they attack to destroy the other to death. This time when Barry and Larry make contact they do not take flight.

Instead they grab the other and trade punches, then they both change their fists into claws. Bloody rips and tears appear on Barry's and Larry's bodies and faces. Larry backs away and screams out a rage he can't slate. Larry takes flight making blood fall on top of Barry's head.

Barry wipes his head and spreads his wings. Up into the air Barry chases Larry. Larry looks behind him and knows that Barry is faster than him. Larry damns the universe as Barry grabs a hold of him with his razor sharp claws.

Slice, slice, slice, Barry strikes with his claws very deadly fast. Larry snaps a little bit more and fights back in a bloody rage. This in flight battle has turned from painful and bloody into bloody carnage. Pieces of flesh and pools of blood fall to the ground as Barry and Larry rip into each other's bodies both trying their best to make the other disassemble to death.

Sam watches as his body is healing. Sam wonders to himself which one will win as Larry stops fighting and flies away from the pain of his wounds. Barry roars out in pain, "Coward fly away as fast as you can, the only thing you do is give yourself a few more minutes to live."

Larry yells back, "Stay away from me or I'll kill you."
Barry's pause in waiting is over as he flies after Larry to end this nightmare battle to the death. Sam is still watching as wings appear on his back, Sam cannot wait to give Barry the kind of pain that he has never given to anyone before.

Barry in mid flight hears wings flapping behind him, he knows deep down that he has put up the fight of his life. He also knows that he has only enough strength inside him to be victorious over only one of his enemies. If he strikes Larry with a lethal strike before he can die, Sam will strike him from behind with his own lethal strike.

If Barry turns around to confront Sam, will his lethal strike even be enough to kill Sam? A strike that in the end would leave him open for Larry to gather his calm and strike him from behind. If Larry's strike is not lethal enough to him, he would still have to take his attention away from Sam to stop Larry's assault, which of course would leave his back open for Sam to strike at his pleasure.

Barry to himself, 'I'm going to die. No choice really in what to do, if I'm going to die in my sleep, then the least I can do is take one of them with me. Tina I love you, I'm sorry I was not strong enough to win.'

Barry picks up speed, faster and faster he flies taking more of a lead in front of Sam. Sam is about to pick up his speed as well when he suddenly stops himself and comes to a very quick stop in mid air.

Sam to himself, 'I don't know what's wrong with me? For years I have been friends with Larry, I want him to follow me to the other side. This is my duty. This is my honor, yeah right. I do not know why but the blood that has been spilled here today cannot be for nothing. Barry deserves his chance to fight until the end, one on one. Good luck Larry. I hope you win. If you do not, I will miss you and carry forth with my duty."

Barry is flying so fast that the speed he is traveling is causing his eyes to water and his ears to bleed. In five seconds Barry will make contact with Larry. Larry knowing that he cannot defeat Barry has only one thing in his mind and that is to get to Barry's mortal shell. For Larry hopes maybe Sam will be wrong and he can escape to safety by flying into it.

Barry closes his eyes as he makes contact with Larry. Larry with the will to live turns his body at the last moment causing Barry's lethal strike to make only half contact with him. Barry's strike may not be a killing strike but it is hard enough to knock Larry out of the air and make him land on the ground.

Barry opens up his eyes to see Larry falling, without hesitation Barry flies towards the ground and Larry. Barry lands on top of Larry with claws in the ready to kill. Larry still not ready to die fights back to save his life. Larry with the last inside himself pushes Barry off of him. Larry quickly takes this opportunity to run towards Barry's mortal shell. Barry suddenly realizes what Larry has in mind to do and goes after Larry to stop him.

Barry tackles Larry, knocking him to the ground, they roll around and slick Larry gets away from Barry again. This time Larry decides to take flight and join Barry's mortal shell by descending down upon it. Barry follows Larry into the air. When Barry reaches Larry, they fight to the death until Barry is about to win and with one last hope Larry grabs a hold of Barry and takes off flying downwards.

Barry and Larry crash into Barry's mortal shell and with contact there is a loud explosion with the brightness of a star.

Singularly these two winged warriors have become larger in stature. Together they have become too large to fit back inside Barry's mortal shell comfortably. Now what once was two has become one. Sam the stranger watches in wonder not knowing what is going to happen because this has never happened before.

Barry wakes up in pain, then falls back asleep and dreams of hardly anything strange.

Six days later when Barry wakes back up a second time, something is very strange. Barry does not know where he is. As Barry stands up and tries to find the lights something else is on his mind. When Barry turns on the lights, he turns and stares into a mirror, with confusion in his voice he says out loud. 'Who am I?'

A Strange Case Of Amnesia

Chapter One:

Tina pulls into the driveway, 'Well Barry's car is here, I wonder why he didn't answer his phone. I hope he's alright, calm yourself there has to be a reasonable explanation, it is just so unlike him not to answer his phone for almost a week.'

Tina turns off her car, opens the car door and steps out of it. In her mind any minute Barry is going to open the front door, he's going to walk over to her and give her a very loving hug and kiss. Tina waits in her mind as she walks to the back of her car. She slowly presses the button on her car remote to open up her trunk. Tina is starting to get more upset as she leans into the car's trunk to remove her suit cases.

'Damn it Barry, you better be alright. I have a very bad feeling about this.' Tina closes her trunk and not wanting to she picks up her suit cases and carries them to the front door.

'I have a man that is suppose to carry my bags and open up my door. If I open up this door and find him with another woman, I will. Well I don't know what I will do. Yes I do know what I will do, I'll cut off his pecker and throw it at his slut. I hope it pokes her in her eye, damn man stealing, home wrecking slut. Why me? I don't deserve this shit.'

Tina unlocks the front door with hands shaking so badly she missed the lock twice. Tina pulls the key out of the lock, picks up her suit cases, walks into her house, and after setting the suit cases down on the floor, she turns and closes and locks the front door.

Not one sound does Tina hear coming from her silent home.

Tina takes a deep breath and counts to five instead of ten and yells out to her silent home. "Honey I'm home, come and greet me." Nothing no response. "Barry I'm home, where the Hell are you?"

A man named Barry that does not know his name is Barry, just got finished taking a very long piss. He is walking out of the connected bathroom when he hears a woman's voice coming from outside this bedroom door that he has not yet had the courage to open up.

'Damn what the Hell am I going to do? Do I know this woman? Does she know me? Man do I have a feeling like I am in the wrong place at the wrong time. I wonder if she's good looking? What the Hell am I going to do?'

'Do I open up this door and say hey baby want to join me in the sack? Please let this woman know who I am and not scream her head off when she sees me. I don't feel like being picked up by the cops and trying to explain to them that I do not know who I am and I do not even know how I got here. Where ever the Hell here is.'

Barry walks over to the bedroom door and opens it up. He walks out of the bedroom as he hears footsteps coming up the stairs, 'Well 1-2-3 who ever I am, I guess it's showtime.'

Barry watches as a very good looking and very mad looking lady steps up the last step and into the hallway. Tina looks at Barry and feels relief instantly, "There you are, Barry why did you not answer me?"

'My name is Barry and this good looking lady knows me.'

"Well are you going to answer me Barry?" Barry stands there silently not knowing what to do next.

"I've been gone for six days and when I get home the first thing you do is give me the silent treatment?"

Tina for some reason feels like she is the butt of a bad joke and this makes tears come flowing from her eyes then just like that they freeze solid as anger rises out of control.

"Okay you cheating bastard where the Hell is she?"

Barry nervously asks, "Who is she?"

"Good you're talking, now tell me what is going on Barry. Please my heart cannot take anymore."

Thoughts go through Barry's mind a million miles an hour as he finally says to this pretty looking lady that appears to be his wife, "Sorry honey, I'm just surprised to see you, I wasn't expecting you home until tomorrow."

"Is that it? You freak out because I came home early? Oh Barry, what is wrong with you? Sometimes I feel like I'm in this marriage all alone. Well just don't stand there looking at me, come over here and give me a kiss."

Barry says beep it to himself and walks over to his wife. When he reaches his wife, she reaches out and grabs a hold of him and says to him, "Barry you ass, you scared the Hell out of me, for the life of me, I thought for some reason that you were dead and I was going to find your dead body lying on the floor somewhere. Now give me a kiss."

Barry gives his wife, who he wishes that he knew her name a little kiss on her lips, "Is that it? That's not a kiss hello, here let me show you how to kiss someone hello."

Tina pulls Barry closer to her and gives him a kiss that should make him want to take off her clothes. Barry is enjoying himself as Tina stops kissing him suddenly. Tina looks deeply into Barry eyes and says, "Who are you and what did you do with my husband?" Tina looks at Barry expecting him to laugh instead she hears her husband say to her this.

"I'm sorry, I don't know..."

"What?" Tina says surprisingly, not understanding this joke that Barry is pulling on her.

Tina then gets really worried when she hears coming from her husband that she loves with all her heart, "I'm sorry, I do not know where your husband is, um."

"Tina? My name is Tina." Tina looks into the eyes of the man she has been in love with all these years and discovers that he does not know who she is.

With her heart beating out of her chest, Tina says, "Stop it Barry, stop this this instant. This is not funny anymore."

Barry and Tina stare at each other for a few minutes without saying a word or even blinking. Tina blinks first, "Barry, here let me check out your head maybe you have been in an accident."

"I do not feel like I've been in an accident."

"Well since you do not know either of us, I think it is for the best if you let me check out your head for some kind of wound or something. Follow me to our bedroom."

"Sit down on the bed Barry." Tina gently rubs her soft small fingers over Barry's head softly, "Damn."

"What? What is it?"

"Nothing, I found nothing wrong with your head on the outside. Now if I only could check out the inside of your head and fix your problem for you. Wait a minute, let me check on the floor."

"Check the floor? Check the floor for what?"

"Well Barry it's a long shot but maybe just maybe, I will be lucky and find the screw that came loose and fell out of your head on the floor."

"Is that a joke Tina?"

"Yes that is a joke Barry. What, along with losing your memory, did you also lose your sense of humor?" Tina says to Barry with a worried looking smile on her face.

Barry looks at Tina and smiles, then says to her, "I don't think so." Tina and Barry share a small laugh together and then Tina grabs Barry tightly and gives him a big hug.

Tina gets a thought going on in her mind and decides even though it is bad, she feels like she has no choice but to go for a shock to Barry's mind to perhaps snap him out of his amnesia, "Barry, I know that you do not know this but you and I have been talking awhile about, well..." Tina nervously stops talking.

"About what Tina?" Tina shakes her head no, she gets off the bed and takes a few steps away from Barry, "Please Tina tell me what we talked about."

"Well, you and I. I can't say it to you, it's embarrassing."

Barry stands up and walks over to Tina, "Tina, you can tell me anything. I have to say to you, when I look into your pretty brown eyes, I trust that you will tell me the truth."

"Okay, here it is. For awhile you and I have been talking about changing partners for a night. And, well, I'm thinking that this can be just as good. So handsome take off your clothes and join me back on our bed and I will give you loving like you have never had before."

"What? Are you serious?"

"Yes I am stranger but before we get started you have to promise me that you will never tell my husband."

40

Tina takes a few more steps away from Barry and takes off her shirt. Barry watches as Tina then removes her bra revealing to him a pair of beautiful perfect hand sized breast.

Barry looks away from Tina and looks down to his crotch. He is happy that he is already ready for action. When he looks back up at Tina, she is taking off her pants. Barry's heart is pounding fast, he tries his best to tell Tina to stop, but all he can silently do is watch as Tina takes off her panties.

"Well Barry do you like what you see? Hang on a second before you answer me and let me turn around and show you one of my best, and soon to be your favorite, features that I have."

Tina turns around and says to Barry, "And that as you can tell Barry, for yourself is my fine looking ass." Tina is scared and shaking, with all her heart she prays that what she is doing will snap the man of her dreams back to where he belongs.

"Damn Tina you have one very, fine looking ass." Barry can think of nothing but grabbing Tina by her fine ass and then picking her up and placing her on the bed to make love to her. With his right hand grabbing Tina's ass Barry somehow regains control over his limited mind and pulls his right hand away from Tina's fine looking and fine feeling ass, "I can't do this. Can I? No, I can't do this."

Tina turns around with tears in her eyes, she blinks three times then she starts to cry out loud, "I'm sorry Tina, I'm so sorry, I just could not help myself."

Tina slows her crying, "Barry, You don't know who I am. My body that you have made love to more times that I can remember, did not make you remember me. I thought for sure since we have such a great sex life together, you would at least remembered that..."

41

"But no, you look at my body like it's the first time that you have set eyes upon it. Oh Barry what are we going to do?"

"I don't know Tina. But I have to know one thing, were you telling me the truth about switching partners?"

"No you dumb ass, we have never talked about switching partners."

Barry looks at an about to start crying again Tina, "Well good, because if you are my wife there is no way that I would let another man have you and if I did it would be over my dead body."

Tina looks into the eyes of the man she loves and knows that he loves her and in all this heaviness and awkwardness of this bad moment there is still hope. Tina tells herself, 'No matter what I have to do, I will get Barry's mind back to where it belongs.'

"I love you Barry." Barry reaches out and gives a naked Tina a giant hug. Moments later they are kissing. A few minutes later they are making love to each other like it's their very first time.

When they are through making love, an embarrassed Barry says, "I'm sorry, Tina."

"Don't be Barry, you have never been any better." Tina can't help herself and starts to laugh.

A surprised Barry asks questioningly, "Really, I was better?"

Tina still laughing says, "Sorry Barry but you were lousy."

"Lousy? I was lousy? I can't believe this. I can't even fuck as good as I did before. I'm in worse shape then I thought I was."

Tina laughing even harder grabs Barry, "I'm only messing with you Barry."

"Really, I was good?"

"No Barry you were great just like every time you make love to me."

Barry calms down and starts to laugh aloud with Tina. Husband and wife get dressed and walk out of the bedroom together, "Are you hungry Barry?"

"Yes I am."

"What do you want to eat?"

"I don't know. What do I like to eat?"

"Well you're favorite is raw meat on toast with mayo and cheese."

"Yuck, no thank you, I think I'll just go hungry."

Tina laughs, "Come on man of mystery, let's see if we can find you something that you like to eat."

"Sounds great as long as you make it, I'm too tired from making it."

"Well Barry, you may not know who you are but you seem like a normal man. Hear you roar, I have sex, I sit down too lazy to move, while my woman brings me my meat and mead."

"That sounds good Tina, yes I think I'll have a sandwich and a beer, and please sweet hot Tina, do not forget to add some chips beside my sandwich."

Tina, who was smiling looks at Barry without that smile on her sweet little lips anymore. Instead they are trembling.

43

"Barry you don't drink beer!" Tina with hope of playing this twisted hand that fate for some reason had decided to make her play, has given up. Tina's mind cannot handle that her husband is now a total stranger and she made love with him.

In her mind this keeps on repeating, 'How could I do this? How could I do this to my husband? But he's my husband! I cannot take this anymore.'

So suddenly to Barry's eyes he watches as Tina's smile fades away, becoming a confused look as she collapses on the floor unconscious before Barry can get to her.

"Tina, Tina are you okay, please Tina wake up. 911, I have to call 911." Barry picks up the phone then thinks to himself, 'I don't know the address to this house, I don't know my address. Will my wife die because I am lost within myself and too confused to snap myself back in control in time to save her?'

'Dim wit, check your wallet, you must have an id, with your full name and address for you to repeat.' Barry gets ready to dial 911 but looks at Tina lying on the floor to see if she is awake. The answer is no, Barry makes his call.

Barry waits, with the front door to his house open up wide for help. Barry still has hope going for him, for Tina is still breathing with a strong, pulse and heartbeat. She just will not wake up.

"Tina everything is going to be fine, I hear them coming now, they will help you, they will make you wake up. Tina please my heart tells me that I love you, please come back to me, I love you."

A few hours later Barry is sitting in a waiting room with what just happened going through his mind over and over. The paramedics got there, they rushed to Tina and checked her out.

They discovered she was in good health. They looked at Tina's head and body for any signs of a wound or trauma. They found nothing. They looked at Barry for answers and all he could give them was his name and address from a card that he was holding in his hand.

'Damn me, I did this to her, if she dies, I hope I never remember myself. Damn me, I hope I can forget this as well. What happened to me? What did I do to make this happen?'

Barry tries his best, his mind has no choice but to shut down or snap. Sleep over takes Barry, a few minutes later he's dreaming.

DreamVerse:

Barry is walking alone in total darkness, there are no sounds except for the sound of his footsteps upon the ground. Barry's dream mind is in a dulled state from taking on the task of smoothing out the complications of two minds transforming into one. Barry just keeps walking thinking about nothing but reaching the blue door that lies miles away in the distance.

(Fast forward five miles of dreamland walking by Barry and he has now reached the blue door.)

Barry looks at the blue door and a flash of blue light shines into his eyes making his dreaming mind feel more stable. Barry takes a deep breath and tries to open the blue door, but the knob is so freezing cold that it makes Barry shiver with coldness.

Barry's hand has become frozen to the blue door's knob. Barry tells himself to calm down, that the freezing intense coldness engulfing his hand is all an illusion. Barry calms his mind and focuses on eliminating the coldness his hand is enduring, 'I'm dreaming, I'm in a dream and this freezing pain is only an illusion of my dreaming mind.'

45

Barry repeats his saying, in his mind until his hand and door knob is at room temperature. In a grand gesture, Barry proclaims, 'Fuck yeah, no door knob will freeze my hand again.'

So proud Barry turns the blue door's knob, which opens up, without delay. Barry strains but it does no good, he cannot see what is beyond the blue door unless apparently he steps through it. Barry shakes his head and walks through the blue door, 'Here I go.' The blue door's frame looks only a few inches wide but looks are quite deceiving, for it takes what seems to Barry to be an hour before he finally reaches the other side of it.

Unknowingly to Barry, hours dreaming is exactly what his mind needs. So Barry can recharge and make his conscious self ready to cope with the mental strains of having amnesia.

Behind the blue door that Barry unknowingly created for himself as a place to escape and relax, is a place that resembles paradise. Staring at beautiful, clear blue water while standing on a warm sandy beach is what Barry finds himself doing after his long trip in between the blue door's frame. Barry tries to remember his hour, passing through the blue door's frame. All that comes to his mind is thousands of flashes from his past life that he does not remember living.

A warm breeze comes blowing from behind Barry, making him wonder to himself, 'Why is this breeze not coming from the direction of the water?' The warm breeze stops as quickly as it started. Count to ten and here comes another warm breeze. This time the warm breeze comes from the direction of the water.

Barry closes his eyes and enjoys the scent of sweet water as it makes his body feel like it's floating with the breeze. Barry opens up his dreaming eyes to feel himself floating across the beach.

46

With the feeling of freedom in his mind Barry wishes to himself that he could fly. Pain suddenly shoots out from both of his shoulders, Barry wonders to himself, 'Why am I feeling pain in paradise?' More pain as two rainbow colored wings appear on his shoulders.

'I can fly!' Barry sings out to his paradise and flies straight up into the air. Barry is having the time of his life when he looks at the sun and decides that he wants to fly straight to it. Barry flaps his rainbow wings faster and faster and with each flap Barry feels more at peace and stronger and freer within himself.

Flying within the skies of paradise is magic to Barry. Barry's smile turns to a frown when it starts to feel like there's a weight on his back. To Barry's displeasure something is pulling him backwards. Barry wonders what it could be as he looks at the Sun he is flying towards. Barry knows something is off as the Sun starts to shimmer then just like that it disappears right before his eyes.

Barry is all alone in darkness with no sight of his paradise around, when he hears in his dream, "Mister Goldrum, wake up Mister Goldrum."

Reality:

Barry awakens, "What, what is it?"

"It's your wife Mister Goldrum, she is awake and asking for you."

"Thank you nurse?"

"Robertson, follow me Mister Goldrum and I'll show you the way that will lead you to your wife."

"Thank you Nurse Robertson, lead the way and I'll follow." Barry follows Nurse Robertson with what she said to him going on in his mind.

47

Barry shakes his head and says to himself, 'What Nurse Robertson said was a weird way to say it but it is time to let that pass because I have a lot more important things to think about.'

Nurse Robertson stops in front of a door, she opens up the door and stands aside and says to Barry looking him in his eyes, "Inside this room is your wife, take your time, give her your love but do not make her upset. For just like that Mister Goldrum, your wife could snap back to unconsciousness and who knows this time she may not be able to snap back out of it and she will have to stay forever lost in the darkness of her secluded mind."

Barry says to himself, 'What the Hell?' But says to nurse Robertson instead a simple, "Thank you."

Barry enters the room that Tina is recuperating in and keeps on walking until he is six feet away from her bed. Tina looks into the eyes of her husband and says, "Damn, what do I have to do, die for you to remember me?"

Barry looks at Tina with disbelieving eyes as Tina waits to hear the words from her absent minded husband that will mean nothing to her in the state of mind that she is in. Tina waits and instead of his words she hears and watches Barry laugh his ass off, with tears of laughter included to make Tina's mind start to tick with extreme anger.

"What the Hell are you doing you asshole? Stop laughing like that." Tina gets more and more angry as Barry keeps on laughing. Then within a blink of an eye Tina feels like a feather has just tickled her heart which makes her laugh instead of yelling at Barry. Tina and Barry stop laughing, "I love you Barry and you are an asshole for losing your memory. Now get me out of here and take me home. You do remember how to drive?"

"Yes I remember how to drive, but I did not drive here I came in the ambulance with you."

48

"How are we going to get home? And how do you know that you can drive?"

"I just know I can."

"Well then Mister I don't know who I am, get your ass back to our house and pick up your car and drive it back here and pick me up."

"Is that all? How about if I pick up some dinner on the way back here to pick you up?"

"Take your dinner and cram it Barry. I want the Hell out of here and I will not leave this hospital in a taxi."

"Why not?"

"Why not? Don't you remember Barry I hate taxis. You don't remember and I'll never forget. Barry one day, years ago I was in a taxi, everything was going nice and normal when the taxi driver decided to have a heart attack while driving me home. It was dark and rainy when my heart stop beating as I watched this taxi I was riding in go straight through a stop light..."

"In horror I watched as a giant truck drove towards the taxi and collided with it. Smash went the front of the taxi from the passenger side all the way through to the driver's side. The back half of the taxi, the part I was sitting in, spun around, causing sparks and smoke to fly into the damp air. I prayed for my life as I finally came to a stop, I grabbed my purse and stepped out onto the road and stood there in the rain until someone came up to me to see if I was alright. So Barry I say this to you, no fucking taxis."

"Damn, that's awful, too bad you can't forget that."

"Yeah too bad."

"I didn't mean it that way, I don't know what to say to you.

I'm sorry this happened to you but it's like a stranger telling me. I'm sorry for them but it has no impact on my life. Was I good to you after this accident?"

"Yes Barry you were great, you gave me so much love and attention that you almost drove me crazy. You could not help yourself especially since this happened not too long after..."

Tina goes silent and becomes very sad. Barry knows that he should just let this go but he knows nothing at all which is making him crazy so he says to Tina, "After what?"

"After nothing."

"Please Tina tell me, I need to know."

"No Barry what you need to know has to be kept from you for awhile longer. If I tell you this story right now it would break my heart in two, just like it did when it happened."

"Okay Tina, I'll let it be for now."

"Good now come over here and give me a kiss."

Barry and Tina are kissing when Tina's doctor walks into the room, "Now, now let's have none of that."

"Doctor Abbot come in, this is my husband Barry."

Nice to meet you said twice, "Doctor Abbot how is my wife?"

"Well it's great that she is responsive now but something happened to her brain. It's like her mind shut down due to some kind of trauma, perhaps brought on by a huge fright."

Barry is about to tell Doctor Abbott what happened, when Tina says, "No Doctor Abbott there was no huge fright.

Everything was going nice and normal for us, in fact we were just about to make ourselves something to eat."

"Then what happened Tina?"

"Then nothing, I woke up here."

"Barry what says you."

"Well Doc, Tina just passed out while we were talking."

"And nothing else was going on that caused her to be frightened, like a loud noise for instance?"

"No Doc, nothing else happened."

"Okay we will just have to go on from there then."

"Like what Doctor Abbott?"

"Test Tina, more tests I'm afraid. I have a few of them scheduled for you first thing in the morning. So I want you to get some sleep, I've ordered a mild sedative for you."

"Is this necessary Doctor Abbott, I feel great, I'd like to go home?"

"I am very glad to hear that Tina however tests are the only way to make sure your health is as great as you feel and more importantly that this shut down of your mind does not happen again. So no going home, you must stay the night and get some undisturbed rest."

"Okay Doctor Abbott, if you think it's for the best, I'll take these tests tomorrow and get some rest, I am kind of tired."

"Barry I'd like for you to say your goodbye and let Tina get some rest. The best thing is for you to go home and get some rest yourself. This cannot be easy on you as well."

"You are correct about that Doc."

"Okay then I will leave you two in peace to say your goodbyes, please don't take too long. Good night"

"Okay Doctor Abbott, good night."

"Good night Doc."

Barry looks at Tina, "I know what you are thinking Barry, but I feel that the best thing for right now is that we keep your amnesia to ourselves."

"You're right Tina. How do you really feel?"

"I feel fine, I don't think I need these tests tomorrow, but I'll have them just to make sure. Now do me a favor my husband?"

"What is that my wife?"

"I want you to go home and remember who you are."

"I'll do my best. If I don't do you still want me to come see you tomorrow?"

"You better."

"I will then don't you worry, I have a feeling that my dreams are the key to me remembering."

Tina looks at Barry strangely, "Not your dreams again."

"What do you mean Tina?"

"Tomorrow Barry, I'm too tired to tell you now."

Barry leaves and as he walking he wonders to himself, 'Now what?'

Chapter Two:

Barry gets out of the taxi and walks to his house. So many thoughts are going through his mind, with just as many questions as well. Barry stops to stare at his house that he does not remember living in. Barry takes a deep breath and begins walking again, with ten steps forward his belly begins to rumble like a beast that has not been fed for a week, 'I don't even feel like finding out if I can cook.'

Barry decides to take a drive, when he comes to the first restaurant that looks interesting enough to check out he will order himself something.

One by one Barry drives past big named restaurants until he sees a sign that reads, 'Welcome to Grubs, home of the famous big beefy and onion burger.'

Barry enters Grubs not knowing for sure if he wants someone to recognize him or not. Barry is seated by a good looking and tired looking waitress, "What would you like to drink?"

"I'll take a coffee, no I'll take a beer. Wait, go ahead and bring me both."

"Both?"

"Yes both." Barry's waitress walks away saying something to herself.

Barry picks up the plastic coated menu. Barry reads the creation of Grubs famous big beefy and onion burger. Barry's tummy rumbles even more as he pictures in his mind, seasoned fresh ground beef stuffed with sauteed onions formed into a pattie then grilled to perfection. Barry goes for the double deluxe with everything, including bacon, and Swiss and cheddar cheese. Now for his two sides? Home-made potato salad and cinnamon pear compote.

Barry is brought his beer and coffee, in his mind he remembers the words that made Tina's mind snap, 'Barry you don't drink beer.'

Barry slowly takes a sip of his beer and notices his waitress Mary watching him with a expression of, 'What, is it going to bite you?' Barry smiles and drinks half his beer down with one drink, 'Damn that was good.' Barry cannot help himself as he drinks the rest of his beer down with one more gulp. Barry holds back a loud burp and tells Mary to bring him another beer.

Barry drinks this beer and one more with his dinner. His burger is outstanding and so are the sides. Barry finishes the last drop of his beer and notices that he has a good buzz so he picks up his coffee but before he can take a drink he hears Mary tell him, "Let me get you another coffee, that has to be too cold to drink."

Barry is drinking his hot, bitter coffee as Mary brings him his bill. Barry pays for his meal and leaves Mary a ten dollar tip. Barry gets up to leave when his bladder reminds him, 'Three beers and one coffee.' Barry is walking to the restroom when a memory comes to his mind of a very painful piss he took one day some time ago.

Barry hurries his steps as he hears Mary laughing in the back ground. In Mary's mind, 'This man is very much so in the need of a pee pee break.'

Barry with the painful, pissing memory in mind holds on to the wall in front of him and lets it go. Barry laughs out loud with a little buzz in him, that everything is just fine. No horrible pissing just a very long and normal release of unwanted toxins.

Waiting to finish makes Barry's smile fade as he looks down and notices that his piss is staring to turn blue, the same color blue as the blue door in his dream that leads to a perfect paradise.

54

'I'm drunk or I'm pissing blue? Why did I drink three beers? My body tells me that it is not used to drinking beer but my mind is clear with a little buzz for some fun going through it...'

'In my dreams is my answer. I feel this, my dreams are telling me while I'm conscious that I am correct. Or damn it, is it a simple case that the reason that I do not drink beer is due to the fact, that the after effect of it makes my piss turn blue? No brew, no blue, ha, now it is all clear.'

Barry walks out of the rest room and looks at Mary. Grubs is empty of costumers and for some reason Mary has a small smile on her faces as she waves Barry to come to her. Barry does as he is commanded to do, "Hello, I don't know your name, is this your phone?"

Barry looks at the phone and replies confused, "I don't know."

"You don't know if this is your phone or not?"

"Nope, not a clue Mary, I'm Barry, wait let me check my pockets."

Mary puts the phone down and rubs her hands together, "Barry, there is no need for you to go to all that trouble."

"There's not?"

"No there's not, not when I would be glad to search your pockets for you. Especially your front pants pockets if you know what I mean?"

Barry's face reddens, "Thank you Mary and that is very hot of you but I am married and I don't fool around. Well at least I don't think I do? I have a hot looking wife Mary, can't wait to enjoy making love to her again."

"Well Barry you don't have to brag about it, a simple no

would have been just fine." Barry looks at Mary and laughs, then he walks up closer to her and gives her a very surprising hug.

Mary at first starts to pull away from Barry then the firmness of his body feels so good to her lonely and wanting body that she hugs him back very tightly, "Why are all the good men married Barry?"

"I don't know Mary, maybe it's our peckers." Mary steps away from Barry and laughs harder than she has laughed in years.

Barry laughs in return, enjoying himself watching Mary break out of her emotional cage that she's been hiding in for four long years now, "Thank you Barry, I haven't laughed like this in years. The last time I laughed like this was with my husband four very long and sad years ago. Barry you do not look like my late husband but some how, some way you remind me of him."

Barry looks at Mary, then turns around and walks over to a table and sits down, "Come Mary, tell me your sad story and I'll tell you mine."

Barry listens as Mary tells him of the day her and her husband went sailing out on the ocean blue. The day started out so very nice, they sailed out into the ocean and stopped in the perfect spot for lunch. They ate, they drank wine and then they made love out in the sun on the deck of the thirty foot yacht they had rented for the weekend.

When they finished they drank more wine as they sailed further out into the beautiful blue ocean. When it was getting dark Mary and her husband were hungry so they stopped to eat. But the look of love and lust in their eyes caused them to go to the cabin and make love. What a perfect first day to start the weekend it was as husband and wife made love together.

When they finished making love for the second time in one day, they grabbed a hold of the other and fell asleep holding each other in the embrace of love. Mary pauses.

After a few moments, Mary continues her happy story that is about to become very sad. "I had to pee, it took awhile for me to peel Andy's arms and legs from around me. I finished my business and went back to bed to lay next to Andy. We held each other, I was so tired, Andy told me to stay laying down and covered up that he would serve me dinner in bed..."

"Andy what a man, what a husband, left me there to sleep some more. I grabbed the covers and pulled them closer to me to keep me warm from the sudden icy chill that was flowing through my body out of nowhere." Mary pauses again.

"I woke up the next morning all alone in a strange bed. I peed, I got dressed and went out on to the deck. I called out, 'Andy, Andy.' I received no answer, in panic I yelled out, 'Andy where are you?'

I searched the yacht as I cried out in fear until I ran out of hope. Andy was missing, Andy was not on the yacht anymore. I looked out into the ocean for Andy's body it was no where to be seen. I called for help, an hour later I was being questioned like I'd murdered my husband. Barry I felt so weak and alone as I cried my eyes out in front of eyes that looked at me like they did not believe me. I got angry, I was sedated, I was put away for some rest for a week..."

"I was a foster child, I never had a family of my own and Andy's family, who took me in and treated me like I was part of their family turned their backs on me. I was the monster woman who took their precious Andy from them all. My broken heart tuned to icy steel as I hated the world more and more every day. That was four years ago, I still love my husband, I miss him every day..."

"I'm so tired of being so sad Barry. I want to live and I hate working here. Thank you Barry for making me laugh, I've needed to laugh for so long now. Tomorrow Barry, tomorrow I will start my life over. This is my last night working here."

Mary reaches out and takes hold of Barry's hand and squeezes it tightly, "Thank you Barry for not using me like so many men would have done, even many married ones. Your wife is a lucky woman, tell her this for me when you go home to her tonight."

Mary stands up and walks away taking off her apron. Barry watches as she throws it on the floor and walks into the kitchen. A few minutes later a unhappy man follows Mary out of the kitchen, "Mary you cannot just quit like this on me. Mary what about tomorrow, who will take your place tomorrow night?"

"I don't care Fred, that's your problem for you to figure out yourself. My tomorrow Fred is going to happen many miles away from here." Mary with her jacket on and her purse in her hand walks to the exit of Grubs.

When Mary reaches the door that will lead her to the rest of her life she turns around and looks at Barry and then she throws him a kiss and says, "Too bad for you Barry, for you'll never know what you missed out on."

Barry smiles and says in return, "I bet, goodbye Mary have a great life you deserve it."

Mary still with the rush of freedom in her mind says, "Goodbye Barry, I know I will think about you once and awhile during my life, do me a favor will you, Barry?"

"What's that Mary?"

"Remember me."

"I will Mary, I will."

Mary walks out of the door of Grubs without looking back. In about a year from now Mary, falls in love with a great man that loves her with all his heart. Mary still loves Andy and will go to her grave not fully knowing what happened to him that day long ago. On the day that she dies she will be surrounded by her family, all her children and all her grandchildren. Her family will mourn her loss but with the love she taught them, they will go on and stay strong living the rest of their lives knowing the fact that she loved them all with all her heart.

Barry in his car talking to himself, 'Damn what a day. Tina, she seems fine but what a shock to her system. Damn I almost fried her brain from the shock of her not being able to deal with the fact that I have amnesia.'

'Mary, What a trip. I don't even know why I gave her that hug. Can't help wondering what she would have been like? Mary has a great looking ass, better get her out of my mind. When I go to sleep, will I dream of the blue door again? Paradise sounds nice for a repeat dream.'

Barry starts up his car and drives back home, thinking the whole time about paradise. Skip forward one hour and nineteen minutes and Barry is getting into bed to go to sleep.

DreamVerse:

Barry is all alone again walking in total darkness, there is still no sounds except the sound of his footsteps upon the ground. Something is new instead of five miles away like the last time the blue door is only one mile away.

Barry starts his walk, then he decides to run the rest of the way. When Barry reaches for the knob of the blue door, he remembers the coldness from before, 'I have control of my dream and the knob will not be freezing cold to the touch.'

Just like Barry commands for his dream the blue door's knob is normal temperature. Barry opens up the blue door and looks at its door frame, nothing special just like the last time, it's just a frame.

As Barry walks through the frame of the blue door, memories come flashing at him. They are fast, way too fast for Barry to make a recollection. Barry closes his eyes and calms himself, when he opens back up his eyes the memories that are flashing at him have slowed down considerably, 'This is more like it.'

Barry watches as birthdays and Holidays come to him from all the years that he has lived. Then they pass on as Tina makes a more dominate impact in his memories. Barry watches as he and Tina meet for the first time. Barry watches as they make love for the first time, he watches as they laugh, he watches as they argue. He watches as they make up and make love. Barry smiles as Tina tells him that she's pregnant, they go out to dinner to celebrate.

Barry wants so bad to remember these memories that his dream is showing him, when everything becomes silent and still. Barry wonders what is going on as a single memory starts to come to him very slowly, like it is giving him time for him to ready himself...

Barry and Tina are in their car, it's a snowy, cold dark winter night. Tina looks so beautiful. They are talking about things that they need to do before their baby is born. Everything is going fine when the car skids off the road...

Barry holds his breath as he watches the car straighten out and continue down the road. Then like a nightmare, their car skids off the road again. This time there is no stabilizing for their car, no this time it goes completely off the road and races down a snow covered hill. The car keeps on driving itself down this large and steep hill until it crashes into a huge oak tree. Barry keeps on watching as he bites down on his bottom lip making it bleed.

60

With the taste of blood in Barry's dreaming mouth he crosses through the frame of the blue door and out into paradise. With tears in his eyes Barry remembers for himself the accident that took the life of their unborn baby.

The next day the nightmare continues on when Tina is told that she can no longer have children. A month and a few days later Tina has turned cold and does not want Barry to warm her. Separation for their marriage, Barry left for two weeks, staying in a hotel to give them the space that they both needed. Tina one night came to Barry's hotel room and they made love like they hadn't done in months. The next morning they went home together and have stayed together in love since then.

Barry starts to remember the accident that Tina told him about when she was in the taxi and the driver had a heart attack. Barry is almost to the end of remembering this memory when a knock from the other side of his blue door makes his heart skip a beat, 'What the Hell?'

Barry looks at his blue door for a moment, then some more knocking starts to come from it. Barry walks up to his blue door that is closed and opens it up and says, "Hello?"

There is no one there then poof a stranger walks through his blue door and into his paradise, "Hello Barry, I am Sam, we need to talk."

"What is this?"

"This, this is your dream, Barry."

Barry looks at Sam and for some reason he does not like or trust Sam, "Welcome Sam to my dream have a look around then get the fuck out. I can tell you're a nightmare creature that has come to inject some of your nightmare terror into my calm paradise."

"Damn Barry, you figured that out, all by yourself?"

61

"Yes Sam, I'm quick like that. Well Sam, thank you man but I have to tell you I do not have the time to be involved in a nightmare. Why you ask? I'll tell you Sam, because I have to find out who I am and the more that I talk to you the more pissed off I'm feeling."

"That makes a lot of sense Barry, no big secret here I am your enemy. I've come to kill you. So die Barry. And Barry, die with your boots off."

"Sam that was stupid, almost as stupid as you look."

Sam looks at Barry all pissed off then laughs out a little bit. "Okay Barry here it is. I have not come to your dreaming paradise to turn it into a nightmare. No Barry, I've come to your paradise to do so much worse."

"How much worse Sam?"

"Just to give you an example of my power Barry, here are a few nightmare creatures that I have created in the past, to scare, to strike out at and to kill dreaming mortals."

Barry watches as monsters appear in his paradise. Barry starts to count, when he gets up to thirty he stops counting and instincts come to him to get ready to battle to the death. Very cool thing Barry thinks to himself that he is not scared just primed and ready to attack the massive amount of hideous monsters that have taken over his beautiful paradise.

"Just like magic Barry, all the monsters go bye, bye. Before we go on I feel like a beer, how about you Barry, do you feel like a having a beer?"

Barry thinks, 'Strike or wait and let Sam tell me what's he's all about before I strike.'

"Don't do it Barry!"

"Do what Sam?"

"Do not test your strength against mine, for you will lose and lose bad."

Barry looks at Sam and thinks, 'Bullshit, this Sam whatever he is, is scared of me or really leery and giving me the sad, I'm the bully and you're my prey bullshit scenario. Why do I feel like I can smack him around like he is my prey?'

"It's all cool Sam, I'm in my paradise and as soon as you split I can go back to having a great time."

"Then Barry, I'll go on. I am a proud member of the Gemini Dream Legion."

"You look like a member that is for sure, a very small one I might add."

"Silence this chatter of yours that you are spewing out, I will hear no more of it."

"Damn Sam, you don't have to be so harsh, I'll just lock my lips and throw away the key then."

"That is the first thing Barry that you have babbled out that has made any sense to me. So yes Barry, shut your mortal mouth and listen very closely to what I have to inform you of, what is to be."

Barry grinds his teeth together and keeps his mouth shut. "Very good Barry, who says there is no hope for you? Surely not I." Sam laughs out loud like he is in total control. However in his mind he is saying to himself, 'That's it, you have this stupid mortal right where you want him. Stay strong, show no weakness keep up this high level of complete control. Barry will fear you and not have the balls to rise up against I, the mighty Sam.'

Sam stops laughing, "First of all Barry let me tell you this, I and every member of the Gemini Dream Legion hate you and everyone that is like you. You and everyone like you are murderers."

"Murderers? I've murdered no one Sam."

"Yes you have Barry, For yourself to live a mortal life you absorbed another that was your twin. You Barry are a creature that is so foul that you killed unconsciously someone weaker than yourself just so you could live."

"You lie... That's insane."

"I speak the truth. Barry you did not have to do this but you did it anyway just so you could be stronger when you were born. Just like your twin Larry, I was murdered before I had the chance to live one day. We the Gemini Dream Legion accept this for we have no choice, it's the way of the universe..."

"However Barry, what we will not accept is you. For you Barry are the most horrible mortal that ever lived. Once was not good enough for you Barry, no you are so sick that you out of greed of more strength you absorbed your twin Larry twice."

"That's insane, okay maybe once but how could I possibly absorbed my twin Larry twice?"

"Like I said, you murdering mortal, out of greed of more strength. You Barry, you figured out how to gain control over your dreaming mind after stumbling one day upon your twin Larry and myself talking before you woke up. Like a predator Barry you kept coming back day after day while you slept and attacked Larry until you killed him..."

"That Barry was your last, the last that the Gemini Dream Legion will let you obtain. What is next for you Barry, jump into other mortal dreams and murder their dreaming twin?

64

All in an effort to gain even more power? You sick sadistic monster!"

"That's enough Sam, I have no memory of this. I listened as you told me your grand tale and I'll tell you this nightmare creature, I do not believe you."

"It's the truth word for word. Larry was your victim twice. If what I say is a lie, where is Larry now?"

"Gone?"

"That's right, Larry's dead and gone."

"So what's the deal Sam? What is this Gemini Dream Legion you're boasting about going to try to do with me?"

"Try Barry? Fool you are so lucky that I don't strike you down right now. If I did not have my orders I would do just that. For some reason unknown to me, The Elders find you interesting. For being so sick and twisted Barry you have now become the very first of your kind. So you are to come with me to The Elders so they can judge your fate."

"I don't think so Sam, I'm good where I'm at."

"I'm sure you are Barry but If you do not follow me to The Elders, your precious Tina will have a very unfortunate nightmare. Will she survive? I do not know. But I can tell you this Barry, if you come with me, Tina will have nothing but smooth dreams..."

"What do you say Barry, are you going to be a stubborn mortal and take the chance of losing the only person on Earth that you truly love? All because of this pesky amnesia that you seem to be having."

"Yes pesky, that's what my amnesia is. It's just so darn unfortunate."

"You've been doing fine so far Barry, do not be stupid now. Your woman means nothing to us, she is simply the weight we place on your back to make sure you stay civil and obedient, like the worthless mortal that you are."

Barry has had enough and decides to be an asshole. "What's wrong Sam, did you go and lose your friend? Well boohoo for you."

"How dare you mortal? I loved Larry like a brother, you fiend."

"Good, I hope his memory haunts you forever. Because I have a feeling it's you that is to blame for Larry's death. What Sammy, were you lying down on the job and could not get up in time to save your friend from my wickedness? Or Sammy were you too damn weak to save Larry?"

"I'll show you how weak I am Barry, you lousy stinking mortal." Sam screams out in a rage, not for the memory of Larry but because of the fact that no mortal as ever spoken to him like this.

Barry has to know where this feeling of power in himself is coming from. Barry stands still and strong as Sam attacks him with vicious fury. Sam's first hit hurts Barry like a dickens, Barry bleeds at first contact.

Each hit Sam delivers to Barry, Barry fells stronger. In moments Barry no longer bleeds. In a few more moments Sam's hits felt like taps to Barry's face and body. Sam stops hitting Barry and looks at him like, 'Oh shit, I think I just fucked up really bad.'

Barry smiles at Sam, "Ouch that really hurt Sam, please no more. I don't know Sam tell me if I am wrong or not, but I think it's my turn to bring my pain to you?"

"Please Barry stay calm, I made a mistake. I wasn't thinking straight..."

66

"It's really your fault Barry, if you hadn't pissed me off so bad, I wouldn't have hit you."

"I believe that Sam, for if you were not pissed off your weak pathetic self would have not dared to strike me, let alone try to beat me down. Whatever I have become Sam, I do not know but I know I am stronger than you..."

"I just gotta know how much pain I can give out, I hope, oh do I hope Sam that it is as much as I can take. For Sam I feel like I can take off your head with one strike from my mighty fist. What do you think Sam? Shall I'll try it?"

Sam stares at Barry with the fear of dying in his eyes compared to a rabbit that is staring at a wolf. Then through the still opened up blue door that leads to Barry's paradise comes ten or more members of the Gemini Dream Legion to save Sammy from the doom of an upcoming death.

Barry watches as winged warriors come flying to him for battle. Barry closes his eyes and concentrates on what he wants for himself to become, 'I'm the hero of my dream. I have to be more powerful than my evil attackers.'

Barry sprouts wings of steel and takes off flying into the air in a battle of one man verses a small army of dream invaders. Barry does not pause as he makes his enemy's scream and bleed and scream and bleed until they all finally fall to the ground. With victory in hand Barry circles his down and out enemies, like a bird of prey.

'What have I become, I do not know but damn I'm powerful. This is happening in my dream. Is all this blood for real or is it just part of the dream?'

'I don't know, yesterday I would not hesitate to answer this question with a fast dream blood is only dream blood it has no comparison with reality living blood. Now as I fly above in my dream that I dreamed to be paradise that is now covered in blood and butchered dream warriors, I wonder.'

Barry descends to the sandy beach of his paradise, he picks a spot that is not covered in blood to land on. Barry looks around at dead and dying beings covered in blood and this scene is now making him feel ill.

'What have I done, am I the monster of this dream, of my dream? My paradise has become blood soaked by my very own blood covered hands. I'm the monster, I'm the monster that kills in his own dreams. No more blood, I want to wake up now, please universe help me out of this nightmare.'

Barry's wings disappear as he becomes weak from feeling so sick from looking at all the blood that he made splash around so thickly everywhere. Barry collapses on the ground defenseless as Sam, the only one that did not fly against Barry in battle, decides it is his time to create a more warrior version of himself. Sam thinks to himself, 'I could create the monster of monsters to kill Barry in his dream, but I want a more hands on version of Barry's death.'

Sam jumps on top of Barry and begins to slice down upon his flesh with thick, long claws that are designed to rip chunks of meat out of a carcass. Barry feels this pain and his blood flowing out of him and landing on the ground in different ways. A splat here, a few drops here with globs of his blood soaking into the sand, 'I'm sorry Tina, I was not strong enough to...'

'Wait a minute, I've done this before. This strange deja vu is making my mind feel like it's thumping. Like before, I do not want to die, if I die in my dream, I die in real life. I have to fight back, fight back now, then fly away so I can have some peace for I feel in my mind that this is it. These final memories that are trying to consume my mind will be my awakening to end my strange case of amnesia.'

Sam is still attacking Barry with victory in his mind. He cannot wait to kill Barry so he can fly back to The Elders, telling them how wrong they were. That yes many family members died but not him, the strongest of all, for he did all by himself what the the others all together could not. Kill a monster that is one of a kind because it has the power to kill one like themselves. Which of course since the dawn of the time of The Gemini Dream Legion, this has never been done before. Not until Barry the mortal monster, invaded their domain.

The domain of Dreamverse where they rule supreme, doing as they wish with any dreaming mortals dreams they choose to enter and make it become a nightmare. So they can feed themselves large amounts of pain and fear which when combined becomes what is known as their dream food.

Barry gathers his strength and rises up to strike Sam. Contact is made sending Sam off his feet. Barry like he commanded himself to do, now flies himself away to safety. Barry looks at his wings in confusion, what once was wings of steel have been replaced with falling off, soft, rainbow colored feathers.

Deep in the sky, Barry looks around, trying to find solitude for himself within his paradise. There is none so the decision to fly to and out of the blue door has been made by Barry. The blue door that is not wide enough for his wing span to pass through, 'This will not do.' Barry shouts out loud and through deep will of thought Barry changes his blue door to accommodate his width.

Once out of the blue door Barry flies among the dream waves by himself for the first time. He does not know this as he enters a sleeper's dream to stop his flight, to hide himself so he can let the memories that he's keeping barely at bay finally let themselves be known.

Twenty minutes later Barry is standing proud and bold as he remembers everything, 'I remember now, I remember everything. I'm not the monster, I'm the hero.'

'Now I know that I am much more than that.'

Barry looks around the dream and he notices that it's a very boring dream. Some guy that he does not know cannot even score in his own dreams. So out of the kindness of his heart Barry helps this poor sap out so he can get past the obstacle that stops him from getting laid in his dreams every single night. The way Barry finally got through is when he told this man not to fear it, just fuck it.

Barry satisfied that he has done some good, flies out of this dream back to his blood covered paradise. Sam is still there in waiting like he has nothing better to do. Barry lands twenty feet away from Sam and says to him, "Hello stranger long time no remember."

"So you remember Barry? What are you going to do?"

"Well Sam the stranger, I would very much like to go to the meeting you had planned for me with your Elders."

"You do? What are you going to do when you get there?"

"How about this Sam? I'll introduce myself as the new ruler of DreamVerse. And maybe Sam, if your Elders don't piss me off, I'll be nice and let them live."

"Watch your grasp Barry, for no matter how mighty you are there are millions of us that feed off of mortal dreamers and there is no way that We will surrender to you."

"Maybe, maybe not but there is no reason for me to discuss it with you any further Sam. For you are a nothing, just a simple soldier so take me to your leaders."

"It's Elders, Mortal."

"Sam relax, I was only kidding about killing your Elders. I'm just a simple and great man that lives his life free and wants others to do this as well, even you..."

"Well I would have if you didn't try to kill me twice. You really liked telling me that I was going to die. I would have died if myself and Larry hadn't combined into one being. Now I'm a little mortal and I'm a little Gemini Dream Legion."

"That's not true, is it? It can't be and yet here you are living dreaming proof that you are what you say you are."

"How you like me now Sam, now that I'm stronger than you?"

"Just like before Barry, not at all."

Barry laughs, "That was cleaver."

"Too bad you're not."

"Now you've turned into a dumb ass. Back to the facts Sam. You tried to kill me twice, but I did not die, did I Sammy? You tried and you failed now I've become what is to be known as The King Gemini of The DreamVerse. How does that title sound to you Sammy?"

"I do not like it."

"Well good for you and since you do not like it, I guess I have myself a winner. Now before we fly to your Elders, I want to know something and I want the truth, not your twisted one sided looking at it. Just give me the facts and none of your commentary is all I'm asking."

"Asking? You seem so civil with your words Barry but in your eyes, I see a mortal monster that will beat me down for fun if I lie to you."

"Well there you go Sam, tell the truth and feel no pain. Lie to me and I'll knock you down and kick you in your head. That's funny Sammy, come on give me a smile."

"How about if I give you my finger instead?"

Barry looks at Sam and then laughs out nice and hearty causing Sam to calm down a little bit, "See Sam, isn't it better to make fun than it is to kill?"

"No Barry I would rather kill a mortal in their dreams than make them smile and laugh. For what I am is not a joke."

"Meaning?"

"I was never born, yet I was an entity that grew from baby to adult during my time with my living twin mortal host. Until his death, I fed off of his nightmares and pathetically even his normal boring dreams. I did not ask not to be born, I am what I am, the universe made me what I am. I have to eat and nightmares are my meals. I am not evil even when I kill a mortal in their dreams, I just do what the universe planned for me to do."

"You're a Parasite Sam. You feed off living hosts. First your twin, then mortals through their dreams."

"Barry, I am a perfect product of the universe, just like millions just like myself that never die until you became what you are."

"And what is that Sam?"

"I do not know."

"Doesn't matter Sam that is for another dream for myself to discover. Now I want you to tell me what I want to know. What I am now, is one of a kind in the universe, correct?"

"Yes that is correct."

"What about before, when I was just a singular that followed you and Larry into dreams?"

72

"What about it?"

"Were there many like myself that could do what I did?"

"Yes."

"Give me more than a yes Sammy."

"What do you want from me?"

"The truth, just the truth."

"Yes there have been many like you before that's traveled with others like myself and their dream twin."

"What do you do with them?"

"Usually we just kill them after they fatten themselves all full with dream food. I tell you Barry what a treat, just a pure delight it is to devour a mortal that was like the way you were before. It's about the only time I ever feel stuffed."

"I get it, you're trying to piss me off Sammy. I just don't understand why you would chance it, I'm your monster remember."

"Fine mortal. Sometimes on rare events we The Gemini Dream Legion will welcome ones like you were before into our legion."

"Why would you do that?"

"Because every once in awhile there is a dream twin that gets the sickness. The sickness that eventually causes that poor dream twin to die."

"You told me that ones like you do not die?"

"Yes and that is correct, if ones like myself do not catch

the sickness before our mortal twin dies, then we become an immortal after their death. If we catch the sickness, we die before our mortal twin dies, we do not become immortals. On rare events the dream twin that has the sickness somehow switches places with their mortal twin."

"How does this happen?"

"We don't know how or why. We have no control over this. This switch either takes place on its own or it does not."

"They just switch places? What about the sickness?"

"The mortal becomes the dream twin, who does not have the sickness."

"Ever."

"Yes every time the switch takes place the sickness is gone from the new dream twin. Then we have the task of training a past mortal to become a member of The Gemini Dream Legion. Sometimes this takes no time at all, sometimes it seems to take forever to train them."

"What about the dream twin that is a mortal now?"

"They receive the sickness, then they die as a mortal."

"I still say you're all Parasites."

"I have to say this Barry."

"What is that Sam?"

"We the Gemini Dream Legion, we are the chosen ones."

"And who chose you?

"God."

"God?"

"Yes God, we are his Creation. First there was Angels then came us."

"Bullshit."

"Bullshit?"

"Yes bullshit. How can one like yourself become immortal without having a mortal host to live off of first?"

"Chicken or the egg Barry? We came before mortals, end of story. All mortals were created as an after thought by God."

"Told you this himself, I suppose?"

"Well no but..."

"You're telling me that God does not talk to you Sam? That is a shame, to be left out like that. So sad to be one that has to rely on others that talk to God to give you the big scoop."

"Blasphemy you mortal monster!" Sam screams out.

"Stuff it Sam, I am mortal and this mortal does not believe in God. But I do believe in the universe. Where it came from, I do not know, nor do I care for right now. All I want now is to meet with your Elders so I can wake up, shower myself clean from dealing with all this and go see my beautiful wife that I love with all my heart."

"Typical mortal, only thinking about yourself."

Barry ignores Sam, "I cannot wait to see her face when I tell her I remember myself, probably won't even have to. Tina will just have to look me in my eyes and see that sparkle of recollection and a very heavy weight will be lifted from her mind and being."

"Her soul Barry, from her soul, she will feel that relief."

"You say tomato, I say tamato. Now let's fly far away to the dump you live in."

Barry flies close to Sam with wings of steel in the ready if there is to be an attack on him. Miles and miles they fly so very fast. Barry still portraying his mightiness keeps on flying but in his mind he cannot believe the speed that he is flying.

Barry to himself, while flying, 'My life has changed, well the dreaming part of my life. I can now go into other mortal's dreams and change them. I'm no stranger to dream food, before I just consumed small amounts while watching dreams and entering dreamer's memory dream doors. What will I consume now? What will I allow myself to consume to gain even more power?'

"We are here. Take a look ahead mortal, feast your eyes on true paradise."

"Not too bad Sammy but how does it look on the inside?"

"Just as grand as the outside mortal." Barry and Sam land on the outer walls of The Gemini Manor.   Sam pushes a button on a console and a female voice says out loud, "What is the password?"

Sam looks at Barry, he smiles then says, "Mortals suck."

"Enter and rejoice brother you are home once again."

Sam with pride for his home is still smiling at Barry, when Barry says to him, "She sounds ugly, is she your girlfriend?"

Sam's smile fades fast from his face, "Just follow me mortal."

"Lead on Sammy."

Barry follows Sam miles and miles through labyrinths of walls filled with holes in them that Sam's people use as a space of their own. Sam's people are crammed like sardines and they do not seem to mind, or do they? Do they just not know any better?

Sam leads Barry to a giant dark purplish door and stops, "Behind this door Barry lies the oldest, the most wisest and the most powerful of my family, The Elders. Watch your words, for they may be the death of you."

"Well open up the door Sam."

"No, you go in alone."

"Very well then. And Sam, I'm going to miss you."

"Mock me all you want mortal, one day things will be different."

"Just keep on telling yourself that Sammy."

Barry reaches for the door knob and there is not one to be found, "Trickery Sam? Open up this door or I'll kick it in."

"Hostile mortal, we do not need knobs to open doors here in The Gemini Manor. As you can tell mortal we have perfected our doors, see how they stay nice and closed together perfectly yet when you push them like so. Wa-la, there you go able to walk through without any effort. If you want mortal, I can hold open this door for you, if my instructions were too difficult for you to follow."

"Brave immortal, when you're alone, you bark only. Yet when you are with your pack, you think that you can start
77

biting. Sammy I got to tell you, you portray the role of a great big old, stinking asshole to the extreme, oh yes you do. Wait for me here, don't know how long I'll be, try not to play with yourself like a pervert while I'm gone."

"Kiss your ass?"

"I don't think you said that right?"

"Yes I did, I wouldn't want you kiss my ass."

"Sam, for fun, you better keep one of your hands in your mouth and the other in your ass. (Laughing) When you take a break and remove your hands (More laughing) Try to remember which hand went where and you'll be just fine. If you taste shit, you might want to switch hands."

"You bone headed Mortal twit. I hate you Barry, I wish I could kill you."

"No Sammy, what you meant to say, is that you wish you had the power to kill me. Vice versa Sammy, I do not have to wish, if you get what I'm saying? Good, now be a good dumb ass while I'm gone."

Barry halts for three seconds then he pushes open the door that leads to The Elders of The Gemini Dream Legion. Barry walks into this giant room that is filled with thousands of Elders. All of whom are sitting in chairs that are hovering about everywhere.

Barry is noticed as he enters the throne room and very quickly they all fall in line leaving a space for the top of The Elders to make their way through. Barry thinks to himself, 'How dramatic.'

Barry stays silent and still watching as a larger looking man comes floating to him at a very slow speed, "Come further into the room mortal, Barry Goldrum, I am Grover. How was your flight?"

78

Barry takes five steps then stops, "Here have a seat."
Grover gestures to his right as a empty chair comes
floating to Barry.

"No thanks Grover, I'll just stand."

"Very well mortal, Barry Goldrum."

"Barry will do just fine, Grover."

"Let's get started then, shall we Barry? Barry you have
seem to have gotten yourself into a lot of trouble."

"I do not think that is true Grover."

"Well none-the-less, you have. It's as simple as time itself
Barry. We the Gemini Dream Legion, we are what you
refer to as Immortal, we are forever. Even the doomsday
that your Earth will finally meet will have no effect on us.
We are special, God loves us. Unlike his Angels that came
first he asks nothing of us. We were created just to live in
peace together."

"Seems good, fate shines down on you, Grover?"

"So it does Barry. I am the first of my kind. Before me,
there was no Gemini Dream Legion. Barry, I created
everything you see from power handed to me by God. For
almost eternity I have ruled here and as every year goes
by my family gets larger and stronger."

"As it shows Grover, by the size of your manor. There's
plenty of space in here."

"I, Barry demand a lot of it. Let me continue. Myself and
those that I rule over are damned by not being born.
Myself and those that I rule over are also blessed with the
power of immortality. Can you conceive the fact that we
never die? Until you were created Barry."

"So the unwritten tale describes as to be truth, Grover."

"Yes indeed Barry. You so far have killed thirty nine members of my family. I have only two courses for you. Kill you as punishment for your crimes against The Gemini Dream Legion or make you one of us. Either way Barry you must die. I will give you one minute to give me your answer. Just kidding Barry. I just wanted to let you know that I have a sense of humor. Ha,ha,ha. No Barry you have more time than one minute, you have 'til tomorrow's dream and then I want your answer."

"I have to die to join you and your family Grover?"

"Yes that is correct. When you agree to join us, we will end your mortal life of existence. Then upon your death, Sam will be there to guide your soul safely out of your mortal shell before it has a chance to go to Heaven, Hell or Purgatory. So wake up mortal Barry Goldrum and enjoy your last day living on Earth for no matter what your choice is, tomorrow you will die. Goodbye Barry see you in your dreams."

Reality:

Barry wakes up pissed off and remembering what happened while he was dreaming, like it just happened in real life. Quickly Barry thinks to himself, 'I didn't get to make a response. Grover just blinked me away and awake. I didn't even fly back to my body. Did I even go back to it at all?'

'No forget that. I'm in my body and Grover is one strong immortal overlord. There was no fear in him, his eyes were clear and sharp with a little no soul added to them for shock value...'

'All others I have no fear of, Grover gives me a fright. What was the reason for such a short meeting? What did he have to lose if it went longer?'

'The size-up. Grover is not one that is use to making mistakes, he is in total control over all The Gemini Dream Legion. Grover did not give me long, but I learned some. Like what I was not suppose to notice. When Grover came floating in all slowly and slightly bumped into one of his other Elders. The look of fear in this Elder's eyes was a tell, that Grover is very evil, a killer of mortals in their dreams and even perhaps a killer of his family members?'

'That's it Grover has to be different, like myself he is the first of his kind. He is a monster. What will I become? Our comparisons are eerie. Like I am the other side of the coin. He is the dark, I am the light. Yeah just keep on putting thoughts like that in your mind and watch you become a tyrant of light and pureness after you defeat the dark...'

'Keep it together Barry. You do not want to own The DreamVerse. You just want to become stronger so you can protect yourself better and maybe help some good people from dying in their sleep unjustly. Fool, a hero dies a hero's death, the bad guy gets arrested if he gets caught.'

'I feed off dream food just like The Gemini Dream Legion. That is where we split, I'm alive, I'm mortal, they have never been mortal...'

'Before this amnesia, I was on a path to making money from some very, very bad people, after discovering what lies behind one or more of their memory dream doors. All I had to do was gather together their information and figure out a way to use it against them. Making them pay me to keep their information a secret.'

'I don't have to be greedy, there is no reason to go back into their dreams after a big score. Not when there are billions of dreamers on Earth and almost all of them with memory dream doors for myself to enter and discover their wickedness and sins.'

81

Barry stops thinking to himself and thinks of wanting to see the smile on Tina's face. He gives himself a few minutes with the picture of Tina's smiling face in his mind before he begins his second wave of thought process. A process that will keep him alive and on his way to financial stability.

'No I will not give this up, I worked too hard to be where I am now. How do I fight and survive against millions of immortals? Hiding and striking out only when I know I have the advantage. Big bonus for me if I die, only my mortality dies. I have another life, an afterlife, where I become an immortal. Grover and all of The Gemini Dream Legion only have one life, an afterlife that makes them an immortal...'

'They are souls that were never used inside a mortal shell. So no Heaven or Hell. Can this be true, what I am thinking now? The universe is not perfect, it makes mistakes or to be more precise when it creates life sometimes there are flaws unknowingly in the design. Is Grover and all the Gemini Dream Legion nothing but flaws? Souls that have no place in Heaven or Hell for they have never not sinned or sinned...'

'God? Satan? That's more thought than I have the time for right now. I have to get to Tina. I have to think how to survive when I sleep. I guess I can never dream again, I have to hide in dreamer's dreams. Then again when I change things in dreamers dreams, am I not using the power of dreams to do it? Yes that is it.'

'How will I get the REM's that my sleeping mind needs so I don't crazy? Is this true? Or am I just trying to give myself something? For I'm all alone, no way that I can tell Tina?'

'Imagine this, hey Tina I remember you, I remember the love we shared. But unfortunately there are millions of immortals waiting to kill me when I go to sleep. Her mind would fully snap. Can't take the chance of that happening to my beautiful and loving wife...'

82

'I will keep it to myself and try not to let it effect my mind. Life, I need to do nothing else but think about what I'm going to do when I go to sleep so I can save myself. But of course today that is the only thing I cannot think about. I gotta get going, time to see Tina.'

Barry enters Tina's hospital room, where she's sitting on her bed fully dressed, talking to Doctor Abbott, "Hey honey."

"Hey sweet thing, how are you?"

"Going home is that not right Doctor Abbott?"

"Yes you can but I highly advise against it. Mrs. Goldrum, Tina, you need to take these tests. They are the only way to rule out things that might be life threatening. They..."

"Like I have told you Doctor Abbott, I feel great, too damn great to be hanging around here. This bed that I am sitting on is for someone else that needs it. I'm fine, I've signed the papers that you need so I can be released today."

"Alright Tina, but you make sure that if for any reason you feel any symptoms like before you come back here without haste."

"That Doctor Abbott, I will make very sure of." Barry says joining in on the conversation. "I plan on propping my beautiful wife up in bed so she can get lots of rest. I will bring her her meals in bed, I will..."

"Like Hell you will, you're taking me out to brunch as soon as we leave here."

"Brunch?"

"Yes brunch, you do remember brunch don't you?"

"Yes, and I remember even more than that."

"You do? Come here Barry, look into my eyes and give me a kiss."

"That My Sweet, I can do and would very much like to."

Doctor Abbott watches as Barry and Tina stare into each other's eyes. Then he watches on as they both begin to laugh and Tina then begins to cry out of sheer happiness. Finally Doctor Abbott watches as Barry and Tina kiss each other like they haven't kissed in a week or more. Doctor Abbott thinks how strange to himself as things are just about to become even stranger for him to witness.

Barry and Tina stop kissing and Tina says, "There's my Barry Man Pie, in all your splendor. Forget brunch take me home and make love to me, make what happened rewind like it never happened at all. Can you do that Barry? Is everything back to normal?"

"Well as normal as I was before. If that's what you want back, my sweet Tina lady, you got it, with all moving parts nice and aligned back to full perfection."

"I love you Barry."

"I love you Tina, let's get out of here."

Doctor Abbott interrupts this strange moment of husband and wife by saying, "Hold on there are rules, Tina you have to exit this hospital by wheelchair. I will tell your nurse to have one brought here so you can leave. Remember you two, take care."

"We will Doctor Abbott and thank you." Tina replies.

"You're welcome Tina." Doctor Abbott walks away shaking his head and thinking to himself, 'Patients, they just don't understand. I'm trying to help. I just know that she will be back, for what she went through, I feel has that big repeat very soon feeling to it.'

"Barry I've missed you so much. You are back?"

"I'm back baby. Where do you want to eat?"

"Someplace different sounds great."

"I know just the place." Barry tells Tina with a smirk on his lips.

Barry and Tina eat at Grubs. Barry looks around not expecting to see Mary but looks for her none-the-less. Barry and Tina talk until Tina is satisfied that Barry is back to full mental capability.

They go home, Tina takes a shower and when she is out of the shower and standing there with a towel wrapped around her, she looks at Barry then lets the towel fall to the floor. Barry and Tina make love and later that night they go to bed together to get some sleep.

Barry does not know what he is going to do when he falls asleep. Barry is wondering this when Tina looks over at him and says to him. "I'm bushed, I didn't get a bit of sleep last night."

Tina rolls over and then she quickly rolls back to look at Barry, "I kept on having this same nightmare every time I fell asleep. It was about this man named Sam, he kept showing up and hitting on me, when I told him no, he got mad and made a monster appear, then I would wake up. Weird huh?"

"Yes that is very weird Tina. Here's to you never dreaming about him again."

"That would be nice, Good night, Barry."

"Good night Tina."

Barry Goldrum Verses
The Gemini Dream Legion

Chapter One:

(Reality: 2043, Three Years Later)

Barry is drinking bourbon by himself in a loud, crowded bar named 'Have A Drink Or Two.' He watches as two very disturbed and sick people interact with the other. The first is a bartender, the second is a waitress. They are cold blooded murderers, that kill for the thrill of it and of course, lots of cold cash taken out of cold dead hands. They have been running their murdering scam for years.

Barry to himself, 'The waitress looks like she would wear a shirt that reads "I Fuck Lots And Lots". Nothing wrong with that if she wasn't a murderer. But she is, so the murdering bitch is going down, along with her stupid looking and stupid minded wrapped around her crotch bartender boyfriend.'

Actually there are four people involved in this whole nasty business. These two and two more men that come and pick up the mark for the night. One man drives the unconscious mark in a truck to their home while the other man drives the mark's car.

In case you are wondering who this waitress sleeps with, well she sleeps by herself, but she does fuck all three of them. One man a night only, while the other two wait for their turn the next night or the night after that. No matter how much they beg the answer is always no.

When the mark is a female that means it is her night off from fucking and her three stupid men get to have fun with the woman until they kill her. She has to bring her whip out many times and beat the hides off them when they start fighting.

It's always the same argument, 'You killed her too soon.'
'I wasn't done with her yet.' 'Now what am I suppose to do,
I can't fuck her when she's dead.' Then like a pack of dogs
they attack the other until the alpha which is the waitress
comes running out of the house with whip in hand pissed
off because they disturbed her solitude once again.

Oh yeah, she doesn't allow them to bring their woman into
her house, so all this happens outside even in the dead of
winter. This all starts with something dropped into a glass
or a bottle. Tonight Barry is going to be their mark, he
made himself become that by showing off the thick wad of
money he has in his wallet.

Tonight Barry is going to make four murderers lives come
all apart at the seams. Barry was handed his drugged
laced bourbon, one bourbon ago. He acted like he
downed it but actually he dumped it under the table.

Barry is just about to finish his last bourbon so he can start
acting like he is totally out of it and ready to be gotten.
Barry knows the names of these sick four but he doesn't
care to say them in his mind.

Waitress comes up to him on cue, "You okay there honey,
looks like you drank too much tonight."

"I guess I did drink a little bit too much." Barry responds
acting like he's nice and drunk.

"I'd say honey you drank more than a little bit too much.
Here give me your hand and I'll take you to a place in back
where you can sleep it off until your ready to drive home."

"Thanks hottie that sounds great, wait a minute, you're
going to be laying down beside me aren't you?"

Waitress looks at Barry like she has him right where she
wants him, "Sure honey, I'll lay down with you if you want
me to. But it will cost you."

"No problem, I'll give you a big tip if you can get me off before I pass out. What's your name?"

"What is a name stranger? Just call me hottie."

"Hottie it is, come on Hottie, let's get it on."

Barry is led to a cot in the back of the bar. He grabs a hold of the waitress by her waist and acts like he is going to give her a kiss but instead he falls backwards on the cot all passed out drunk. "About damn time, I actually thought I might have to kiss you, you piece of shit."

Waitress makes herself feel better by kicking Barry a few times. She rolls Barry over so she can get to his wallet. Waitress opens up Barry's wallet and takes about a third of his money out of it and sticks it into the right front pocket of her too tight pair of blue jeans. She's putting Barry's wallet back into his back right pocket of his pants when there is a knocking at the back door of 'Have A Drink Or Two.'

Waitress opens up the back door and starts right in on her two stupid men, "About damn time you two showed up, the place is packed tonight with all kinds of marks. This is just our first for the night and the night is still young. So hurry the Hell up and take him home..."

"Do not kill him just tie him up. We're going to have some major fun tonight boys. We will wait until we are done for the night and how ever many marks we collect tonight, we will wait and kill them all at the same time. How does four marks sound to you two tonight?"

Both men look at Waitress without answering her, "Well answer me you stupid fools."

Waitress gets tired of waiting, "Never mind, I don't need your answers. I say four and it's four. Yes four is the perfect number for tonight, it feels lucky to me.

Hurry up and grab him. Make sure you keep your phones with you so you don't miss my call. I mean it, either or both of you piss me off tonight and I'll make you take off your clothes so I can whip you really good and hard. Do the both of you understand me?"

Both men say a simple yes at the same time, "Good now get the Hell out of here."

Barry is riding tied up and hooded in the back of a full size piece of crap truck. Time is up. Barry who is so much more than he was three years ago is getting ready to demonstrate just how much more powerful he is now. Barry now can tap into The DreamVerse at will. Which means all Barry has to do is bring out his dream twin into reality to untie himself.

Here is some very cool facts to be known about Barry's power level. Before, Barry's mortal shell was useless while his dream twin entered The DreamVerse, this has changed. Barry's dream twin now does not have to wait for Barry's mortal body to fall asleep to enter The DreamVerse. He uses it constantly doing whatever he wishes to do until Barry goes to sleep.

When Barry sleeps he takes over his dreams while his dream twin hangs most of his way outside Barry's body to stand guard against the mortal dangers of Barry's life.

(Barry has become two once again. This other that is his dream twin is not Larry. Who this is will be forth coming, to answer this mystery.)

Barry's mortal shell cannot enter The DreamVerse for it has substance. Barry's dream twin does not have substance so for Barry, the only human on Earth that can do this, brings his dream twin out of himself just far enough to untie him. As long as Barry's dream twin keeps in contact with the outside of Barry's body, he has substance, that can effect changes on Earth, good or bad.

89

No one but Barry can see his dream twin when he's hanging outside of his body. Which makes great offense and defense as well. Since his dream twin is part of The DreamVerse and the fact that Barry's dream twin controls his own dreams and whomever dreams it chooses to enter he can bring that power with him to the mortal side of life.

Like the power to create a three headed dragon for the driver of this beat up truck to see come flying down to him breathing fire. The fright that Barry's dream twin has effected on the minds of evil awake mortals is outstanding because of the sheer beautiful, horror of his imagination. Barry's dream twin's creations are only an illusion, they look as real as life and can make an evil awake mortal pray to them like they are a God or a Devil.

These creations cannot physically touch mortals, their only ability is to alter their minds. By achieving this this makes these evil awake mortals experience a day-mare that their soon to be fragile minds cannot handle. Their minds become putty for Barry's dream twin to sculpt into a very manageable mortal that is under complete control.

Barry is untied, he un-hoods himself as his dream twin stands up to check out what is going on with their surroundings. Barry's car is following behind them driven by who is to be referred to as Number Four, "You ready Barry for me to do my magic?"

"No wait until we get to their home."

"You still want me to create what you asked for me to create for these two stupid murdering mortals?"

"Yes I do, I want to have some fun with these two monsters before they pay the price for their sick murdering ways."

"Yeah damn murdering mortals, who needs them? Mortals, not one of them is worth a damn."

90

"I'm a mortal."

"Yes, but you're my mortal, which makes you okay."

"Wow, I'm okay. Man you better settle down before you get all emotional."

"Funny Barry."

"Why ain't you laughing then?"

"I never laugh, I only bring down the pain of justice on sinners."

"My ass, you're a horny immortal that spends most of your time entering beautiful women's dreams and having dream sex with them."

"Is it my fault that I'm lustful?"

"It is when you spend too much time getting dream laid instead of finding out what's behind a sleeper's memory dream doors."

"Hang on Barry we're slowing down, we're getting ready to turn onto a gravel road up ahead on the right." The ride down this gravel road is about ten miles until the gravel road turns into a hard, dry, dusty dirt road that leads through some very beautiful woods.

When the ride is over the piece of crap truck comes to a stop in front of a small nice looking house with flowers, bushes and trees spread through out the property that surrounds it. This helps give the house the appearance of nice and normal, with no bloody murderers living here just good, God fearing folks that give the Lord our prayers.

"Now Barry?"

"Fuck their minds up and then it's my turn to bend them to my will." Barry watches while still laying down in the back of the truck as a Heavenly cloud shaped UFO descends from the sky. It is loud, sounding mean with intense powerful brakes slowing it down for it to hover, thirty feet in the sky above the small out of the way house in the woods.

Number Three jumps out of the truck screaming out loud that God has come to Earth to pick him up and take him to Heaven. Number Four jumps out of Barry's car screaming the same thing.

It only takes twenty two seconds for these two buffoons to run into each other and knock the other to the ground. 1-2-3-4. Numbers Three and Four start fighting like God loves one of them more than the other. The UFO in the sky suddenly and eerily stops making a sound causing the fighting to stop as both buffoons stand up trying their best to get the best look they can at their savior in the sky.

In a few seconds both Number Three and Number Four will fall to their knees when they hear coming down to them from the sky, "You two, down on your knees!"

"You two, whose names are not worth speaking out loud, your souls are damned. You have murdered and murdered so many of our children, Hell will be your home after your deaths for your sins."

"Please forgive us. Please forgive us. Please forgive us." Number Three and Number Four shout out to the empty sky hoping beyond hope to save their souls from damnation.

"Silence, you two are pawns, however there may be hope for one of you murdering party of four. You two get in your truck and drive back to the bar where you collect your victims and pick up the waitress and bartender."

Number Three and Number Four, "Yes God."

92

"If they do not wish to come back with you, then you have our permission to bring them back to us for judgment by any means necessary. One thing you fools, do not kill them, bring both of them back alive. Until then the man you have in the back of your truck now has some of my power inside him so hands off him. Do you understand us you fools?"

Number Three and Number Four scream to the sky, "Yes Lord of Lords."

Number Three and Number Four are walking to the piece of crap truck as Barry is getting out of the back of it. Barry shouts out to the UFO, "Hey God can I show these mortals my power?"

"Yes chosen one you may." The UFO replies back to Barry.

Barry walks up to Number Three and Number Four and says, "Watch me hurt you without moving my hands, if you strike back I shall end your lives."

Number Three and Number Four stand still, stupefied as Barry without lifting a finger and with the help of his dream twin, punches them both in their faces causing them both to bleed. Barry is satisfied for now, "Now take the Hell off Fools and do as you are commanded to do."

Still begging for forgiveness Number Three and Number Four jump in the piece of crap truck and speed off as if death is chasing them.

Barry and his dream twin have a good laugh as Barry walks to the house after he first retrieves a bag he has stowed away in preparation from the trunk of his car. Barry walks into the unlocked house and looks around. Barry knows who is in charge of these four murderers so he looks around the house until he finds the waitress' bedroom.

Under the mattress is thousands of dollars that Barry puts into his empty bag. Barry walks out of the waitress' bedroom and looks around and spots a baseball bat lying in a corner.

"This is going to be fun." Barry says to his dream twin as he picks the bat up and starts smashing everything that is breakable in the house.

Barry and his dream twin wait patiently while Barry drinks a beer. Barry walks out of the house when he hears the truck coming up from the distance. Barry now walks to the side of the house just out of sight to wait to see what happens when there is no UFO in the sky like Number Three and Number Four told the waitress and the bartender there would be.

Barry holds back his laughter as a tied up Waitress screams for herself to be untied. As soon as Waitress is untied she begins to smack Number Three and Number Four in their dried bloodstained faces. As soon as Waitress gets tired of smacking them she runs into her house where everything is busted to pieces.

Waitress looks around at all the damage holding her breath. She lets out her breath then she begins to scream and cry, screaming, "All my shit is broken."

In shock Waitress remembers her bedroom and all the money that lies under her mattress. She falls to the floor crying saying, "Why me?" over and over again after she discovers all her money is gone except for one single dollar bill, laying on top of her pillow like a slap in the face.

Waitress stops crying, saying why me and gets off the floor. She walks over to her bedroom dresser and pulls out her .45. She then walks her .45 out of the house where she uses is to shoot Number Three and Number Four to their deaths.

Bartender still tied up stares at Waitress with fear in his eyes as she points the .45 at him and opens fire. Then in the sky the UFO reappears. Ten minutes later Waitress puts her .45 in her mouth and pulls the trigger.

Barry walks around to the front of the house straight to his car and drives away laughing his ass off, while his dream twin leaves him to go back into The DreamVerse. On the way home having a beer jumps into Barry's mind and he feels like obliging it, so he does and he makes a stop at 'The Perfect Place'.

Barry changes his mind from beer to scotch, he is on his second one as he decides to look around to check out all the wealthy, divorced ladies. All these divorced ladies are looking for something dumb, young and hung to help spend some of their ex-husband's money.

Some know nothing about Barry but a few ladies here tonight have had the delight of meeting Barry Goldrum. Sex, all these ladies came here tonight to find it until the few that know Barry come at him full speed like junkies willing to pay him any price for what he is selling.

Hot blond and built Karen is the first to spot Barry in this mass of rich Cougars and Beefcakes bar party. When Karen is three steps away Barry puts up his left hand for her to pause what she has to say. Barry drinks his scotch slowly, loving his power, the only power on Earth like it, over Karen and the other three ladies that are standing behind her. The only concern on their minds is how do I get the bitch in front of me out of my way, so I can get closer to Barry and his perfect dream tool for having lots of dream sex with.

Barry finishes his scotch and puts down his left hand, no need to count any seconds before Karen starts with her opening bid of one thousand dollars. It gets up to five thousand very fast with the bid from Miss Fourth in Line. Karen quickly takes top bid with six thousand.

Barry puts up his hand, Barry feels good, Barry wants to make more money by charging one of these ladies a heavy price to moan perfectly tonight.

"Ladies ten thousand and not one penny less."

"Ten thousand and Barry's mine."

"And the winner is Karen, I moan the hardest and best because I am richer than all of you other ladies, Roberts."

"Yes." Karen shouts out in victory.

"You know the way, pay into my account by noon tomorrow or dream your own sex dreams forever."

"I'd rather die than let that happen Barry."

"Would you Karen? Life is until you die, my dream I create for you is only an hour."

"Yes one hour, one hour that is perfect."

"I say sad and I also say the customer is always right. So let's find a table so you can dream your perfect dream."

Barry and Karen walk to a table and before they sit down Barry says, "My money?"

"Tomorrow I promise."

"Okay then, let's have a seat Karen, let me try to remember what you like your perfect dream to consist of."

"Yes remember what I want Barry, also remember not to start the count down before I start dreaming."

"I remember Karen, you want giant beast men all over your body, who are hung and seven foot tall.

You're rich and powerful and want to be used like a little plaything that is not allowed to say no to whatever they want to do to you."

"Um, that's not me, however if you change the men from seven foot tall to six foot tall that would be great for starters."

"Then what?"

"Well I do not want my six foot tall men to look like beasts, I want them sexy looking and hung, all four of them."

"Any thing else?"

"Yes one more. You have it switched around."

"I do?"

"Yes most definitely. My men cannot say no to me, not I can't say no to them, got it."

"Yes Ma'am."

Karen's dreaming mind is dreaming about four sexy men caressing and kissing her naked body, compliments of Barry's dreaming twin. Karen's mind may be dreaming about four men but it is solely Barry's dream twin who is making love to her dream body. Every paying lady gets the double loving impact of dreaming mind and dreaming body, without taking their clothes off.

Barry is drinking another scotch as Mandy who was third in line a moment ago is negotiating her chance to have an hour of dream sex herself tonight, "Please Barry, I'll do anything."

"Anything Mandy?"

"Yes and you know it."

"That's why you're my favorite Mandy. Okay, why not. Mandy if you get under the table and make me smile, I'll only charge you five thousand."

"Is that all? Barry I was going to do that anyway."

"Once again, that's why you're my favorite Mandy."

Mandy gets on her knees and looks up at Barry, "You know Barry it's a shame this is all you want from me. I would love to make love with you."

"Thank you Mandy... I'm like any man, I need the release. Making love to you or anybody just is not in my heart."

"Well Barry, you're a fool then, for I'm not after your heart, I just want your body. You have a great body and pecker."

"Thank you Mandy."

"Now if you'll excuse me Barry, I've got work to do."

"Please, by all means Mandy, get to work."

Karen is sleeping and moaning out loud, like she's having hot sex. Barry is kicked back and smiling as a fine looking, red headed, waitress walks over and notices Mandy's legs sticking out from under the table.

With her mouth open in shock, this hot red head, looks back and forth at Karen and a pair of legs until she finds the words to say, "Look here people, you can't do that here."

"It's all right beautiful, here take this." Barry pulls out his wallet and hands this sexy red head a thousand dollars to walk away.

Quickly Lacy grabs the thousand dollars out of Barry's hand.

Lacy puts her thousand dollar tip away and asks, "Which one?"

Barry is smiling bigger, "What beautiful?"

Lacy waves her hand, "Never mind, I know what I'm to do."

Barry watches as Lacy disappears under the table with Mandy. Barry waits a few moments to see if there's a change with his smile. Nothing changes but for some reason Mandy stops what she's doing and moans out loud, "Don't stop."

Barry looks around, with his smile becoming a frown. Mandy for some reason now says, "Stop, I can't take any more."

Barry listens harder as Mandy now says, "Make him smile for me beautiful, I can't move."

To make a long story shorter Barry finally gets to smile as big as he needed to. After that Mandy and Lacy start walking off together.

Barry, while zipping up his pants, interrupts them with a simple, "Thanks Red."

"No problem Dude. I'm Lacy, you have a great pecker. Now if you'll excuse us, it's my turn to smile."

Barry looks at his watch and crosses his legs because he has to take a piss and Karen still has fifteen minutes left. Barry passes the time by thinking to himself, 'What a place, what a day. I scored over seventy thousand from the sick, murdering four and ten thousand for just an hour of my time. Mandy and wow Lacy, they were so kind, thank you ladies, I feel great.'

Barry looks at his watch again, 'Damn only a minute has gone by.'

Barry dream's twin to Barry, "I've been through pleasing Karen for awhile so I checked out the remaining of her dream doors I haven't gotten to yet."

"And?"

"She clean, she's never taken a life."

"Are you sure? What about her husband? Whatever his name was. Karen had nothing to do with his death."

"Nope, she's clean."

"Well good. I thought for sure, she had her husband killed."

"What do you want me to do Barry?"

"Leave her in peace. Take all the memories of us away from her mind."

"What about the money she owes us?"

"Let her keep her last payment to us, for not being a murderess. Besides she's paid us enough over the past few months."

"Give me a minute."

"Hurry I have to take a piss."

Barry walks away to take his piss. A moment later Karen wakes up and looks around. Karen does not know why but she feels great. She grabs her purse and gets up and walks away. On the way out the door a young good looking man asks her if he can do anything for her.

Karen smiles and hands him, her car keys, "Drive me home stud."

Karen is nowhere in sight as Barry heads for the door, "Hey Barry, Lacy and I have been talking and thinking."

Mandy stops talking and gives Lacy a kiss. After she's through she continues on, "This is new to us, neither of us has done anything like this before..."

"Yes?"

Lacy finishes what Mandy was going to say, "We want you to join us. If you're up for it, that is?"

Barry's dream twin to Barry, "Don't let this pass you by, if you do you'll hate yourself forever. And like a good friend, I'll remind you every day how bad you fucked up."

"It would be my pleasure ladies, do me a favor, take it easy on me."

"If you want easy, find a girlfriend Barry. We're going to use you until you can't move." Lacy proclaims.

Barry's dream twin to Barry, "Barry you lucky bastard."

Barry, Mandy and Lacy leave together. As the the three of them are at the door, Lacy's boss ask her where she's going. Lacy smiles, turns around and says, "I'm out of here, I quit."

For the next three hours Mandy and Lacy make Barry go and go some more until Barry can't help himself anymore and falls asleep.

Lacy to Mandy, "Men, they can never keep up."

"You're so right about that Lacy. Great thing about men now, we only need them when we want them from now on."

"Smart and beautiful, Mandy I think I'm in love with you."

"You better be Lacy, without you, I don't know if I could do this."

"Don't worry Mandy, I'm all yours."

The next morning Barry finishes the breakfast that Mandy and Lacy made for him in bed. Mandy hands Barry the morning paper and pulls the covers off of him. Barry shakes his head, "Life is so great sometimes"

An hour later Barry takes a shower and puts the clothes on from the bag he always keeps handy in his trunk for reasons like last night. Barry gives Mandy and Lacy a thank you and a goodbye hug and walks out the door.

Barry gets in his car and drives downtown to a children's shelter and gives the seventy thousand dollars to the couple that owns it, with the only agreement that Barry's name is never mentioned.

Tears in Mrs. Williamson's eyes roll down her cheeks as she is pouring Barry a cup of coffee. "Mr. Goldrum thank you so much," Mr. Williamson says as a crying Mrs. Williamson repeats three times thank you to Barry.

"My pleasure, I know you are good folks that spend every day of your lives taking care of homeless children of all ages. I was homeless when I was a punk kid and your father took me in Mr. Williamson, right here in this very same shelter. I look around and great memories come racing back to my mind. I was ten when your father arranged for the Goldrum's to adopt me. After that I lived a good life with the Goldrum's maybe not the grand one I dreamed about having before I was adopted but one that got me off the streets and on my way to where I am now in my life."

"Is there anything that we can do for you Mr. Goldrum?" Mr. Williamson asks.

"No nothing. Wait there is one thing. I want the two of you to take some of that money and spend it on yourselves. I know you two, so what you spend on yourselves does not have to cost much."

"It's a deal," Mr. Williamson says with a smile on his face. Barry leaves the shelter after one quick look around.

It is almost lunch time and Barry's kind of hungry so he drives to Grubs for a burger and a beer. When Barry enters Grubs he hears his name being called out from a voice he has not heard in quite some time, "Barry!"

"Hello Shelly, it's been awhile."

"Too long, come on over and sit down with me." Barry walks over to Shelly, who just happens to have been Tina's best friend and was a big support for Barry after Tina's death.

After a few minutes of casual conversation, Shelly moves on to how long it has already been since Tina died. Barry agrees out loud but in his mind is the knowledge that when he goes home and is all alone the memory of Tina's death, three years ago, will occupy his mind until he relives the whole bloody story from start to finish.

Shelly looks down at the table upset with herself, she wanted to have a nice talk with Barry, "Barry I'm sorry, I don't know why I brought up Tina. I'm ashamed about what happened between us."

"Shelly you were my savior. I just woke up from a coma that lasted for six months. My last memory was going to sleep one night six months ago with Tina. Then I wake up in a hospital, I asked where's Tina. They asked me questions, not giving me the answer to the only question I asked. I asked again, this time adding my wife. The Doctor starts to talk then stops herself. Then tells me that there is time for that later, Mr. Goldrum.

She continued on, right now you need to get some rest, you have been in a coma for six months. I jerk away from the needle saying I've slept enough, where the Hell is my wife..."

"The next afternoon you came to visit me after I found out that Tina died of an aneurysm the same night six months ago that I fell into a coma. I was down, like my life was nothing but a bad dream. The smile on your lips with tears in your eyes as you gave me the love of friendship..."

"Holding your hand was a slice of nice warm reality my lost in my dreams mind needed to help me keep a balance with reality. I was slow recovering, you kept coming back, my anchor as I fought a war in my mind, (In his dreams.) until I won."

"It was the least I could do for Tina, I loved her and I loved you as friend. You were so sad, I was so sad, we needed each other to lean on."

"One month later I left the hospital, I had no home, you took me in. We lived together for a month as best friends."

"Then one night we made love for hours until we fell asleep embraced like lovers. I woke up the next morning and you were gone, leaving only a note simply saying, 'Thank you and I'm sorry'. Barry I was so confused and angry that I lost my best friend and new lover after sharing only one night together."

"Shelly, what we shared was soft, tender hours that both of us wanted and I needed to help me be able to finally move on with my life. At first I felt like I betrayed Tina, that is why I took off and didn't call you."

'Can't tell her the truth, that it was not my choice to leave but God's. And it was more than one time we made love together.'

"Yes then ten months later we bumped into each other, we had drinks, we drank them, I thought you wanted to get something slowly started together. We kissed and you were to follow me home. And then you never showed up."

"I'm sorry Shelly."

"Barry, I was so angry with you, then my mind cleared. I could not believe that what I wanted with you was so strong in my heart. Then it came to me that I was in love with you.

"I didn't know. In my heart, I felt love for you but..."

"But that is over with now?"

"Yes."

"Good, I'm in love with someone and I just want to be your good friend."

"That's great Shell and here's to friends." Barry lifts his beer bottle up as a salute.

Barry and Shelly eat and drink another beer together before saying goodbye with a big friend hug. Barry goes home and takes a shower then he sits in front of the TV and starts to think of what happened that strange and sad night three years ago.

Chapter Two:

"Yes that is very weird Tina. Here's to you never dreaming about him again."

"That would be nice. Good night, Barry."

"Good night Tina."

'This is the last thing Tina and I said to each other before we fell asleep. I rolled over behind Tina and squeezed her. I laid there holding Tina in between being wake and falling asleep until my left arm fell asleep, then I turned around and a few minutes later I was asleep.'

'I entered The DreamVerse ready for war and all I found was Sam.'

"What's going on Barry? Are you ready to follow me to see Grover?"

"Sure Sam let's go."

'I let Sam fly about a thousand miles in front of me before I attacked him without warning. I sliced and beat him down, then flew away. Another thousand miles I flew as fast as I could until I found a nice dream to hide myself in and gather more strength from my consumption of dream food.'

'The sleeper's dream that I entered first was a very boring little man that was dreaming of people being nice and talking to him like he did not receive while he was awake. I could only take about ten minutes in this man's dreams before I changed it.'

'I took example from Sam and Larry and changed this little boring man's dream into a nightmare. A nightmare filled with growling, large fury, four legged beasts that were running around everywhere fighting each other out of wildness and anger.'

'Boring dreams, bland dream food. Nightmare's make dream food so much more tasty and satisfying. They build strong dream bodies for flying around The DreamVerse.'

'I was feeding fast and hard on this man's dream food, not caring what was happening to him when his intense scream brought my mind back around.'

'His scream, in his eyes there was terror. Like this was the first time he'd ever seen, nightmare creatures like this before in one of his dreams. No nightmares?'

'My beasts wait for their cue of the first scream then they spotted the dreamer. I erased my beasts from sight when they were half way to getting to this dreamer, for fear of the dreamer having a heart attack in real life.'

'I tried something a little less scary and no good, this boring man's dream food was stale. So I slipped out of his dream to find a better and more stronger sleeper whose dream that I could turn into a nasty, bloody nightmare without them dying on me.'

'I found a man that liked to play the hero of his dreams, when I watched his dream of himself killing a dragon. I stayed for about an hour creating monsters and beasts for him to slay. Just like a game every new monster or beast was stronger and more vicious than the one that came before them.'

'I ate good, this dreamer's dream food was chock full of dreaming vitamins that was so good for my dreaming mind and body. A body that is only a frame my mind creates as I go dream hoping or flying through The DreamVerse.'

(Everybody that dreams creates a dream self for their dreams to interact in and with. Some mortals can altar their dream selves here and there but nowhere even close to what Barry can do.

107

In a dream, the only limits are the dreamer's limits that their conscious sets up for their dreaming minds to reach before a danger alert wakes up their mortal body.)

'I jumped out of this warrior's dream but not before I found out his name, Michael Mellow. It's funny, just like the saying the voice does not match the face, it's the same here, a dreamer's dream self doesn't always match his awake self. I found out this was the case with Michael Mellow a few days after the last night I spent with Shelly.'

Michael's dream self was pumped up extra compared to his mortal body. Which means that through mental will only, this dreamer was getting closer to stepping out of his dreams more so than any other dreamers I had made contact with so far.'

(Michael Mellow was hit by a stray bullet. In an attempt not get shot again Michael took off running, unfortunately he did not check both ways before crossing the road and got ran over by a car doing the speed limit but the driver had no chance to step on their brakes before bumping over Michael twice making him paralyzed from the neck down.)

Barry stops thinking about Michael Mellow and takes a pause. Barry might have stopped thinking about Michael but his part in this story so far has only just begun.

'I was pumped and ready for some more dream jumping. What came next was something that I was not expecting. I was fresh out of Michael's dream, I looked around, I was all by myself within this part of The DreamVerse.'

'I knew I had one maybe two dreams that I could get to until I spotted several of The Gemini Dream Legion flying around trying to find me and take me to Grover. Or perhaps that had ended and now was to be killed on sight.'

'I flexed my powerful dream self like bring it on, I'm a one of a kind that will not be stopped, I will take over instead.

I flew three hundred miles and inserted myself into a dreamer's dream. There I stood frozen, hating what I was watching but I could not stop myself from watching.'

'I felt ashamed for thinking to myself that I did not have the time for this, to give this lady a helping hand. A helping hand that might just end the same constant true to life nightmare that she dreams perhaps every night. One of her Memory Dream Doors is wide open, feeding her, painful memories that she does not have the dream strength to close and lock forever to end her pain.'

'I will not say her name, she has suffered enough. I will call her Blossom. Blossom was laying on the floor, then on a bed, then she was on a table. Every time with the same faceless man that is used her for his sexual pleasure. All Blossom did was say no please don't. Please no more. Please kill me, I don't want to live like this anymore.'

'I was sick and feeling pissed so I created a hero to save Blossom from her endless torment. The hero rose and with sword in hand he struck the beast. Nothing happened. I stepped closer to Blossom's dream self until I was standing right above her and she could not see me.'

'I brought forward the hero I created for her to see. Nothing she just laid there on this ugly green couch saying no please stop, to this faceless man that never stopped having sex with her like he owned her. Then Faceless says to Blossom, say you like it Blossom, tell me not to stop, tell me you love me, tell me that you love it that I own you as my sex slave.'

'Blossom for the first time showed a sign of anger and told Faceless that she hated him and that she would never love him. Faceless said yes but you love this I know and then he started to sex Blossom as hard as he could until Blossom's no's turned into a yes.'

'With a to shock to my ears Blossom said things to Faceless that I do not want to remember. I thought about walking out of this twisted dream that seemed to be what Blossom wanted? I stopped myself and looked over at the opened up Memory Dream Door then I looked back at Blossom pinpointing my eyes to her face. There I saw tears falling from her eyes and running down her face.'

'I walked over to her opened Memory Dream Door and stepped in. Blossom was abducted by a man whose face I still cannot see, even in here. He did not want money, he did not want to kill or hurt Blossom, all he wanted to do was to own Blossom for sex. Faceless kept Blossom as his sex slave prisoner for two or three years before she escaped one day when he was away at work. The night before the morning of her escape Blossom was put back into her sound proof hidden room, untied to go to sleep.'

'Earlier that night Faceless was having her any way he wanted and while he was enjoying his lust, Blossom was taking the ropes that were tied around her wrists and making them rub harder and harder against her flesh. Moments later Blossom was bleeding and crying. When Faceless finished he looked at Blossom's wounds and could not believe what he had done to her. Quickly Faceless apologized to Blossom telling her how sorry he was and how much he loved her and could not live with himself if anything happened to her.'

'With lots of pain showing Blossom convinced Faceless not to tie her up that night. The next morning as Faceless was eating the breakfast Blossom cooked for him, with lots of throbbing pain still emitting from her wounds, Blossom convinced him once again not to tie her up before he went to work, just to put her in her room so her wounds could heal faster. She had secretly hidden a key in her room for her escape that Faceless knew nothing about.'

110

'Blossom, one night a few months ago, had grabbed the key to her room's door lock off the table and held on to it tightly until Faceless was done with her for the night. Blossom went to the bathroom, she cleaned herself up and hid the key the only place she could. Painfully, naked Blossom walked to the kitchen and made Faceless a sandwich. She watched him eat with a smile on her lips and hate for him running through her mind until she felt the pre-ecstasy of her upcoming escape.'

'Faceless took this feeling away from Blossom when he said to her.'

"Blossom you were great tonight, how great was I?"

Blossom held her breath and cleared her eyes of hate and responded calmly back to Faceless, "You get better every day. I'm already looking forward to tomorrow. What do you want me to wear for you tomorrow night? Do you want me to wear something you want to tear off me? Or do you want me to wear something you want me to wear all night long?"

Faceless wants all night long and then he says to Blossom, "Why wait for tomorrow, I want you again right now. Come to me my Blossom and lay yourself across this kitchen table in front of me."

'Blossom knows Faceless so well, that he's just boasting and cannot go again. He's through for the night. Blossom made sure of that by making him wait and wait 'til he exploded so she could enjoy him more. Lies mixed with truth. Blossom hates Faceless but she cannot stop a part of herself for loving the way he treats her. That she is so beautiful and sexy that Faceless had no choice out of want and love for her to grab her up and keep her all to himself and away from the rest of the world.'

"I would love that. You tell me when, you tell me how baby and I'm all yours."

Blossom walked over to the kitchen table and laid down on top of it all naked and sexy looking. She looked at Faceless who was still eating his sandwich and said, "Stop eating that damn sandwich and please me again like only you can, please I want you so bad."

'In the back of Blossom's mind was the thought of what if she is wrong and Faceless can go again. What is going to happen when he feels the sharp key that is hidden in what faceless loves so much.'

'This thought made Blossom laugh out loud causing Faceless to get mad.'

"Are you laughing at me?"

Blossom stopped laughing quickly and said, "No Faceless, I'm just so happy that unlike most nights you can go more than once. You know that I want you to enjoy me as much as you can every night. You just love it when I tell you no please no more, I cannot take anymore. And that Faceless is the truth, you are just too much man for me to handle all by myself, I think you need to bring us home another lady just like me so you can enjoy yourself even more. You know you deserve it. Now please, please me all night long."

'Blossom waited to see what happened when Faceless stood up on his feet. Moments later out of frustration Faceless tells Blossom to get off the kitchen table that it is time to go to sleep. Faceless walked Blossom to her room, when she was safely inside he reached into his pocket for the key to Blossom's door so he could lock them both in until she was safely tied up.'

'It wasn't there, so Faceless had Blossom follow him back to the kitchen, but he couldn't find the key. Then Faceless had Blossom follow him to the living room right up to the ugly green couch.'

'Blossom stood naked and shivering from being cold but on the inside she was calm and cool, as Faceless searched everywhere for the key, even taking the cushions off the ugly green couch to look under them.'

"I don't remember, did I wave the key to your prison in your face as I made love to you Blossom?"

"I don't remember. I was so into it, all I could think about was how great your manhood is. I'm sorry you can't find your key to my prison. Would you like for me to help you look?"

"Yes that would be nice."

"You know Faceless, I think this is a sign."

"A sign?"

"Yes a sign. You have always told me since you first decided to own me that when you feel that you can completely trust me you will allow me to sleep in the same bed as you. Can tonight be that night? I would love to be held by you when I sleep, I get so lonely without you."

"Yes I know and I love you for that. I almost feel that very soon you will be able to take your first step at eventually becoming my wife."

"I cannot wait for that Faceless, it's all I can think of. I mean me and only me that you chose to become your wife. At first and forgive me for this, I thought you were crazy until I finally realized that you were right. If you love someone enough the only way that you can make sure that they love you as much as you love them is to force your love on to them. I love you now, let's sleep to together tonight as future husband and wife."

"I love you Blossom but no. I have to put you in your room tonight.

I need some sleep and I cannot have any distractions."

"Of course you are right what was I thinking? I do not want to be a distraction to you, so yes I agree you should tie me up and put me in my bed to sleep tonight."

"Yes Blossom I am always right and never am I wrong. I am so glad you finally figured that out. Wait a minute, do you have my key?"

"No."

"Are you sure?"

"Yes I'm sure, look at me, where would I have a key?"

"I don't know, maybe someplace that you think that I would not look."

"Gross Faceless, I would never do that. You hurt me so Faceless, you know how bad I feel for letting all those men that came before you have me. You know how much I would love to go back in time and stay untouched for you."

"Yes I know. But I told you not to mention the other men anymore that you defiled yourself with."

"I'm sorry, can I please you now?"

"No not now, I need to find my key first."

"Goody, goody."

"Why did say that?"

"Because after we find your key I get to please you."

"No you don't."

"Yes I do, you told me that I could."

114

"Well never mind Blossom you have to wait 'til tomorrow night. Now stay here, I'm going to get my extra key so I can lock you up for the night."

"Okay Faceless anything you say."

'That night Blossom had her hands tied together and was helped nicely into bed. When she was alone with only the light of a small nightlight shining she removed the key that would very soon lead her to her freedom. Blossom cried from the pain of the damage the key did to her most tender spot.'

'Every day for the next few months Blossom became stronger inside herself until the night before her escape. That night she wanted Faceless to tie her back up for sex after he untied her when got home from work. Greedy Faceless complied with Blossom's wishes and tied her up real tight.'

'Tight enough to hurt her and make her bleed he thought. The next day, the day of her escape, Blossom was let out of her room to make breakfast for them and she convinced Faceless not to tie her up for the day. It was one hour after Faceless left for work that Blossom walked out of the house that she had been a prisoner in for three years, four months and sixteen days.'

Blossom's skin was so pale in the sun. The sun she had not felt since the day she was abducted. Blossom walked away from Faceless' house of dirty sex and on down the sidewalk. She thought to find a cop, tell him or her what this monster did to her. They would ask her why did it take so long for her to escape. How could she tell anyone that she liked it? The sex was great just being a prisoner sucked really bad.'

'She asked herself am I warped now? Can I ever go back to how I was before? But she did not wonder for too long because she heard a man's voice coming from a car that had pulled up beside her.'

"Do you need a ride pretty lady?"

Blossom looked at the male driver that was already taking off her dress in his mind and said, "Yes I do."

'They drove for thirty eight miles before this horny man pulled over to a hotel to get them room to have sex in for the rest of the day. Blossom so used to playing whatever role that Faceless sent her way had now discovered that with little effort she was in control of this man. She made him beg, she made him bark, then she let him have her, while she told him to please her more.'

'This man was so enthralled with Blossom that he did not even see the ashtray coming to the back of his head. Blossom took his wallet and his keys and drove two hundred miles before she pulled over at a diner where she waited until she found the next Mr. Right to drive her far away from there.'

'Blossom did this over twenty times more and every time these men got the lay of a lifetime. So many of these twenty plus men fell in love with Blossom as she used them for a ride and their money until the last man that gave her a ride. He was perfect, weak and harmless so Blossom made him marry her a week later. This is where this Memory Dream Door's story ends.'

'I stepped out of this Memory Dream Door and into another one that was only ten feet away. In this Memory Dream Door I discovered that Blossom used her husband, even to the point of bringing men home with her to have sex with in front of him.'

'One day Blossom came home with a man in hand to have some fun with, but both of them were turned off when they discovered Blossom's husband dead from putting a bullet through his brain.'

116

'Blossom's husband left a note that read.'

'I loved you at first sight. I loved you even more after we got married. But now you have turned into a slut that I do not want to live with anymore. So I end my life, I hope my blood stains your soul forever.'

'The unlucky man that came home with Blossom ran out of her house never to be seen again.'

'Blossom sat down next to her dead husband and cried. Slowly her mind started to remember all the things that her husband did for her. Like bring her home flowers and take out food from her favorite restaurant just in case she did not feel like cooking that night. Her husband loved her with all his heart and Blossom loved him in return however she was warped which made her love turn into something that did not resemble love anymore until he took his own life because of it.'

'How far has she fallen Blossom asked herself as she reached for the pistol that ended her husband's life. With tears in her eyes and very shaking hands, Blossom put the barrel of the pistol in her mouth and squeezed the trigger.'

'Nothing happened, Blossom was still alive so she squeezed the trigger of the pistol again and again until she discovered that there was only one bullet put into the gun, the bullet that ended her husband's life.'

'Hours later the police took Blossom to their station where they tried to get answers from her for hours until they gave up and took her to a sanatorium. There Blossom has stayed until the night I showed up in her dreams.'

'I walked out of her Memory Dream Door and back to Blossom's dream self where she was still being used for her body by Mister Faceless.'

'What could I do for her, I did not know. I tried to grab a hold of Faceless and pull him off of Blossom but my hands went straight through him. Then I got it, Faceless was not real, he's just the nightmare that Blossom created for herself so she could never forgive herself for what she made her husband do to himself.'

'I didn't know what would happen but I tried anyway. I put my right dream hand on Blossom's forehead trying my best to enter her dream. It was hard as Blossom resisted me until I finally broke through into her nightmare.'

'When Blossom noticed me in her nightmare that changes but never ends, she screamed at me to get out and stay out. I did not comply as I walked closer to her. Blossom got so mad at me that she sicced Faceless on me. Faceless came at me trying his best to destroy the man that entered his creator's nightmare. He hit me and I knew that as long as I remembered that he was only a creation that his hits would have no effect.'

'Being one of a kind, the same could not be said for Faceless when I grabbed him and knocked him on his ass. Blossom stopped screaming and looked over at Faceless. Blossom closed her eyes and when she opened them back up again, Faceless was not faceless anymore. No, now plain as day was the face that abducted her and had dirty sex with her over and over again.'

Blossom screamed at her creation, "I know you, I remember you now, I will make you pay for what you did to me for I remember where you live."

Blossom smiled as she walked over to me and gave me a great big hug. I didn't know what was happening at first until I discovered what I was feeling in my dream self was a different kind of dream food. A dream food that only I have access to. A dream food that made the other kind of dream food I ingested seem like only the appetizer before the main course.'

118

'It's the sweet and the bitter. The Gemini Dream Legion, ingest only bitter, just like myself at that point. I felt so powerful as I left Blossom's nightmare. A nightmare that had now become just a simple dream where she was standing on top of a mountain. With tears drying Blossom looked down at her past life of horrors that would no longer have the power to effect her life.'

'Full of hope I stepped out into The DreamVerse where there were thousands of the Gemini Dream Legion looking for me. They spotted me and hundreds of them attacked me. I fought for my life as I became a monster to them, one that could not be defeated or destroyed. My steel wings sliced the air as my claws ripped the heads off of every member of the Gemini Dream Legion that flew up to me for battle. In just a few minutes hundreds of them were dead as I grew stronger and not weaker.'

'The rest of the Gemini Dream Legion that didn't attack me flew away to safety. I gathered up my speed and flew straight to my mortal shell. When I got within ten miles of it, I spotted Grover there in waiting. I flew faster and harder straight at Grover, he didn't move an inch. In his eyes there was no fear as I collided with him. The pain I felt was like nothing, I could ever imagine feeling before that day.'

'Grover did not move as I bounced off him in tremendous pain. Grover laughed and called me a weak fool that was way out of his league. Grover stopped laughing and flew towards me to take my life. I watched as he got closer and closer to me until I finally told myself to get my ass flying to safety. Just in time I moved before Grover could strike me down and dead with his immense power.'

'Everyday for the next six months I gathered my strength until the day I was strong enough to knock Grover the Hell out of my way so I could finally reenter my mortal shell. During my six months of gathering strength I entered many dreams of good and bad people.

I helped some with the power from my dream power by creating in their dreams what they needed to free themselves. Others I helped like I did with Blossom.'

'During my six months stuck inside The DreamVerse I would enter the dream of a dreaming child time to time. I would look around making myself invisible as soon as I discovered I was in a child's dream. After my look around I would leave causing no harm or help. A few times I could not help myself, these few children that I helped needed it.'

'They were helpless inside their nightmare confronting their monster let alone defeat it. All the children that I helped were not only having nightmares they were living them in reality as well and so sadly just as helpless. I did some good I know but every time I think of why I had to help, it pisses me off and brings me down.'

'These memories are in my mind, so to help push them to the back of my mind, I will think of only one. Not too heavy, I got it. I'll remember a young boy of the age of seven named Tommy that I helped him get out of his dreaming and living nightmare.'

'Tommy was the name his mother called him but his name was not Tommy it was Tony and she was not his real mother. When Tony was four years old his real mother had the fear of fears come at her. Diana took her son Tony to the park where he played with the friends of the mothers that she was friendly with. It was just a slight moment when she was not paying attention and when she looked back at where her son was suppose to be, her son was not there, he was being taken out of the park in the other direction.'

'Diana in panic yelled out for her son to call out to her. When Diana did this everybody looked at her and finally when everyone knew what was going on it was too late. Tony along with the woman that abducted him, named Diana as well, was out of of sight.'

Diana screamed, "Where's my son?" As her son was softly, forced into the back seat of Diana's new car.

"Buckle up sweetheart, Mommy has to drive us away from here in a hurry."

Tony screamed, "Where's my mommy? Mommy please help me."

With a soft and calm voice, a very confused Diana said to Tony, "I am here sweetheart. Now please stop crying because on the way home we are going to stop for ice cream."

"You're not my mommy."

"Don't be silly sweetheart, I'm your mommy."

Tony kept on crying for his mother as Diana said, "Hush Tommy everything is alright."

Tony yelled at Diana, "My Name is Tony not Tommy."

Diana said, "Don't be silly Tommy. Wait a minute are we playing a new game Tommy, where you play that your name is Tony?"

'Before Tony could answer, Diana told him that she did not like this game and they were no longer going to play it. No stop for ice cream because Tommy was being such a bad boy by continuing to say that his name was Tony.'

'By the time Diana and Tony pulled into Diana's driveway Tony was not crying anymore, his young mind was so confused. Diana was already inside his mind making him question already what was real or not.'

'Diana was so happy that she sang out loud, softly some old love song that Tony never heard before but liked.

Diana still singing got out of her car and opened up the back door and helped Tony out of her car. There she took him by his hand and led him to the front door of her house. She did not let go of his hand as she unlocked her door with the key ready to use in her other hand.'

When they entered the house Diana told Tony, "Go to the bathroom and wash up Tommy, while I fix us some lunch."

"I am not Tommy, I am Tony."

Diana got mad and said to him, "Enough of your stupid game Tommy now go wash your hands."

Scared Tony asked, "Where is the bathroom?"

Diana shook her head with a smile, "It's where it's always at sweetheart."

Tony to himself, 'This is a bad dream and very soon I will wake up and my real mommy will be here to hold me tight.'

It was later in the evening of the same day while Tony was watching TV and Diana was cooking dinner that Diana's husband William walked into the house just a little late from work, "Hello Darling, Diana, I'm home, something sure smells great, I'm starving."

Diana walked out of the kitchen to the front door to welcome home her very soon to be confused husband, "Hello William it is so good to see you, I missed you. I want you to go up and take a shower then come back down here because I have a very big surprise for you."

William laughed and asked, "Did you buy a new new pair of shoes or a new dress?"

Diana just smiled and laughed saying, "Much better than that my dear, now please go clean up for dinner."

122

Before William did what Diana told him to do he asked her, "Why is the TV on?"

"You have to wait until later because why the TV is on is part of my big surprise for you."

'Twenty minutes later William walked back into the kitchen and gave his loving and beautiful wife a hug and a kiss. Diana asked William if he was ready for his surprise. He nodded his head yes while smiling loving that his wife was in such a great mood and was glad that whatever it was in their living room made her so happy. He could not wait to find out what it was so he could share in her enjoyment.'

William hand in hand with his wife walked to their living room, when they reached it they walked into it together still hand in hand. William said, "What the Hell?" As he spotted a young boy that he'd never seen before sitting on their couch watching TV.

Diana not pleased with her husband, "Watch your language William!"

"Who is this young boy Diana?"

Diana did not answer, she just looked at William. William not knowing what was going on looked over at the boy and asked, "Who are you son?"

Tony looked at William and felt like he could trust him, "I am Tony."

Now it's time for Diana to speak, "Do not start that again, Tommy, mommy told you not to play that game anymore."

William, looked in confusion at his wife, "What is wrong with you my dear? This is Tommy, I found him. I told you he was alive, I told you someone took him. Don't you feel the fool now for burying an empty coffin? Well what do you have to say for yourself my dear?"

"Diana my darling, your mind is very fragile right now, but I need you to understand me and be calm when I tell you this little boy is not our son, he is not Tommy."

"No that's not true, he's my Tommy."

"No Diana, this boy is someone else's son. Now tell me my darling where did you find this boy?"

'Diana did not answer, she just looked at William once again with eyes of disbelief, she couldn't believe the words that her husband was saying to her.'

William said, "Tony come to me son, let's get you home, back to your mommy and daddy."

'Tony smiles and got up really fast and started to walk just as fast to William. William did not even think about whether he should turn his back to Diana or not which was a very big mistake.'

Diana eyes turned darker as she grabbed a lamp and broke it over her husband's head, "I love you William, with all my heart but I will not let even you, stop me from having my son back, my Tommy back."

'William knelt on the floor, holding his bleeding head as Diana picked up a very sharp piece of the broken lamp and plunged it deep into his throat. William couldn't believe what his wife had just done to him and he tried his best to ask her why but due to his wound all he could do was gurgle blood out of his throat.'

'William laid dying on the floor as Diana walked towards Tony who was frozen in fear, "Tommy you need to be strong my son, that was not your father. It may have looked like him on the outside but on the inside that creature had the Devil in his soul.'

Tony looked at William without saying a word in response,

"Tommy my one and only son, I know this is so very hard for you to understand. On the day you were born as Tony, my son Tommy's body died, from a defective heart. With great enjoyment my son's soul did not fly to Heaven his soul flew straight into your body where no soul laid. Tommy I know you don't remember the life you lived before but with my help in time you will remember everything."

Tony continued to look at William still not saying a word in response, "Now if you have to go to the bathroom you better do it now because we have to leave here in a few minutes. Tommy I love you so much."

'Three years have passed, as Diana day by day, made sure she took the very best of care of her son while they have been on the run. A son that now remembered the past life they shared together.'

'Tony has kept this Memory Dream Door ajar so he will not forget even though when he wakes up he only thinks it is the same nightmare he dreams every night. Poor Tony I had to help him. What kind of creature could I create that would not snap his fragile dreaming mind. A cute talking dog was my choice.'

'Tony's nightmare is on replay every night, it gets to the point where he finally believes that he is Tommy and it starts all over again. He is on the part where William lies dying on the floor when I send in Rover to talk to him."

"Hello Tony I am Rover come over here and pet me please." Rover had to repeat this three times before Tony looked over at him. In the back of his mind Tony knew that he was supposed to stay there frozen in fear but Rover was so cute and cuddly looking, that for the first time in three years he broke the cycle of his nightmare.'

"That's it Tony pet me, I am a good dog, I am your friend. Now look at the woman that thinks she is your mother. She has no power over you here if you do not want her to.

125

Watch as she still thinks that she is talking to you. If you want her to stay out of your dreams Tony all you have to do is wish her to disappear. Just keep on petting me Tony use my friendship for you to help her disappear. Now Tony give me a great big hug and close your eyes and when you reopen them she will be gone forever from your dreams."

'I watched as Tony gathered his strength making Diana disappear from his nightly nightmare.'

"Open your eyes Tony you did it, she is gone. Now Tony you have to be very brave when you wake up. Can you do that for me Tony?"

'Moments later Tony woke up full of confidence and grabbed the phone of a still sleeping Diana and called 911. A few days later I re-entered Tony's dream, what I found was a young man that found his way home but was still so mixed up. So I recreated Rover for him to talk to and within a few minutes after I made Rover go away Tony had the power enough inside him to create Rover all by himself to help him deal with all that he was going through. I wish Tony my very best and I believe that eventually he'll put his mind back together.'

'There are so many dreamers that had something so very bad happen to them in reality. Something that they could not stop or control coming at them like a living nightmare. In some cases like Blossom and Tony they have Memory Dream Doors that are opened up. Doors with memories that are suppose to be locked away so the dreamer can dream normally.'

'These unfortunate dreamers open up these doors themselves to punish themselves even if they do not deserve it. The bad, the killers, the rapist and the extremely sick, I did not help them. I gave them nightmares that fit their crimes. Almost every one of these dreamers worst fear was to have happen to them what they did carelessly to others.'

126

'Then there are some that got off on it. Their true to life nightmare had no effect on them no matter how far I went. If I had no mortal shell or no conscience, living an afterlife like this would be so compelling and free to take whatever I wanted from dreamers no matter what the cost it would be to their lives.'

'Fortunately I have both so I didn't push myself past the limits when it came to taking a life. Sure I fucked with their minds making them scream and bleed but before their hearts stopped beating I would stop and then I would take a piss on the floor or on the ground next to them, then I would leave just like that.'

'24/7 being in The DreamVerse started to take a toll on me. I guess it was a week or so after Grover stopped me from reaching my mortal shell when I first started to feel like the life I was living was my reality. I needed to dream within someone else's dream without even creating a fly on the wall.'

'Every dreamer's dream that I have entered in the past has a blue star shaped symbol on the outside of their dream barrier. Making it easy to remember where I have been. So out of all the dreamers that I have met, I chose Michael Mellow's dream self to enter as a link to his mortal shell. This provided me the REMS that my mind needed so I didn't go crazy. Every day for two hours I would do this and it became the balance I needed to survive The DreamVerse until I could escape it.'

"When I woke up I was told that I had been in a coma for the past six months and my wife that I loved with all my heart had been dead the same amount of time. I won my battle but it felt like I had already lost the war. Until Shelly slowly helped me rediscover the importance of life and that my war with Grover and his Gemini Dream Legion was far from over with.'

Chapter Three:

'The confinement of being in the hospital for another month after waking up from my coma was Hell on my awake mind. I thought if only I could get the Hell out of there it would make it so much easier for me to fight the war I fought every time I went to sleep. Given sleeping pill after sleeping pill almost cost me my life a few times that first month. Before the end of my one month stay in the hospital I was tossing my sleeping pills in the trash.'

'When I was given something by needle to make me fall asleep after they say I got out of control when I woke up from my coma was easy on me. I was knocked out hard even making my dream mind so sluggish that it stayed inside my mortal shell until I woke up.'

'The Gemini Dream Legion came knocking and I just ignored them. It was wild that I never thought what would happen if I just stayed inside my mortal shell and stayed out of The DreamVerse. What could they do? And the answer was nothing. Sure they could bark loud but all the dogs were behind a fence and helpless to get to me.'

Then Grover spoke to me, "Enjoy your safety coward. You now know that you can hide inside yourself from me every time you go to sleep but know this the longer that you stay away from The DreamVerse the weaker your dream mind will become. Right now you have enough power to keep me out of your dreams but as every day passes the day that you are too weak to keep me out anymore comes closer. And that day is coming sooner than you think..."

"I will destroy your mind then I will take your life. Goodbye for now Barry Goldrum. Have a good night's sleep and I'll see you again in your dreams tomorrow and the day after that and the day after that until I make you dead."

'I told him to fuck off then I began to wonder if he was telling the truth.'

'I found out the truth on the fifth day I kept my dreaming mind inside my mortal shell when I went to sleep. I could feel Grover's banging at the outer walls of my dreams even more. I knew that in three maybe four days tops Grover would invade my dreams.'

'I would be weaker than I was right then, perhaps too weak to fight off Grover from killing me. I gathered up the power of my dream mind watching Grover through a peep hole I created. The old powerful immortal was taking a few steps away from the outer walls of my dreams when I struck out at him from behind. My steel wings sliced the air as my mighty clawed right hand hit and ripped open the back of Grover's head just a little bit.'

'Yes a little bit was all it took for Grover to freak out that he was bleeding and wounded. Yes, I knocked him out of my way and on his ass that day as I forced myself back into my mortal shell. But that day all I did was hurt Grover's pride and piss him off even more.'

'The next day, the sixth day, I was weaker than I was the day before. I said fuck it and struck out at Grover from behind again, causing the same wound as the day before. The look in Grover's eyes as he was holding the back of his bleeding head and looking at me, made me thirst for more blood and I attacked him. Grover with his mouth opened up wide as a snake swallowing a fat rat just stood there frozen as I hit him with every bit of powerful rage that I have inside my heart for him.'

"You killed my wife!" I screamed out loud at Grover as I hit him and hit him. Making him scream out a sound that is very similar to a squealing pig that is in the process of being slaughtered.

"Get him off me you fools!" Grover yelled out to the members of his family, that were standing there silently and watching dumbfounded as their leader was getting his ass kicked like none of them has ever seen before.

'Grover pushed, trying his best to get away from me. Still in a rage I reached out and grabbed Grover by his cheek. When I had a hold of it real good I squeezed down as hard as I could and pulled away. I can still in my mind hear the sound of Grover's right cheek sickly being ripped off his face. Like a beast that is getting ready to strike its death blow, I stared at my prey with no mercy. Grover begged for me to stop as I dropped his cheek down into The DreamVerse where it dissolved to ash.'

'I was one breath away from justice when some members of The Gemini Dream Legion grabbed me and stopped me from striking Grover with my death blow. They held on to me without trying to hurt me long enough for Grover to gather himself up and make his escape.'

'When Grover was out of sight I was let go. I turned around to look at the ones that stopped me from my final justice with Grover. The look in their eyes made my dream self feel like icy fingers were rubbing down my back.'

Then one of the Gemini Dream Legion that looked stronger than the rest of those that surrounded me said to me, "I am Ivan, are you any different? Will you kill as many of us as it will take for you to get your justice over Grover? You are a powerful, new, one of a kind, is all you want to do now is kill?"

I looked at the warrior named Ivan and said, "No."

Ivan relaxed, "Good for there needs to be a change in The DreamVerse. There are many members of the Gemini Dream Legion that are tired of all the constant killings and want for them to be stopped."

'At this point many of the members of the Gemini Dream Legion that surrounded me flew off to return to Grover's side. Many did not fly away. I stood still feeling safe as they closed the gap that their family members left behind.'

'Ivan told me of how the members of The Gemini Dream Legion that no longer killed the dreamers whose dreams they entered were punished by Grover and the rest of The Elders. Those members found it brought them peace just to eat dream food without killing the dreamers at the end. I could not believe what I was hearing and a different kind of rage set itself up in my heart.'

'I told Ivan and the rest of the Gemini Dream Legion that surrounded me that I would be their leader and that if they helped me kill Grover and the rest of The Elders I would set them free to live the rest of their immortal lives at peace without ever having to kill again.'

'Ivan turned towards his family and looked at them but before he could speak a word every male and female voice said the same thing to him. That it was up to Ivan, whatever he decided to do they would follow him and they would fight to their deaths for him.'

'Ivan looked at me and asked me if I would betray him and his family. Actions I knew would speak louder than any word I spoke so without saying a word I took eight steps towards Ivan until I was five feet away from him then I dropped down to one knee and bowed to him.'

'Ivan surprised, asked me what does this mean? I said I am no longer interested in being the leader, that he is now the leader, the leader that I will win our war for. Ivan stood up taller and told me to rise up as one of them. I stood back up, Ivan and I looked each other in the eyes as around us cheers of happiness came roaring out of our army of soldiers that would very soon would be fighting to the death against their former family members.'

"Ivan, I have to ask you something."

"I will tell you the truth Barry no matter what."

"I need that Ivan, I'm putting a lot of trust in you and your band of dream invading warriors and unlike Grover I am not going to be the one that is holding the back of his head wondering who did that, who hit me from behind."

"I have a lot of respect for you Barry, what you did for me. I never would have thought you would do that."

"Ivan I am not interested in running The DreamVerse, that you can do and best of luck. I want my revenge, I want justice. I want Grover's head on a spike that I carry around with me until this dark damn hate expels itself from my heart."

"You mean your soul do you not Barry?"

"Soul, maybe there is such a thing but I do not feel it to be true. If there are souls in the universe then there are many in this universe that do not deserve to have one."

"Good and evil Barry are part of the universe and as well in individual life. It is what you do with that life that matters. If you want to know the truth whether there are souls in the universe all you have to do is take a closer look at me. Barry I am a living soul."

"A living soul?"

"Yes I was never born inside a body, the attempt was there but I and everyone like thyself was pushed aside by a stronger twin that did not want to share its mother's womb."

"If what I understand about souls Ivan is that they cannot die."

"You are talking about transcended souls Barry, souls that either go to Heaven or Hell after their mortal shell dies."

"They cannot die?"

"That Barry I am not positive of but I rely on my faith to believe it to be as truth."

"Faith, the Gemini Dream Legion has faith that there is a God and a Devil?"

"Yes we do, as it is told to us by the The Gemini Dream Legion member that is chosen to be our guide as we grow our living souls to their final maturity."

"What happens when a living soul does not develop to maturity?"

"You remember Grover's cheek? Same goes with that living soul it dies and becomes ash. Have you asked me what you wanted to know yet Barry?"

"No, I want to know why Sam not only told me but also believed it as truth that no member of the Gemini Dream Legion died before I took the life of the first one?"

"Simply put Barry, Sam is a true believer in Grover and his Elders. His words, his truth comes from God. Just like so many of The Gemini Dream Legion they have only faith in Grover because he was the first, who came to be what he is, way before any modern mankind."

"Before we walked out of our caves huh?"

"Before that Barry. Grover came here when mankind started to walk on two legs."

"What is Grover, Ivan?"

"No one knows Barry and in my soul that I am, I believe that Grover does not even know. Barry my army of the new Gemini Dream Legion needs a fortress, a home."

"Sorry can't help you out Ivan, I don't own any property in The DreamVerse."

Ivan looks at Barry like he does not understand why he said that. "That was a joke Ivan, not a very good one but a joke none-the-less. What, does The Gemini Dream Legion not have a sense of humor?"

"No we just kill mortals in their sleep."

Barry and Ivan look at each other then before either one can crack a smile they both start laughing their asses off. "Thanks Ivan, I needed that, I haven't laughed like that in a long time."

"Tell me about it Barry. Try living your life with blood on your hands at all times and still it's not enough to satisfy Grover, the blood and death hungry prick. I hate him. He should have not been allowed to be the first of my kind."

"Yes Grover sucks, he must die."

"Barry I'm going to give you the big know it all now. We, the non-elders of the Gemini Dream Legion, are all workers. We consume as much dream food as we can then we fly back to our home where we give most that we consume to Grover and The Elders."

"Lucky you."

"Barry we are so lucky that Grover allows us just enough to feel barely full. He would lessen even that if he could but he knows that we need this much so we can be strong enough to consume maxim amounts of dream food..."

"At first I felt like all the rest that this was the price of life handed down by the words of God told by Grover. Until I saw what I was not suppose to see, what I could not believe to be true, while I was walking around bored and being nosy in places I was not to enter for fear of punishment..."

In The Gemini Dream Legion there is what as known as the Chosen, everyone wants to be a chosen. What a honor it is to be a Chosen. When you find out that you have been chosen to be a Chosen you get to meet Grover and The Elders in person which is very rare unless you work directly for Grover as one of his support staff."

"Chosen for what?"

"Check this out Barry this is when the story gets really good. When you have your meeting with Grover and The Elders they give you a very special mission. A mission that is so very special that you are never allowed to return home again. You get to travel beyond our domain to another realm where all the other Chosen just like you are building a second home to house all the living souls that will come home to The Gemini Dream Legion when the end of days comes to be on Earth."

"It's always about the end of days."

"Of course Barry, Grover so proudly told us that this is what God wants us to do. So no questions asked when one of us is chosen we comply to whatever orders we are given. Here comes the kick to the ass Barry."

"Let me feel it Ivan."

"There is no other realm that the Chosen travel to. No they are fed on by Grover and The Elders until that Chosen one turns into dust. Grover needs us, his family, to stay strong and in power, he also needs us to eat to stay alive."

"Grover and the Elder are parasites."

"Yes they are Barry. I heard that Grover was the only one that could do this until he changed one of us regular members of his family into the first Elder member. Then just like him they become living soul eating vampires that hunger for more and more."

"Is that it Ivan?"

"Walk away and come back to kick you in the ass once again. This is priceless Barry. Grover feeds on his elders not too often but often enough to have to create a fantasy sickness that some of The Elders catch and they have to be put to death for there is no cure."

"Parasite to cannibal."

"Of course no one but Grover is allowed to witness these mercy killings for even their ash can transfer the sickness to another Elder. Grover is so quick in spotting the sickness in his Elders that before they can become contagious to other Elders the sick Elder is quickly taken away by Grover and mercifully transformed into ash. I hate The Elders, they receive back what they deserve."

"How do you know all this about Grover, Ivan?"

"There is someone very special named Sloar, that very soon I will let you meet, that will enlighten you to every horrible act that Grover has committed."

"Who is Sloar?"

"Sloar is one of the very first Elders that Grover created. He is very old, very sick and lucky to be alive. It was not too long after I witnessed what I wish I did not witness when I came upon Sloar. He was bleeding and hurt, all his wounds were given to him by Grover himself. I helped him escape from our home and hid him in a dreamer that cannot wake up."

"That was great idea, Ivan."

"He is safe but growing weaker everyday. As my reward for helping Sloar he told me all about what Grover has done over the years to his family."

136

"You trust Sloar?"

"With my life Barry. I think that is enough for now Barry. Now you have to help us build our new fortress."

"How can I do that?"

"With all the power you wield Barry. It will take a lot out of you. After our fortress is built, you will need to leave the war to us your new family and enter dreamers' dreams and consume as much dream food as you can so you can grow big and strong again, ha ha."

"I guess, I can do that?"

"Barry I feel the longer you consume dream food the better our chances of winning this war. One month of just consuming and not expelling any power by creating anything and you will be ready to join our war."

"I don't want to wait, can't we build our fortress after we attack Grover and the G.D.L."

"The G.D.L.?"

"Yes the Gemini Dream Legion. I have to say Ivan, that name sucks. Fucking Grover, fucking Elders, let's get it on. Grover is bleeding, the time to strike is now."

"Please Barry give me a month."

"I get it Ivan. Loss on both sides cannot be felt sad and hard until the loss of family members starts to rise higher and higher."

"Yes Barry, I hope some of the members of the G.D.L., decide that Grover is the wrong side and come over to our side."

"Don't hold your breath Ivan, you are a heretic just like all our family members."

"Yes this is true, still when word spreads across the G.D.L. that we are with you, those that don't want to kill anymore will escape or try to join us. I feel positive that at least a million or more will join us by the time you are ready for your strike on Grover and The Elders. Without them and their show of unity after Grover and The Elders are ousted, civil war will continue on until both sides are depleted."

"Seems like you have the same shit here in The DreamVerse, as we do on Earth."

"We are a proud people that believe in what we do. There will be so many that will never join us. I don't know what to do with them after we win the war."

"Okay you need time Ivan. I'll give you your thirty days but no more."

"Agreed Barry. Thank you for your loyalty."

"Well then Ivan, how do we get started on our fortress?"

"I'm not sure, I think the best thing to do is join hands and together you and I and all our warriors will concentrate together."

"And that will work?"

"I pray that it does. Before we get started Barry you have to promise me something first."

"And what is that Ivan?"

"That you will not kill Grover until I have had the proper amount of time to question him."

"About what?"

138

"I want to know if it is true that God talks to him or if this whole thing is just a means to make life more comfortable for him. Barry will you do that for me?"

"Yes I will give you your time to question him. But you have to make me a promise as well Ivan."

"Anything Barry."

"I want your word that no matter what Grover tells you that after you get your answers his head comes off."

"I promise you Barry with all the living soul that I am you will have your revenge."

'I thought to myself how was I going to create a fortress for my new family without being inside a dreamer's dream. It took awhile, damn thing kept on appearing then disappearing until I sent so much power out of myself that I knocked my dream self out from the sheer intensity of it.'

'Ivan and my new family safely carried my dream self back to my mortal shell for safe keeping. As I slept Ivan had one hundred warriors guard my mortal shell from the possibility of an attack on me in my weakened state. I woke up and had my just another day in the hospital until I went back to sleep.'

'When my dream self stepped out of my mortal shell there was one hundred warriors waiting for my return to The DreamVerse. Lucky for me they were all members of my new family. They followed me for the next thirty days of my sleep as I dream jumped non-stop until I found dreamers that were strong enough to help me with thick meaty portions of dream food that I needed so badly.'

'On the thirty-first day I was a powerhouse ready for war when my dream self came out of my mortal shell. I led my one hundred warriors home to our hidden away fortress in The DreamVerse for a meeting with Ivan on how the war was unfolding for our side. I heard some fucked up news.'

'Sloar was dead. Ivan looked like shit, war was kicking his ass. No where close did a million warriors join us and I had to change things up as soon as I stepped in the door.'

'We agreed that it was up to me to attack The Elders full out, take no prisoners, destroy, smash and thrash myself through Elder after Elder until they were all dead. Then all that stood in the way of freedom would be Grover.'

'Ivan was looking like half the shit that was stuck to him had been wiped off. We were talking, we were walking and the sound of war came to our ears from outside our fortress. Grover, all his Elders and a massive army of the G.D.L. attacked us. Tired of this war and losing too many members of his family, Grover came this day, at this time to end the war by killing every traitor.'

'I roared out for battle as I ran, then somehow, I don't remember how, I was all by myself, like I was placed somewhere out of war's way. I was alone someplace and ready for war when my mind turned on me. This is what my mind asked me to wake me up to, the reality that I was living, while I was sleeping and not living,' "When will you be able to mourn your wife?"

'I could not believe myself. How fucked up I was, was being repeated in my mind. I was so pissed off that I gave myself a war to fight and win instead of facing the reality of losing my wife six months before I could get back to my mortal shell. It's all my fault, I did not pull the trigger but I did give them the gun when I selfishly entered The DreamVerse instead of just going to sleep and dreaming like a normal person.'

'Tina I love you, how can you be dead? I said as I fell to my knees and cried out my pain.'

'Silence turned to the sounds of war outside our fortress. I looked around, I was the only one alive and breathing and it was up to me to help save The DreamVerse from a tyrant? I ran to find Ivan and my new family. As I ran by all I saw was hundreds of dead bodies. I thought to myself that Grover didn't know I was back inside the fortress or did he?'

'By the time I got to the throne room Ivan was being slain. I watched as his body turned to ash. Grover turned around from killing Ivan and looked at me with murder in his eyes. He smiled, said, hello coward, then he charged.'

'Tina on my mind made me weak as Grover got the best of me. Like a smart coward, Grover did not attack me alone. Within a few moments I was on the ground as Grover stomped on my face. I felt my nose bust open, I felt teeth being stomped loose. My beat down went so far that one of my eyes came out of its socket.'

'I was all fucked up getting ready to die when Tina came to me and told me to save my life, to fight back, to kill Grover. Tina had changed, I laughed knowing the truth that Tina was all in my mind, or so I thought then but I'm not so sure now.'

'Tina was the reason I needed to get myself out of this and revenge her death at the same time. I roared out loud. I raged up like a beast and struck at anybody that I could until I was able to stand on my feet again. Grover and all that were still alive around me watched as I put my eye back in its socket.'

'Grover spread his wings, I grabbed them and ripped them bloodily off of him, while he screamed and bled so beautifully. Grover's wings turned to dust as I grabbed hold of his head. Like his wings, I pulled and I pulled on Grover's head until it came off in my hands. I watched Grover's head try to speak as everything went silent around me.'

141

'With Grover's head turning to dust in my hand I attacked every Elder I could get my hands on. They were my only targets as the G.D.L. discovered, so they backed away in confusion or in fear and watched as I changed their lives in a blind rage. By the time I was through, dust was every where and falling down like gray snow covering everybody, making every one of us look the same.'

I screamed out loud, "No more, I want out, you sorry ass bastards fucked up my life."

'The rage inside me felt like it was starving for more pain and death because I felt no physical pain just giant amounts of mental pain. Everybody looked at me with eyes of disbelief as I calmed when I noticed all the ash on everybody including me. I stood there feeling like a monster, wanting nobody to look at me.'

I said, "I'm sorry." Then I flew away to re-enter my mortal shell.

'With tears flowing from my eyes, I flew thinking about nothing but Tina, when someone flew past me on my right side. They were flying so very fast all there was, was a blur then they were out of sight.'

'I kept on flying, when I spotted in front of my flight path Sam. He stood still with his wings spread out waiting for me to catch up to him. Sam, I did not forget about Sam. He was out of sight until then and man oh man did I want talk to him, yeah right, one more to go then I mourn, then I say goodbye to The DreamVerse forever.'

'That was what I wanted. Was that what I got? Fuck no! Sometimes now I wish I would have just kept flying and just gone home but my hunger for revenge changed my life. I cannot believe what I have become. Out of all the people on Earth, me, I'm the one. I'm?

'I need a beer. What a load for my mind to remember.

Need a beer before I remember in detail what comes next, might as well take a piss during my break. Tina I love you, I'm sorry at least I know that your soul is safe in Heaven. I could not die for you, instead I live a life that the universe gave to me. I'm chosen, I feel damned, it's the least I can do, it's the way I pay for my punishment. My reward? Do as I am told to do until I die and I will never be damned, for Heaven will be my after life home.'

'Still I say, I don't know. I am, I was an unbeliever, why was I chosen? Makes total sense if you want something that will stir the pot the wrong way. And most times what happens after that is some of what's in the pot gets spilled over the edge onto whatever surface it can stick to. Then finally at the end there is only a stain that can be ignored, noticeable but ignored.'

'Am I going to become this stain? Heaven help me I feel it to be true. God is going to flick me in my head then kick my sorry ass straight to Hell. What can I do? I have a hand that I have to play to the end, there is no folding for everything I have is in the pot. I lose, I lose the biggest pot in my life, with no chance in Hell of every getting a chance to play another hand.'

The Truth As Only The
Universe Can Tell It

Right at this moment in time in The DreamVerse Barry's dream twin is finding out information on a real rich pig of a man that is going to make Barry a lot of money.

Barry stands staring at his couch, with his mind on auto pilot. This is self done for Barry does not want to remember anymore of what has led him to the life he now has no choice but to live.

Back in focus Barry sits back down on the couch and downs his beer, he grabs another beer and downs half of it, then he lets out a big burp. Barry laughs as the mental pains of remembering are just about to come full throttle to a screeching halt within a heartbeat.

'I was flying to my mortal shell and then there was Sam. I came close to striking Sam before I stopped very close to him. There was something different about him that I noticed when I was flying closer to him as he stood there without flinching. The Sam I knew would know better.'

'Within a moment of still silence, Sam presented himself to me for punishment. I attacked him with my final rage. Sam did not flinch as I hit him with everything I had in myself. My hits made impact, which made Sam move back and bleed still he did not try to stop me from hitting him nor did he strike me back.'

'After about twenty more hits I stopped hitting Sam and looked at him. Sam wiped the blood away from his face as his wounds were already healing. Then Sam with a voice of more confidence said to me.'

"Have you depleted the rage inside yourself Barry Goldrum?"

'I did not answer.'

144

Sam calmly said, "No matter you are through hitting me. I know you hate me Barry, you have good reason to. So you believe."

"I more than believe. Tina, my wife is dead, I blame you. You are the one who said that Tina's life could be on the line. Then she died. You killed her you sorry bastard."

"I did not.."

"Bull shit!"

"No, true shit Barry Goldrum. It was Grover who killed Tina. I left and went to Heaven when he was on his way to do it."

"Heaven, you went to Heaven?"

"Yes Barry, that is where Angels call their home."

"You, you're an Angel? Yeah right, if you are an Angel, you suck as one. Why didn't you help Tina if you are an Angel?"

Sam looked around and away from me then back to me and said, "Saving Tina was not my orders. Making you become who you are now were my orders."

"Were?"

"Yes were. Barry Goldrum you are about to start your journey to becoming more than any other human has had the chance in becoming."

"Not interested."

"What? How dare you?" Sam got mad really quick but tempered himself just as quickly.

"Let me start this over once again Barry Goldrum.

145

I am Sam of The DreamVerse, this is my mission. I am not one of The Gemini Dream Legion, I am an Angel. And not just any Angel, I am the Voice of God. You will listen to what I have to tell you then you will do as I tell you to do."

"No I will not, Sam."

"Yes you will Barry Goldrum, for the words I speak to you come from God. You do not say no to God, you do as he commands you to do. Do you understand me Human?"

'Sorrow and rage still in my mind, I told Sam, I said no and I mean no and in other words for him to go fuck himself. That was a big mistake.'

"You stupid damn Human, you think I will allow you to talk to me like this, to talk to God like this?"

'Sam came at me, I defended myself, damn little did it help. I had my final answer when Sam's hits hit me. This was the same man I fought but only now this man was not holding back his immense power. A power that brought me beaten down to my knees.'

Sam grabbed my face and used it to pull me to my feet, "Human you are special to God, I will not hurt you anymore at this time. What you went through, losing your wife Tina was a lot to ask from you. You have to understand in that frail human mind of yours, that Tina's death was meant to be. There was nothing you could have done to stop it. So now it is over and done with. It is time you gather yourself up and go forth knowing you have a purpose in your mortal human life."

'I was still not willing to bend, I was pissed that I was used like this. Sam beat the shit out of me some more then while I was bleeding and hurting Sam let me see what was happening to my mortal shell. I was dying, my heart couldn't take much more strain from the pain I was feeling in The DreamVerse.'

146

"Barry Goldrum, let God in your soul, let me show you his mercy."

'Sam touched me and my wounds started to heal, I looked over at my mortal shell and it was healing as well.'

"Barry Goldrum you are healed now and I also returned all the strength you lost from the beating you received by my hands. I can hurt you again Barry Goldrum, then heal you and start all over. I am eternal. I have lots of time, you however, do not. If you die before doing as God commands for you to do, your soul will go to Hell."

"Hell, I'm to go to Hell? Will you be joining me, Sam?"

"Funny. However if you do as you are commanded to do to the day you are to die, your soul will come home to Heaven. How does that sound? Could God be any fairer?"

"What does God want me to do Sam?"

"Listen with a sharp mind Barry Goldrum and all will be told to you."

'I was to break the walls down. The fortress that I created and the original fortress of The Gemini Dream Legion. Chaos, shock and awe was on the menu when I went to sleep. Dream food my power source I needed to stay the powerhouse I was, had to be obtained another way. No longer was I to go into dreamer's dreams for dream food. No, now I got my dream food when I slayed a member of The Gemini Dream Legion, both sides.'

'I was told to live with Shelly for one month while I followed my command every night. I asked how I was to convince Shelly that I should move in with her. I was told that she would ask me when she came to visit me later that day. After a month I was to leave her behind and make myself ready to do a lot of traveling, mostly by driving.'

147

'Also after my month was through with Shelly I was to find myself a new dream twin. After I found this new dream twin I would change. My new dream twin would be able to enter any dreamer's dream he chose to when I'm awake. This new dream twin would also do what God commanded for him to do. Simply put my dream twin was to find the worst of dreamers that have to pay for their sins either in their dreams or in awake life.'

'My new dream twin would bring back the information to me and I was decide what to do with it. My only two choices were to eliminate them either in their dreams by scaring them to death, or make them eliminate themselves while they are awake. This is where my new dream twin would come in handy by making them think they were losing their minds when he brought dreams to living reality for the worst of these dreamers.'

'On the plus side this new dream twin when added to the mix would be a power source that would be powerful enough that I no longer had to worry about my mortal heart exploding while I was in The DreamVerse.'

'All caught up in the moment, I was not thinking straight as it came to me, a new dream twin? How could I find a new dream twin? I am my dream twin now, he is I, we have become one.'

"How is this is possible Sam?"

Sam looked at me like I was stupid, he waved his hands in the air and told me, "Barry finding yourself a new dream twin is as easy as wiping your stinking human ass."

'I looked at Sam, while he looked at me like I should be slapping my head any second saying out loud oh yeah, that's how I do it.'

Sam, irritated said, "Damn do I have to pick out your dream twin for you as well. Okay human listen to me closely for I will only be telling you this only once. You, yes you Barry Goldrum, you will enter another human's dreams that does not have a dream twin and make them become your dream twin."

"Just like that?"

"Yes stupid human just like that. It's not like you haven't already chosen in your mind the other human you want to be your dream twin."

'I had no idea who he was talking about and I had just about enough of Sam and his smart ass Angel mouth, when he slapped me across the top of my head.'

"Michael Mellow you stupid human idiot."

"Michael Mellow?" I said in response as it became clear to me, after I said it. Just how far on my path, that was chosen for me, I have traveled to get to this point in my life.

I did not want to hear the answer especially from Sam the disgruntled Angel but I asked him anyway, "What does Michael do? Does he come and go between my body and his own."

Sam laughed, readying himself to enjoy what he was about to tell me, "No silly human after Michael becomes your new dream twin, his mortal shell, his mortal human body dies. When Michael becomes your new dream twin he will do so until the day you die. Then like you he will get to come home to Heaven."

"Just like that Sam, Michael and I are Heaven bound?"

"Yes. However Barry all this is a month away from now. Now Barry, it is time for you to go to war for the next month. This is all God wants you to do now, go to war for one month. After that, well there better be a huge decrease in the population of the Gemini Dream Legion.

Show no mercy and take no prisoners Barry Goldrum. It would be best if you just thought of yourself as a monster that wants to kill anybody you see in The DreamVerse for the next month."

"Fuck that Sam, I can't do that."

"War or burn in Hell Barry Goldrum. If you ask me I hope you choose Hell. In my opinion, there are way too many of you damn humans in Heaven already. And one more would not make a difference, but still it would be one less and that Barry Goldrum I would enjoy very much."

I'd had enough of Sam's shit at this point, "Well Sam if you ask me and you probably don't but none-the-less here it is. Sam, you're one fucked up Angel. I do not know if you know this but this it is very true. Hell? Right now it seems like a better place to be than to be in Heaven with you after I die."

"You are a stupid human, Barry Goldrum."

"At least Sam, I will get that free choice that us humans desire so much. I do not want anything to do with a war, I'm through, no more. I'm going back to my body. The DreamVerse, you and whoever can kiss my soul."

'Sam looked at me saying nothing. The look in his eyes told me that Heaven was no longer my place to call home after I died and that made me feel numb and uncaring.'

I was deep in thought of why me when Sam said, "Say it Barry."

"Say what Sam?"

"Tell God to kiss your soul which I and he knows you mean your ass. Go ahead mortal, I dare you. Come on Barry, you're going to Hell anyway, why not go there in a blaze of glory? I can't hear you, you have nothing to say?"

"Human, shit, scum, on your knees, I'm going to slay you now."

"Put me on my knees you sorry ass Angel, I've had enough of your shit, come on."

"Maybe later Barry Goldrum, right now the power level you are at I would shove your head up your ass then kick it back out again without breaking a sweat."

"Oh yeah?"

"Yes you dumb ass human. Instead of doing this, I'm going to ask you a question instead."

"Well ask away Sam."

"How would you like to have the power level to perhaps kick my ass?"

"I would love that Sam."

"I bet you would Barry. If you say no to me, you are saying no to God and you will never get that fair fight you want so bad."

"That would be a shame, Sam."

"Wouldn't it? Even more, think of this Barry Goldrum, you were chosen for this task by God. If you say no God will just pick someone else, someone that will say yes. Then Barry they would reap all the benefits and all that power. Best of all they would be graced in God's eyes instead of you, you dumb ass human."

"Tina. What about Tina?"

"Your precious Tina, is in Heaven. How do think she would feel, if I told her you told God to kiss your ass? And in doing so you sealed your fate. That you have to go to Hell instead of coming home to Heaven so you can spend forever with her there. She is waiting for you Barry, she misses you so badly. It's almost heart wrenching I tell you."

"Lousy bastard."

"What was that Barry?"

"I said you are a lousy bastard Sam. I think you are fucking with me. I don't believe you are from Heaven."

"You don't?"

"No I don't. I believe you are from Hell or at the least you have spent some time there, long enough for it to corrupt you. You are warped and I am leaving, see you in Hell you lousy Demon."

"That's it, God commands it to be or not. I'm not going to take your filthy human mouth anymore."

"Do your worst Sam."

"I'll do more than that Barry Goldrum. I will show you why Demons fear Angels you stupid, stupid human."

My mind was spinning out of control I was so pissed off I didn't give a shit then my mind cleared and calmed down and I asked Sam this, "Tina, my Tina. She is safe, she is happy in Heaven. Tell me the truth Sam, tell me the truth."

Sam full of rage looked at me with questioning eyes then he calmed down and said, "Yes Barry, Tina is safe and very happy in Heaven and so will you be."

"Okay enough. Sam no more of your shit. I'll do it, damn me I'll do it."

"Very good Barry Goldrum. Now go back to you mortal shell and wake up, you are through for today."

I just had to know, "Sam?"

"Yes Barry?"

"How much?"

"How much what Barry?"

"How much are you going to be in my life Sam?"

"You will continue to see me 'til the day you die Barry."

"God help me."

"Ha,ha,ha, that was funny Barry, keep that sense of humor, it will help from making your mind go snap."

'I went back to my body and woke up and when I opened my eyes Shelly was sitting in a chair staring at me. We said are hellos and then Shelly told me she had a great idea. I asked her what it was. She told me that she wanted me to move in with her until I got back on my feet. I smiled and said yes. Poor Shelly was it her idea? No, it was not.'

'It was weird living with Shelly for that month. Every night when I went to sleep I was in a war that I fought where the other side no matter how much they wanted to surrender, could not.'

'Every morning I would wake up covered in sweat and every morning I felt like I was covered in blood instead of sweat. From Shelly's perspective, I'd get up and she would be cooking us breakfast. As every day passed the more Shelly fell in love with me. We came close to starting something one night after dinner. But I cooled things down by going to bed.'

'Than came our last day together. I was told this the night before by Sam that I had one more day to spend with Shelly and I was to let myself go and have a great time.'

'After Shelly and I had sex the third time that night my conscious came a calling to me telling me that Shelly was in love with me. It was all my fault because I knew better and I didn't care anymore. What I was going through no person on Earth should have to go through.'

'From Shell's perspective, I'm glad that it was only one night that she and I spent together making love, because God help me I wanted to do nothing more than put the war that was over behind me and stay with her.'

'Back to the first night, after I left the hospital and stayed at Shelly's house. I was a nervous wreck, I tossed and turned for awhile until I fell asleep. When I stepped out of my mortal shell to enter The DreamVerse, Sam was waiting for me.'

"Damn it took you long enough to get here. What you do Barry, try not to fall asleep?"

"You know how it is Sam. I tried counting sheep but that did no good."

"What did you do then Barry?"

"I pictured your face in my mind, then I kept on punching it until I finally fell asleep."

"Are you trying to tell me something Barry, like you don't like me or something?"

I was getting ready to reply when Sam stopped me by telling me, "Like I give a damn whether you like me or not you piece of shit human. Why don't you punch me in my face now?"

'I told him maybe later. Sam talked more shit for ten more minutes, until I had enough of his constant bitching and told him to shut his sorry Angel ass up.'

'Sam threatened to kick my ass than he changed his mind and gave me my rules for bringing war to The DreamVerse.

I. Show no mercy, destroy all that get in my way.
II. Do not jump into dreamers' dreams for the next month.
III. My reward, getting stronger after each kill, a power up.'

"Barry there are Elders still alive in this DreamVerse. They like Grover are a scourge on DreamVerse. You did great in taking Grover away from all his power."

"I did not take Grover away, I killed him because he killed Tina."

"Yes very well and I'm damn proud of you for that. Hey Barry check this out, Grover killed Tina in her dreams because and get this human, I told him to. Damn I'm a great Angel, you should be bowing to me right now."

My mind started to go blank with only one thought left inside it and that was total rage, "Get this Barry, Tina was dying."

"What?" My mind came back to me.

"Yes Tina was looking fine but in a short while after that she would become very, very sick and not be looking so fine with her hot, built body withering away to nothing. The night before she died, the night she spent in the hospital, I came into her dreams for a nice little chat."

"Yes I know, she told me that you hit on her."

"Yes I did and I told her to tell you that just to piss you off. Tina went to bed with you her last night alive knowing what

155

was going to happen. That she was going to die."

"Why did she have to die right then? You said she was fine, why could you not give her more time you lousy bastard?"

"Not me Barry."

"Then who?"

"God, did not give Tina more time because that is his will."

"Tina's death, was God's will?"

"Think of it like this Barry. What does one give up if they are already feeling the pains of dying? Heaven for Tina came after belief and sacrifice."

"This is not right."

"Right or wrong are human concepts Barry and they belong on Earth. I'm talking about Heaven and Hell."

"Still Sam, it's not fair. I loved Tina, she loved me. We should have been allowed more time together."

"Barry Goldrum are you so selfish that you would deny Tina Heaven?"

"Go to Hell Sam."

"I have Barry, many times."

"I believe that Sam. I think the next time you go to Hell, you should stay there like forever."

"I stay in Hell as long as God tells me to stay and not one moment longer."

"God sends you to Hell? I bet it's for pissing him off."

"You know nothing of what you talk about human."

"Yes I do, I'm right ain't I?"

"Eat shit human and get your stupid ass off to war."

"Touchy, touchy. What's wrong Sam? Did the flames of Hell singe your wings?"

"The flames of Hell, will singe your head and stupid ass, human, scum."

'I stood there not moving, wanting to punch Sam, in his face. When he couldn't help himself, The Voice of God is a talker and he was not done talking to me yet.

"Barry tonight you leave no Elder left alive. Do not count your kills Barry just do your damn job great and who knows, maybe just maybe I'll get off your back."

'That was that. Sam folded out his wings and flew back to Heaven, leaving me there alone so I could start a war with the whole Gemini Dream Legion, original and new.'

War, DreamVerse Style

Chapter One:

'The DreamVerse was quiet as I spread my wings. I had a long flight to get to The Elders so I turned my wings from soft to steel and I took off. Nobody was around. As I flew by I looked at all the blue stars on the outside of dreamers dreams, I had entered. There are a lot and they are spaced far apart. The thought of dream jumping sounded so much better to me than war but that was not my choice so I flew on faster and faster.'

'I was at the half way mark, the point where myself, Ivan and the rest built our fortress. There it still stood with big pieces missing, making it look like it had been abandoned for years. I was just about to kick my flying into overdrive when out of the corner of my eyes I spotted some members of my past family of the new Gemini Dream Legion. They were talking among themselves without a care in The DreamVerse.'

'I slowed my flight and turned back around not to say hello but to get this war started with blood flowing free. What was going to happen to me? How was I going to take in their power, my new dream food as they died and turned to ash?'

"It's Barry Goldrum!" Someone shouted out joyfully.

'I flew at them like a winged predator that is about to pounce down on unsuspecting prey. I struck out at two at a time ending them to ash before I grabbed a hold of the next two at random. I was on my fifth pair when out of nowhere my power ups, my new dream food came at me like a rush of violent ecstasy.'

'I stopped and enjoyed my power surge as the rest of my prey that didn't fly off to safety attacked me.

They were betrayed, they were in a rage when they hit me with everything they had. I was hit, a wound appeared, I bled and quickly I healed. I struck back turning twenty or more to ash within a minute. I kept on warring as more and more power ups came to me.'

I was well over three hundred when I shouted out loud, "Enough weak prey, live for another day, tell your tale of Barry Goldrum the new warring monster of The DreamVerse. Hope and pray that I don't lay eyes upon you again until my war within the DreamVerse is over with. Now fly away and spread my fear and pain."

'I was out of my mind with power as I told myself to let the rest go. For no matter how much I enjoyed their power ups they were weak compared to Elders. Something I could not wait to prove to myself to be right about.'

'A thought came to me, they were standing there talking and not warring. Was their war over with? Or did they take a day off from warring?'

'I had to know so I spread my wings and flew fast but not too fast. Within a few seconds I caught up with my past family members. I snatched one of them out of the air for a little talk. Before I could speak, while I had one of my clawed hands around my prey's neck, there came this soft, voice out of nowhere.'

"Please Barry leave my lover alive. Why are you doing this? Have you gone mad? We are your family. We love you, you are our savior. Barry how could you kill so many of us?"

'Damn did I feel like a monster. Sam was right when he told me not to count my kills. What could I do? My mind was on fire with power, part of me wondered why I even cared. I did the best I could at that moment. I felt like shit but I could not let that weaken me. On the other side I didn't have it in me to kill these two lovers.'

'I was coming down from my highness of power and rage still having to play like I was ready to kill at the blink of an eye. So I decided on playing the role of sexy, crazy, bad ass that will let some pass if I get what I want first.'

"What is your name woman?" I looked over just noticing that this lady was hot looking.

Like the hot lady, she is, that knows how to play it so well, she spoke to me this, "My name is Arielina." While playing with her hair. I watched as Arielina took her hand away from her hair to bring it down so sexy, slowly down the shape of her body until she brought it to a halt right below her waist, "It's all yours big boy, if you let my lover live."

'Damn Arielina was hot as I enjoyed the size of my dream boner she had given me. In the past I've noticed ladies before while in The DreamVerse. This was different Arielina had really turned me on for the first time since I woke up out of my coma. This is the first time I've been turned on for seven months, from the start of my coma to the first day out of the hospital. And my first day of living with Shelly.'

'Which brought up another thought in my mind. Was Shelly to be my sexual comfort while I was awake during my month of war? By hook or by crook Shelly wanted me to live with her. Shelly is hot and fine and she would be so nice to lay down with. This was what I was thinking as my thought turned to telling myself that I should not use her. I was giving a mental nod to myself as I heard a voice coming from the man's neck whom I had my hand around.'

"Arielina, what the Hell are you doing? Stop that, you will not give yourself to this dirty, filthy betrayer."

"Banack, shut up, I'm trying to save your life."

'Back and forth they went until I said enough when my dream boner went away.'

160

"Enough from you two stupid lovers. Arielina, I'll let your lover live if you tell me what I what to know."

"Anything Barry, I'll tell you anything you want to know." Arielina pleaded, sexily to me.

"What happened to the war?"

"The war is over with, Grover is dead, you made sure of that. The Elders don't know what to do so they called for us to rejoin them to replenish our numbers."

"Where are The Elders now?"

"Hiding in the safety of The Gemini Manor, in Grover's own throne room."

"Good, that's very good to know." I let go of Banack's throat, "You two are free to go without harm coming to you."

'Arielina turned around and asked me one more time out of desperation why I was doing this. I made my answer simple. Because God wants me to.'

'Elders here I come ready or not. Back in flight with wings of steel slicing the air at break neck speed I traveled. Word spreads fast across The DreamVerse. As I flew by I heard many times members of the Gemini Dream Legion screaming to other members, watch out, look out here comes Barry Goldrum.'

'I just flew on by, making them wonder what was going on. I was getting closer to The Gemini Manor, I was in a weird mood not knowing if I had in me what I just had in me minutes ago. Like I had a choice, my mood did not mean a thing, my orders were to kill all The Elders this night.'

'I was twenty or thirty miles away from The Gemini Manor when a wall of tens of thousands members of the Gemini

Dream Legion stretched their way out in front of my path, hoping to be strong enough to keep me away from their Elders. I stopped and looked at so many people that were willing to fight me until they won or died.'

'Like a mob a chant started of go away murderer, you're not one of us, we hate you, we want you dead. I stood still watching as some of them started to get closer, with this chant strong in their voice. Making them stop believing that one mortal man has the power to destroy them all. I waited 'til they were almost upon me when I spread my wings in a flinching gesture making them snap loudly.'

'The chanting stopped and silence filled The DreamVerse. All I could hear was my dream heart beating like thunder, which I know is really my real mortal heart beating way too fast. Fast enough to perhaps cause damage to it.'

'I had to find my calm. This was not easy. I was starring at tens of thousands of people that wanted to kill me. No matter how strong I was, I was human, the urge to take off was present in my mind but painfully I stood my ground and pushed forth.'

'I could count the seconds until I would be attacked. They blinked and I attacked them first. I flew straight at them with my clawed hands reaching out as my sharp steel wings flapped through the air. Hundreds and hundreds of the members of the Gemini Dream Legion, I knocked out of my way as I eliminated as many I could in the process. I was going strong gaining power ups as my enemies surrounded me until they swallowed me all up.'

'So many hands were lost by being sliced off in the attempt and success of bringing my steel wings to a halt. More members finally got a hold of my shredding clawed hands. They had me, there was too many of them as they beat me down. My arms, my legs were broken many times as they kept on healing just so they could be broken over and over again.'

'My face, my face has never felt the kind of pain that it was receiving. Fingers were being stuck in my mouth and ears as well as my eyes in a hope to rip them out their sockets. I tried to fight back but it did no good, I was being held too tight to build any kind of momentum.'

Someone yelled out, "Stop, stop!" And they all did. Then that same voice said, "Let's forget everything else and let's just rip off his head and kill this monster mortal human bastard."

'That's all I needed, that still moment and I broke free. My wings sliced hands and heads off bodies as I built up speed. I flew towards the direction I came from for about a minute or two then I stopped flying and turned back towards my army of enemies. There was no way that I was going to make it through this wall this night.'

'Like a great predator I used my advantages over my prey and struck out at them only a few at a time making myself stronger after each kill. I was way faster than they were.'

'Before anyone could tell my direction of attack, I'd fly up and snag two of my prey turning them dead and to ash. I quickly struck again before the ash could disappear. I did this until it was time for me to wake up the next morning.'

'I was tired, covered in ash and blood, I'd had enough and in my path to my mortal shell was Sam shaking his stupid Angel head at me in disgust. I remember his words all so well. And mine also.'

"Hello there you stupid human. Did you have a bad night in The DreamVerse?"

"Yes I did Sam..."

"Shut up, I do not need or want to hear your excuses."

"Good, cause I don't feel like talking to your sorry ass."

163

'I passed Sam by on my way to my mortal shell, paying him no attention.'

"Get your stupid human ass over here mortal. You do not walk away from me unless I tell you that you can. Do you understand me?"

"Yes I understand. Do you understand this?" I asked Sam, as I gave him both middle fingers.

Sam was shaking from being so pissed, "No human that gesture you have is backwards. I want you right now to point those fingers at yourself. Well I'm waiting, point your middle fingers at yourself or I will kick your ass."

"Nope, their pointed in the correct direction. I don't remember how many times this is now, that I have had enough of Sam the Voice of God Angel? Yet once again like a bad repeat, you come barking."

"Barking? I'm an Angel from Heaven, I do not bark, you stupid ass mortal."

'I could not help myself and I went on telling Sam off. An immortal Angel that I could barely hurt even with my increased power level handed me back my head and ass. I was in a lot of pain, I told myself that I killed way too many people for God and his war to get my ass kicked for not killing those that I was deemed to kill. This was only my first day on the job of war and I wanted to quit.'

"Sam, fuck you. I've changed my mind, kill me now, take me away from this war. Then you and God can kiss the ass of my soul that will be burning in Hell. Find someone else to war for you two and take your shit at the same time. Good luck finding someone else. No forget that, the both of you just go to Hell."

"Human, you sick mouthed, scum filled, waste of God's time, I'm going to..."

'Sam stopped talking and acted like he was hearing something I could not.'

I gave him a few moments then like I knew not was going on I said, "You're going to do what?"

Sam looked at me with eyes filled with rage and with a shaking voice he said to me, "Go back to your mortal shell Barry Goldrum, I will be waiting for you tomorrow night right here in The DreamVerse." He paused to compose himself.

"Well someone will be waiting for you Barry Goldrum. Just be ready for more war. God loves you, you cannot say no. There is no one else for this war than you. If you say no, God will have no choice but to damn all that live in The DreamVerse. Which means they all go to Hell."

"That's not fair..."

"Out of his Wisdom, God gave untouched souls that never had a mortal life a place to call home. This place, this DreamVerse will no longer exist. Barry Goldrum not only will you damn all the millions and millions of untouched souls to Hell here presently. You will also damn every untouched soul that will come to existence in the future for all eternity."

"Don't lay this on me..."

Sam ignored me, "For they will have no place to call home. So on the day a mortal is born and they have a dream twin like all that live here does that untouched soul will be ripped out of that new born and sent to Hell."

"Why can't they just go to Heaven instead of Hell?"

"Barry Goldrum, there is no two for one in Heaven. The only way a soul can enter Heaven is after it had a mortal life no matter how long or short that life is.

That is why God, out of wisdom and compassion created The DreamVerse. He felt the pain deeply of all the souls that went straight to Hell for commenting no sins. It is all up to you Barry Goldrum, kill thousands in this war that will only last one Earth month, so the rest that survived the war will remember that they should feel God's grace more."

'My mind was thumping hard, I had no choice but I stayed silent, waiting to hear more.'

"The Gemini Dream Legion have killed too many mortals before their time out of no restraint. This will change one way or another. Grover was the first, God gave him a consciousness of a man far in the future. This concept of an after life he was living along with Heaven and Hell had no meaning to him."

"I've heard this before..."

"Well hear this then, it took Grover hundreds of years for his simple mind to catch up with his new consciousness. Grover knew of Heaven and Hell thousands of years before living mankind. God in his wisdom brought Grover into this DreamVerse after his mortal twin died. The race of past mankind that Grover lived with were just about ready to become enlightened and journey forth to discover the world they had no name for."

'Millions of afterlives would die and go to Hell if I said no. My mind clicked, my eyes went out of focus and for how long I do not know, I was in my own mind not paying attention to what Sam was telling me.'

"Big shock Barry Goldrum, Earth was not your planet's first name. Barry are you listening to me?"

"Sam all these people's lives are on my mind, no I am not listening to you. This is too much, this is not right, no one should have this thrown at them, especially me."

166

"Well get use to it Barry Goldrum and accept your fate. Now where was I?"

"I don't know or do I care Sam..."

"Oh yes that's right. The DreamVerse was empty, save for Grover. In that time what grew from understanding his place in God's universe turned muddled to Grover's mind making him believe that he was the God of The DreamVerse. God with great patience let Grover have free will over The DreamVerse until his patience declined and that is where you come in."

"Yes me, you want to trade places Sam?"

"Hell no. Thousands of years Barry Goldrum that is how long Grover had to change his thirst for blood and death. You will not receive the same amount of time. War for one month then do as you are told 'til the day you die a normal death or feel the death of millions within the blink of an eye tomorrow."

'I watched as Sam unfolded his wings and took off flying fast enough to make me feel the sharpness of his flight. In my own world again only thicker I did not hear one hundred assassins sneaking up behind me.'

'So silent they attacked. One moment I was all alone deep in thought, the next moment I was wounded and bleeding out from almost all of my body including my face and head. Pain out of nowhere is something to make someone stop what they are doing to protect themselves. Instincts kick in, adrenaline comes up racing to the surface to take over.'

'The pain I felt, felt like enough pain to kill me a hundred times. I did not know what happened when I came back around. There was one hundred dead assassins floating around me instead of just being a large amount of ash. Maybe twenty seconds I looked around before something fantastic happened.'

167

'Out of the corner of my right eye, I spotted a quick spark. This tiny spark just flickered in the air staying still in its position of five feet above its picked out assassin to land upon. Slowly it descended, so slowly that it sort of put me in a trance like state. I had a little bit of consciousness left, enough to be a step away watching but not enough to act if I had to. It felt like an hour I watched as this tiny spark kept its steady downward pace.'

'It was only a foot away from its destination when this tiny spark grew one hundred times its size in a blink of an eye. I have to admit what came next was sick but at the same time it was totally amazing in its execution.'

'Like the dead bodies were saturated in gas with fumes emitting from them and when this tiny spark bulked up to its full size, Boom. There was no inferno of flames only burnt ash everywhere. This ash came flying to me fast with a lingering smacking sensation. I shook my head and coughed out ash. My spit was black and thick when I spat it out of my mouth in a hope to gets its nasty taste out.'

'Blood dries away, ash well normal ash dissipates in time. This ash was thick and hard as coal. I could not rub it off me, my dream self was dirty with no way of washing it clean around. Souls do not need water or soap. Then Boom! Out in the far distance a bright blue light came to life, it was huge, the size of a mountain. Then like an echo I heard the sound of this giant blue light come to life.'

'The giant blue light came racing towards me. Deer in headlights, I was for a few seconds when I snapped out of it enough to make my retreat. Fate or bad luck? I could not move as this giant blue light came speeding towards me, 'til I could not take it anymore.'

I screamed out, "Enough of this shit."

'I heard a deep laugh, as this giant blue light in a instant turned from giant to eight feet in size.'

168

'I looked at this blue cloaked clear looking angel that made Sam the Voice of God look like Mr. Rogers. I was scared shitless as this eight foot Angel just stood there looking at me like I was nothing to him, which humored him. I could tell this from the small sly smile on his lips.'

Startled, I shook as he spoke out to me, "Human, you are damned, I have come to reap your soul and take it to Hell."

'I did not know what to say as this terrifying Angel broke suit and started to laugh hard enough to make his wings flap.'

"Damn Barry, you should see the look in your eyes, they're like, damn I'm dead and going to Hell." This Angel reached out and put his hand on my left shoulder and looked at me all seriously. A moment later he couldn't help himself and he started to laugh again, this time even louder. When he did this he bent himself in two pulling me down with him, only to make us stand up tall again, while he still laughed.

'This Angel, took his big hand, that was full of immense power off my shoulder. He kept on laughing, wiping tears out of his eyes. I did what what any human has to do when they encounter a crazy person, and just laugh along then walk away.'

'I was a mixture of scared and pissed off, I had it for the night so to say. I killed, I did not want to. I got the shit kicked out of me by Sam, a hundred assassins blew up in the loudest bang/boom I have ever heard. Which covered me in ash that stuck to my dream self's flesh like sin and now I had this big ass laughing Angel laughing at me with what seemed like no other interest in mind but to do so.'

'I laughed showing teeth like I was having a great time, then I walked away.'

From behind me laughing Angel said, "Where the Hell you going Barry? What's wrong, do you have to take a shit?"

I could not believe what I just heard. I turned around fast and asked laughing Angel, "What kinda of freaking, flaky Angel are you?" Things changed very fast after that.

"Barry, Barry, dirty assed Barry, your Humanity is showing. Small minded, for you are from simple minded Earth not glorious Heaven. What can I do to help you? I have it, now don't move this is going to hurt you immensely."

'Not laughing anymore Angel opened up his blue cloak which is a extension of himself and exposed what lies within it, within him. A void of nothing that can torture your soul or heal it, in my case my dream self.'

'I was pulled into his void of nothingness with no chance of escaping due to the fact that my strength was as laughable to him as the look in my eyes. Darkness and silence greeted me instantly upon entering this void. A mile in, I think, I stopped being pulled in further, I turned around to watch as this Angel's cloak closed back up taking away all light and sound with it.'

'I freaked out and screamed a few times, knowing I did not have the means to get myself out of this void when I started to calm down. This void of nothing was just that. In there I started to feel more at peace as something soft as feathers rubbed against my body.'

'Before long I felt like I was being cleansed when the urge to puke came to me. I puked and I puked, I think I even puked out more than puke, like blood, like my sins.'

'Light and sound blinded and deafened me as I was expelled out of the void back into The DreamVerse, where I was all alone. I felt good, I was healed, I had to go to war tomorrow night, blood and ash will stain me until this damn war ends. Twenty nine more days of war counting down, just to have my life become something I will never be able to live free.'

170

'I walked over to my mortal shell slowly, dragging my feet, I felt good and I wondered what I was going to feel like when I woke up. I've been drained before upon waking up where coffee was like drinking dark water. I did not know what I was going to feel like when I woke up but I knew my time to wake up was coming soon. So I dragged myself just a little bit slower 'til I jumped back into my mortal shell where I woke up and looked at my clock. It was one hour and seven minutes until my alarm was to go off and with a weak creak the door to my bedroom opened up.'

Shelly was wearing a sexy red teddy. I sat up in bed feeling horny and needing a release, no I can't. This is what I said to Shelly, "Shelly you look so beautiful and thank you very much for your offer but I do not think we should do this."

Like Shelly was high out of her mind she said to me, "Good you're awake, how was your first day at war honey? I hope you killed a lot of your enemies. Now lay back so I can give you a massage so you can be relaxed enough to make love to me at least twice."

"Twice?"

"Yes twice, do you like the color of red I'm wearing? All that blood you saw last night, I know not if it turns you on, so I picked out my red teddy that is the closest to the color of blood."

"What? What is wrong with you Shelly? No blood does not turn me on."

"Well good then, now get up first and go pee and come back to this bed and lay back down."

'My mind was frazzled just waking up and I didn't know for sure if Shelly was messing with me or not so I asked her if I had time enough to brush my teeth as well.'

171

"Do what you may Barry, just know this I have not been touched by a man for six months. I have saved myself for you Barry since the first night of your coma."

"Why would you do this Shelly? I don't understand."

"I was sick, I was dying. In my dreams some Angel named Sam came to me that night, telling me that when I die I will feel a lot of pain. After I'm dead my soul will go to Hell."

"That's a very bad dream, Shelly."

"Are you messing with me Barry?"

"No, I'm being concerned. Look at my faces, can't you see concerned all over it?"

"I don't know? Seems to me, your concerned faces looks a lot like your, I'm being a smart ass face."

"No, I'm being concerned."

"Well good... Hell! Hell Barry, for I am a sinner and that is where sinners go. When I was a teenager, I was drunk and driving myself home from a party when I ran over a man that was walking in the middle of the road and killed him. I drove off because I was drunk, I was pissed off and I blamed the man I ran over for being in my way. Let me back up before I was drinking and driving and explain how I got there."

"Take your time."

"My boyfriend was getting stale and there was this hot guy I wanted to make love to. So I broke up with my boyfriend the morning before the party he was going to take me to that same night. I dolled myself up and went to the party, I drank one no three drinks before we were making love like we were perfect for each other. We finished, I cuddled up next to him and he laughed at me then he told me to get the Hell off him. I was in shock and sobering up quickly when this bastard jumped off the bed and put his clothes back on, and the whole time he was still laughing at me like I was pathetic."

"That's fucked up."

"Yes very... I screamed to him that he was a bastard and he told me that I was a slut and not a very good one at that. I was about to yell at him, when he snapped his fingers at me and coldly said to me..."

"Tell you what, I'm going out looking for another slut to screw, if I can't find one that is better than you then I'll be back to screw you again."

"When he thought he could turn around and walk away, after saying that to me... I got so mad that I threw a lamp at him which broke across the back of his head. He ran out of the door calling me a crazy bitch."

"Damn and good for you Shelly. This guy was a big asshole."

"No Barry, he was a dick."

"You're right."

"I cried feeling just like the slut that he just called me. I picked up my phone, I could not believe what I had done to my perfect boyfriend. He answered. I cried to him that I was sorry and what I just did. Which I told him was a good thing because it made me realize what I had with him was so very special and made me love him even more..."

"He called me a slut and hung up on me. I got so mad, I was out of my mind, the boyfriend that I dropped because he was not good enough for me called me a slut. When I felt he should thank me for going out with him in the first place."

"I was sober, I wanted to become drunk, and I needed to snap. I got dressed walked out of the bedroom, there was this guy standing there looking at me with his mouth wide open holding a glass. I walked up to him grabbed the glass out of his hands but it was only soda which made me even madder so I threw the rest of the soda in the glass straight into his face."

"That's funny, Shelly's gone sexy, crazy."

"Damn straight... I said listen up and listen up good you dog, go get me a drink right now and maybe I'll let you screw me. He ran away so fast saying he'd be right back. I got bored so I walked back down to the center of the party which was a combo of the kitchen and living room. My dog came up to me with two drinks, one was suppose to be his, I drank mine down fast then grabbed his out of his hand and drank it down. I told him more drinks, he walked off like a good dog."

"Then what happened?"

"I looked around, there was this hot guy who had a full drink in one hand and his girlfriend in the other. So I walked up to them and pushed his girlfriend out of the way, I grabbed his drink and drank it down then I kissed him. He kissed me back and I bit his tongue making it bleed. He called me a crazy bitch. I said to him and everyone at the party that's right I'm a crazy bitch that wants to get drunker and if I want your man I'll take him away from you and turn him into my dog."

"I bet there was silence around the room after you said that?"

"Yes and a lot of mouths hanging open. Barry I was out of my mind with regret, fear and pain. What would everyone say about me when that bastard told his tale of fucking me and tossing me away? At least I busted that lamp across the back of his head..."

174

"I know that was a long time ago, still if he would have just held me, we probably would have made love again. I would have not been in my car at that point of the night for what was to unfold for me to make me a sinner with a damned soul with a destiny to burn in flames."

'I watched and listened to Shelly like her eternal being had been tuned down to a nice calm simmer. She said words that were full of emotions with barely any emotion showing at all. Like a person that knows what emotions are, they just do not have it them to bring them out to full bloom.'

'I wanted to interrupt Shelly, I wanted away from this scene of heavy that I knew was about to get a lot heavier. A lot heavier on me for I knew what was coming. Her damsel, me knight.'

Shelly continues, "I was told to leave, on the way out the door I told the whole party to go fuck themselves. I got in my car drunk as can be and not caring one damn bit. I sped off like a mad woman and in a few moments it was all I could do to keep my eyes open then thump, thump, I ran over a man that was walking in the middle of the road..."

"I stopped my car, when I tried to step out of it I slipped and landed on my face breaking my nose. I said forget him, got back up on my feet, got back in my car and drove off calling him a lousy stupid dog for walking in the middle of the road."

"A few days later the news about his death was everywhere and not only that but what he did before he got ran over. He killed his wife and kids in cold blooded murder, got drunk and walked down the road with their blood all over his body."

"Damn... I don't know what to say?"

"It's alright Barry, just listen. The Angel named Sam told me I had one chance not to die in pain and for my soul to go to Hell. You Barry, I belong to you for one month."

"One month? That sounds familiar?"

"Sam explained to me that war is Hell and you needed me to comfort your soul during the times you were not warring."

"Shelly, I don't know."

"If you tell me no again that you do not want me, I will come out of the trance that I'm in right now. I will not know what is going on, I will not know why I am dressed this way and worst of all my deal will be over with and I will become sick once again and die."

"I don't want that to happen, Shelly."

"Good... I agreed to this in my dream Barry, I will not remember what we do. When I am not for your comfort, you will be just my friend that lives with me that I have a secret crush on."

"This part sounds nice, Shelly."

"Please Barry, do not say no to me, please I do not want to die and go to Hell. After you leave me in one month, I will go on with my life until I die years from now and after I die, I get to go to Heaven."

"I don't know Shelly, I'll be using you."

"You do not want to take Heaven away from me do you Barry?"

'I shook my head and told her that I would love to make love to her after I took my piss and brushed my teeth.'

'This first morning became Shelly's and my routine, every morning I woke up after warring myself bloody and numb.

It was weird at first then I became use to it, until it became the only thing in my life that I looked forward to.'

'It was so wild, we would make love, and when we were finished, Shelly would tell me that I was great then she would ask me if I was through with her. I would tell her yes and she would get out of my bed and leave me there alone to go back to her own bed after she cleaned up first.'

'Shelly would wake up not knowing what we did once, what we did ten times, what we did twenty nine times until the last night I was to stay with her.'

'My last night of war was bloody as can be when I was told to go into over drive to make sure God's point stuck forever in the minds of The Gemini Dream Legion.'

'I woke up, Shelly entered my bedroom, we made love, she left me to wake up in her own bed and then got up to make us breakfast just like she did every morning.'

'Well in truth it was one month and one day I stayed with Shelly. That day at breakfast Shelly went for it, to her it had been thirty days we lived together in her home as friends and it was time for us today to become more than friends.'

'Fate was telling her to do this so when I left her the next morning after making love to her for the first time, leaving her just a simple note it would make sense to her and she could go on with her life.'

'It was weird as Hell, I was trying to save Shelly by making love to her then eating breakfast with her like we didn't make love.'

'No going up behind her and giving her a hug or pulling her fine soft body next to mine just to enjoy the feel of it against me after we made love.'

'I still wonder to this day how Shelly could not feel like she just made love after she was back to her normal self. I mean she was not just my lover, I was hers as well. Shelly had needs and wants and she had no trouble in telling what they were.'

'The last time/our first time I just had to know. Was Shelly going to be like she was every day before? No it was like the first time all over again but this time with her true feelings coming forth from her. Which made me know that that last time/first time we made love together every time before that was sex, just wonderful stress relieving sex.'

Chapter Two:

'War, day number two. I packed my lunch and skipped my way to bloody war. Really I was just like fuck it, come what may, I hate my life, twenty nine days to go, bring it on. That was how I was feeling. I mean damn I felt great before I entered my mortal body, like never before, only to wake up having Shelly looking so fine, making me so weak. I'm a man, I get turned on when the wind blows, this is the first time I ever felt ashamed for having sex.'

'Before I was married to Tina, I was a man that sexed a lot with a lot of different ladies. I had two at a time, I had one then the other. Ladies looked into my eyes like I want to be able to control and own you, while they were on top and making love to me. I watched as heart breakers lost control for the first time. When we were done, they were ashamed for not staying in control over themselves making me the one that they looked to for the answers.'

'I always received that I love you, I hate you look from their eyes. I knew who won the sex battle, so did they. I never taunted them for what I did for them, I felt it was a blessing. Something they could put in the back of their minds and bring back out when the man they were getting ready to heartbreak did not have enough in him to please them.'

'Some of them cried, I would bring a tissue to them that I had in the ready. Some would take their tissue out of my hand nice and gentle, holding on to my hand to give it a light squeeze before pulling it out of my hand. Some were different, some used a different approach to take the tissue out of my hand. Saying things like give me that damn thing, then ripping it out of my hand only to crumble it up to give it back to me by throwing it in my face.'

'Some would simply slap it out of my hand and tell me to fuck off. I have a great big heart, I like to laugh, I have a sense of humor that ladies like, sometimes I do not.

When I am told by a lady I just made love to, to fuck off, I always try to lighten things up by saying. What is Off's first name or is that her first name? Ladies like you always seem to want me to fuck her, yet none of you can even tell me Off who is, let alone what she looks like. After this I either get a laugh or I better watch closely for the quick smack to my face.'

'I was the one that waited on phone calls so I could pick out for the night which one sounded better for my best friend, my manhood. So many called me for more loving, while others just called me that bastard. Heads or tails, whichever way it landed I was cool with. I was always in control, that is until I met Tina.'

'Tina and I started our night like I have a hundred times. When sex came around, it was a little bit late and I still had an after date sex to go to after I was finished with Tina.'

'Wow Tina put me in my place, made me fall in love with her, made me call her back for more when she grabbed me by my face, looked me in my eyes and said, no, no, no, that won't do. I was just about to finish, Tina was out of sight so I said hell with it and went for a huge quick release.'

Then I heard what stopped me. "What do you think you are doing? Don't you dare finish until I tell you that you can." Tina said this to me while she was underneath me looking up at me like I was an idiot.

'I could not believe what I just heard coming from the voice of a sweet, little, sexy lady that felt like she'd saved it for long period of time, until she felt like it was time for her to play a little bit.'

Tina let go of my face, while I said not one word. "Off me now man, it is time for me to show you how to have total sexual control over your body."

180

'I told her to go for it, playing along, followed my orders as Tina took control over her sex having for the night. Tina screamed/moaned four times then told me it was okay for me to have mine. I pushed Tina off me, who was shaking with delight and I told her not yet. Tina bit her bottom lip, she closed her eyes and when she opened them back up, she ran her right hand through her hair and told me to take my time.'

'God I love that woman, she was sexy, she was smart, she made me laugh, she made me crazy. I was hers, she was mine, a miracle for a man like me, that is why I married her and never cheated on her once.'

'Back to war day number two, I fell asleep, I stayed inside my mortal shell for a little while, when I brought my dream self out into The DreamVerse, I was greeted by the eight foot laughing Angel from the night before.'

"Hello Barry, I am the Messenger of God. I will be meeting you upon your arrival here in The DreamVerse for the near future. Sam has been going through a little bit of a rough patch and needs some time off to bask in the light of God."

"Well Messenger of God I hope Sam goes blind from staring too long, for he is a lousy Angel. What about you? You seem normal, more than you did last night?"

"Yes last night, that was my attempt at humor, you were so stressed Barry, I thought you could use a laugh, even if it was a little bit at your expense."

"Thanks for the concern but I'm fine."

"Are you Barry Goldrum? You do not look fine. Did Shelly not put your mind back in order? Would you want another lady to do that for you?"

"Yes I would, I want Tina."

181

"I cannot give you Tina Barry, she is in Heaven."

"Then Shelly is the one I guess."

"You guess?"

"Yes, if I choose another lady then Shelly dies and goes to Hell."

"Yes this is true, nothing I can do about that either."

"Then Messenger of God where does that leave us?"

"That all depends on you Barry, on your answer. Will you go to war tonight? Will you go to war every night for the next twenty eight nights after tonight?"

Barry lets the heavy of his answer linger in his mind, "Time is up Barry, no more deciding. War or go home?"

"Damn it, war, I pick war."

"Good you know the rules, you are not to enter any dreamer's dream here in The DreamVerse for extra strength. Your strength comes from power ups after each kill you make. Do not dare go into any dreamer's dream Barry, I warn you of this. If you do you will leave me no choice but to come in after you and rip you out of that dream as violently as I can. My presence in a dreamer's dream will melt their minds and they will die and it will be all your fault."

"What if I accidentally get knocked into a dreamer's dream?"

"Accidentally?"

"Yeah, like I'm battling a group of the Gemini Dream Legion and their sheer numbers are so great that they push me into someone's dream."

"Well Barry in the slim likelihood that happens then I'll give you a pass. As long as you hurry up and get your human self out of that dream as fast as you can."

"What are the other rules Messenger of God? By the way what is your name?"

"Thank you for asking Barry, you cannot speak my name, if you tried your tongue would rip itself out of your mouth."

"I take it Sam's name is not really Sam?"

"That is correct. But I can tell you this Barry, Sam's Angel name is a very sorry one that other Angels make fun of."

"Poor Angel, but still I can't feel sorry for that prick. He hates humans for some reason. He made me bleed Messenger of God, I kinda hate him very much. Now what about the other rules?"

"There's only one rule Barry, kill and gather strength."

"You know Messenger of God, that is sick. Grover, yes I killed him, he was a monster that killed thousands of people and most importantly Tina. But the others of the Gemini Dream Legion..."

"But nothing Barry, they kill as well, many people whose souls were not ready to come home to Heaven..."

"Not all of them."

"What was that Barry?"

"I said, not all of them."

"Yes Barry, now some of them do not kill dreamers in their dreams. Before, yes before, every member no matter how less they kill now has killed before.

Every member Barry, remember this. Their entire race was birthed from the death of living humans."

"Did God know that the Gemini Dream Legion was to exist before he created humans? Or were they an unhappy side effect that was not included in his plans?"

"I cannot answer that Barry. To do so would mean that I am worthy enough to understand God's will, which I am not."

"Any last words for me Messenger of God?"

"Yes Barry, tonight The Elders must fall."

"You mean, I must kill them."

"Yes Barry."

"You do not understand Messenger of God."

"I do not understand what Barry Goldrum?"

"To get to them, I have to get through thousands of The Gemini Dream Legion first. Some who are only there because they are following orders."

"So what? Did I not just tell you that every member was a killer one time or another? So go through them Barry Goldrum by any means necessary to get to The Elders, tonight."

"I can't."

"What do you mean you can't?"

"One night, eight hours is not enough time to make my way through to The Elders. If I did I would be tired and weak from fighting which might make me an easy target for The Elders to kill."

"Is that what you think Barry Goldrum? How wrong you are. Take away from your mind your frail human condition."

"Just take it away?"

"Yes."

"If I die in this DreamVerse I die in real life."

"Yes this is true, make it simple for yourself and do not die here in The DreamVerse. Barry, Barry you are thinking too hard on your mortal limits. You are one of a kind."

"Yes, so was Grover."

"Grover was a killer you are not."

"Yes I am and here in just a little while I will kill again. I don't think I can handle that heavy weight on my soul Messenger of God."

"That is where I come in for you Barry Goldrum. I will cleanse your soul for you just like I did last night."

"Yet I am still a killer, how can I be allowed in Heaven?"

"Because you killed for God's will and not for yourself out of malice. In Heaven Barry Goldrum there are many souls that were covered in blood before they entered Heaven. The great thing about blood Barry Goldrum is that it can be cleansed away."

"I feel that you are wrong, I hope that you are not. I feel that I am signing my own doom with the blood of thousands of people."

"That is why you will be worthy of Heaven Barry Goldrum, for your pain, for your sacrifice you will be allowed to come home after you die to be one among many.

I do not want any failures tonight Barry Goldrum, so I will aid you in your conquest."

"What kind of aid?"

"I'll give you a lift inside my void straight to the The Gemini Manor, where all The Elders are all gathered there tonight, hiding like powerful cowards, while their soldiers fight to the death for them out of loyalty."

"You could do this Messenger of God with little of ease, could you not?"

"Yes Barry and I would love to, but my part does not allow me to do that. I envy you Barry Goldrum."

"What is there to envy?"

"Tonight you change, your power level will increase a thousand fold. After tonight no one in the DreamVerse, no matter how many they are, they will fall to your power."

"That cannot be possible, can it?"

"Oh yes Barry, before long you will gain enough power to be able to battle a Demon, to battle an Angel and perhaps have the power to win."

"That's power."

"Confidence Barry Goldrum, I do not feel coming forth from you. I know a secret about your power level, I thought at first it would be a great big surprise for you to experience your true power level that increased by killing Grover."

"I didn't receive any power level increase after Grover's death."

"Yes you did, it has been suppressed to you for future use. Which is tonight Barry Goldrum.

186

Are you ready to feel power like you never thought possible? Are you ready for power that will be so strong that your soul will feel it?"

"Yes I am, give me my power Messenger of God," I commanded like a great warrior.

'I asked for it and I got what I asked for plus a lot more than I thought possible. The Messenger of God opened up his blue cloak to expose his eternal void and pulled out this ball of glowing green light, with highlights that included red, purple, orange and blue. The Messenger of God looked at me and asked me, who's the man?'

'Next moment before I could answer, Bam! My soul? Was attacked by a entity of power that was as brilliant as it was sadistic. This force of immense power did not just enter my dream self it forced itself into it. It hurt like Hell.'

"I started to convulse making it feel like my dream self was coming apart at the seams. The pain just would not stop and the thought that I was going to die came to my mind. Which for some reason I thought was funny so I laughed out loud. I looked around for Mr. Death knowing I could not take much more, when the pain started to subside.'

'Moment by moment, I started to feel thicker and thicker. I lifted my head back and laughed out loud, only this time I was laughing at the power level I was feeling come to life within my being, within my very soul.'

'Watch out DreamVerse here comes Barry Goldrum, the man with the unlimited amount of power inside him.'

"How's that new power feel to you Barry Goldrum?"

"I feel like I could destroy the world."

"Well jump into my void so you can test your new power level out on The Elders."

"No I'm good, I do not need your ride Messenger of God, I have my own."

'I made my wings appear and snapped them open. They were made out of soft feathers at first. I turned my wings into steel like I have done many times before, then I used my new power level to turn my wings into a metal that would slice straight through normal steel.'

'I looked at the Messenger of God like he was prey, for which he shook his head no to me, I laughed and flew away. I was fast before, the speed I could travel now was God like. If I did not have my strength enhancement, this speed would kill me fast.'

'I came up so fast on the The Gemini Manor that when it was hundreds of miles away it took me only a few minutes to reach it. Thousands of the Gemini Dream Legion were standing in my way again. I did not slow down, I just flew straight through them without any resistance. I sliced myself through hundreds and hundreds of them who all died in a matter of seconds after I passed through them.'

'I stopped at the doors of the The Gemini Manor, I turned around, there was a trail of heavy, thick blood and dust that coated The DreamVerse. I was so fast that it took a few minutes for all my power ups to catch up with me.'

'I grabbed a hold of the The Gemini Manor and shook it, I was strong enough to make it shake like I was an Earthquake. I ripped off the doors and threw them away from me. I roared out my battle cry. With my claws and wings, I marched straight to Grover's throne room killing anyone that got in my path or tried to stop me.'

'My battle plan was simple, charge my enemy and fight them until every one of them was dead. I was a beast from another world that they had never seen before. I was quick, I was deadly, I did not pay any heed to their pleas as I ripped apart to death every Elder that lived.'

188

'Blood soaked every part of my dream self. My mind was not mine any more it now belonged to death and war. After every Elder was dead, I looked around for more Elders to kill. I could not come down, I was out of control to the max.'

'I came flying back out of the The Gemini Manor looking for more enemies to battle. In front of my path was the Messenger of God. He told my not listening to him ears that the war was over for me this night. It was time for me to reenter my mortal shell and dream some soft and safe dreams for the rest of the night.'

'I did not listen to him as I tried to pass by him to get to the thousands of Gemini Dream Legion that I wanted to battle to the death. The Messenger of God's void can become as large as he wants it to be. He swallowed me up into his void which I fought against with every thing I had in me.'

'After an hour I finally calmed down enough to be let out of the Messenger of God's void of nothingness. I reentered my mortal shell and dreamed nicely for the rest of the night. When I woke up Shelly was laying beside me waiting for me to wake up. We made love three times, the third time I cried like a baby, trying my best to get all the pain I felt inside me out.'

Shelly looked so beautifully flushed at the end, still with a pale tone of emotion said to me, "Goodbye Barry, my sexy lover, it is time for me to go back to my bed and wake up feeling so good."

"Goodbye Shelly, see the real you in a few minutes."

"Thank you Barry, for choosing to save my life and my soul. I will always love you for this, even though I will not remember that you did."

Chapter Three:

War, day number three. Dream self out of mortal shell, I walked over to the Messenger of God, "Evening."

"Good evening Barry Goldrum, how they hanging?"

"Large and to the right."

"Your soul looks calmer tonight?"

"Yes, I feel nothing like I did last night, thanks for pulling me out of The DreamVerse. I turned into a blood thirsty monster."

"Yes you did."

"Why?"

"Why what Barry Goldrum?"

"Why did you pull me out, was I not the perfect warring machine last night?"

"Yes quite right."

"Then why?"

The Messenger of God paused his answer for a moment looking away from me, then he spoke his answer while he looked me in my eyes and spoke calmly, "Last night I filled your mind with the glory of war and triumph by giving you all the power that formally resided in Grover. You were the perfect killing machine, which you needed to be. I pulled you out after you were finished with The Elders because last night was the only night of this war you have to be this killing machine."

"I don't understand. I'm glad, but why?"

"The killing machine you were last night was a warning to the Gemini Dream Legion that this unstoppable warrior can resurface if need be. The war changes for you tonight."

"In what way?"

"No longer will you be this killing machine, from now on you are an assassin for Heaven. Starting tonight you will be given a list. On this list will be names. Every name on this list starting with the first to the last has to be marked through by the end of the night."

"Only names on this list, what about other people that get in my way that are not on this list?"

"Do what you must Barry Goldrum. The very worst of the Gemini Dream Legion will be the very first name, then the second and so forth."

'The Messenger of God handed me my first list, I looked at it reading off names that I did not know, each with their own number.'

"There is one hundred names on this list?"

"Yes Barry Goldrum."

"How do I find the people on this list? And I have to find them in order?"

"Yes, in order."

"I'm fast Messenger of God, but how can I find someone that I do not know?"

"That's funny Barry Goldrum, you work for Heaven there is no margin for error. As soon as you take off flying the first person on the list will send out a beacon for you to find. Also when you come upon this person there will be a number one on his forehead, the same with the second.

When you finish with number one their beacon will fade away along with themselves and the second person on that list, their beacon will activate."

"Seems simple enough. I guess I better get started dream time is a wasting."

"Very good Barry Goldrum. Before you fly away to war for the night, there is one more thing that I have to do."

"What is that?"

"This."

The Messenger of God reached his right hand into Barry's chest, like his hand was ghost like and ripped away from him the power of Grover.

"What was that? What did you just do to me?"

"I took from you, Grover's power. You do not need it for right now."

"I don't?"

"No, you do not."

"You leave me weaker? Why would you do this to me Messenger of God?"

"God's orders Barry Goldrum. If I left Grover's power inside you after your first encounter of the evening, you would once again return to the mindless killing machine that you were last night. You still have enough power inside you to complete your task..."

"Remember after each kill you will gain a power up. When you leave The DreamVerse this night you will have gained one hundred more new power ups to strengthen your dream self."

"What about Grover's power up?"

"That is something you will regain someday after this war is over with."

"What if I need it?"

"You will not Barry Goldrum, have faith in yourself and in God's wisdom. When you receive Grover's power up once again, you will have to learn how to use its power without becoming a mindless killing machine. When I give it back to you next time Barry Goldrum it will remain inside you for all eternity. Even when your soul resides in Heaven. In fact it will become part of you that only God will be able to take away from you."

"That sounds heavy Messenger of God, very, very heavy."

"It is Barry Goldrum. The evil that resides inside Grover's power up is that, it is Evil! It will do its very best to turn you into a killing machine and make sure you stay that way."

"How can I overcome this evil?"

"Time and patience Barry Goldrum. You have a good and powerful soul that will be tainted every day this war continues. After the war is over with you will be stronger of soul. If your soul is strong enough it will be able to fight back the temptation of Grover's intense evil."

"If not?"

"God will rip it out of you and in doing so will rip you apart as well. You will die in extreme agony and your soul, your good and powerful soul will be damaged beyond repair making it a soul that does not belong in Heaven. That soul, if it ever comes to be Barry Goldrum, will have only one place to fall to and that is Hell."

"Win the war and control a thick chunk of evil inside me

until I die and I get Heaven. If I lose or if I can't control this evil then I get Hell?"

"Yes that is correct Barry Goldrum."

"Well that is just perfect."

"I am glad that you are happy with your out come."

"Yes I am, I mean why would I not be? I wish I could thank God in person for thinking about me when he decided upon this war and beyond for the rest of my living human life."

"Well good then Barry Goldrum."

"No it's not good Messenger of God, I was being sarcastic."

'The Messenger of God looked at me all serious for a second or two then he started to laugh his wings off.'

"That's the spirit Barry Goldrum, keep that great sense of humor up front and it will help ease your pains and make it possible for you to find your paradise at your end."

"Well until game over then Messenger of God, see you on the way back out tonight."

"'Til then Barry Goldrum, break a leg or two."

"Have I told you lately Messenger of God how much better you are than Sam?"

"Yes you have."

"Well you are but from me to you, I think you suck, I thing everything about this sucks."

"Think this all you want Barry Goldrum just do not believe

this in your soul. For if you do then you will fail and fail ultimately. Have a great night Barry Goldrum."

"You too Messenger of God."

The Messenger of God was about to fly away, when a thought came to me. "Messenger, there's something I need to know."

"What's that Barry?"

"I, with help built a fortress."

"Yes."

"On this side of the DreamVerse, where dreamers do not dwell. Why in all this space does only the Gemini Manor and the fortress we built, that was never named and now lays in ruin, exist?"

"It's all about Grover. Inside The Gemini Manor, there is Grover's castle. Plenty of space provided for himself and The Elders."

"Let me guess, where everyone else finds an uncomfortable place to try to feel comfortable with."

"Pretty much to the fact."

"So no individual housing ever, just one large community building for all to share? Seems to me that freedom is what they need, instead of war?"

"Barry, war will lead them to their very first taste of freedom. After war comes changes."

"So by doing what I'm doing, I'm leading them in the direction of freedom and peace?"

"Yes."

'Surreal, the last two nights were as well but this conversation Messenger and I had, made me understand deeply how insignificant I was. I could deny it as much as I wanted to with things like God thinks I'm special or I am God's special warrior. But no matter what, I'm doomed and I knew that ever so clearly, still do.'

'I've grown a lot harder which has made my good and evil filled soul calm with acceptance of my role 'til the day I die. Which I wonder how much longer will this be? Will I die fairly young, hard and strong, or will I die really old, weak and frail? Will my age of death be reflected in Heaven? If this is the way then I'd rather be a younger soul forever.'

'I'm forty now in the year of 2050. Three years I have done my job, I've had enough, damn the same. I go after bad souls in their sleep, I go after bad souls wide awake making them feel like they are experiencing a waking nightmare that drives them to take their final steps towards their death. Three years I've seen death come up to these dead bodies and reap their souls out of them.'

'Every damned one of them heading to Hell, I could care less. After Death, do their reaping they always look me in my eyes. Three years of having death do this, well what can I say, fuck death they are only cogs in the machine between Heaven and Hell.'

'Maybe it's me but in their eyes I feel either they want to take me to Hell. Or is this their upcoming future obligation to take me to the place a damaged soul like I have deserves to rest in pain and torment. For even though all the souls I have sent to Hell deserve it, I cannot help to feel that my sole purpose is to forcibly push myself into their lives so they can die at a earlier time in their lives.'

'I have at least, helped people, good people sometimes, not as much as I want to, the bad people always come first. Sometimes on the way as I fly by to take out evil, I hear the cries for help from good people to end their pain of what lies behind their open up memory dream doors. Memory dream doors, that eat away at their good souls every time they close their eyes and sleep. Endless nightmares, which I know plenty about for I am a nightmare that was brought to existence by God. Damn that's heavy, woe is me, ha,ha,ha.'

'Back to three years ago. Sleeping, blood, death, waking up to the softness and pleasure of sex. One month, war and sex every day it was very simple and easy to understand. One month my war was over with which has led me to where I am now, three years into my post war life.'

'War days number four through twelve, were pretty much the same, I made good use of my talents by eliminating the one hundred names on my list from day three to day twelve. Day thirteen was just a normal war day going on in my mind as I entered The DreamVerse. Fun to say but little did I know what was waiting for me on this thirteenth day of war.'

'Mister Scratch, Satan himself made a visit to The DreamVerse all the way from fiery Hell. Bastard stinks, Satan is a bastard that stinks to low Hell. I thought my eyes were playing tricks on me. The Messenger of God was bloodily wounded, looking close to death by the mighty evil hands of Satan.'

'Satan looked at me smiling like look what I just did. He was giddy having a great time tasting the Messenger of God's Angel blood that is the color of a rainbow.'

This I did not understand as Satan said, "Hello Barry Goldrum, how the fuck you doing tonight, you weak ass limp, human?"

'I did feel limp, nothing will turn you off more than Satan. Deer in the headlights, damn I was scared. My brain was chattering away at me like a train leading away from Hell to climb aboard and get the Hell out of there.'

'Who was I to fight Satan, did I stand a chance? I could not do what Satan had done to the Messenger of God. How could I defeat him? No way I could I think of, so I took off flying back to my mortal shell which was not that far away.'

'I flew up all fast and furious to where it was suppose to be and it was gone. I looked around all nervously, like where the fuck is my body. Right after that, this wall of fire appeared in front of me, blazing out of control with an intense heat that made my dream self feel like very soon it would start melting to goo.'

'Scratch to the back of my dream self, Satan is standing behind me with my blood on his claw. Evil bastard made my heart stop, when all of a sudden he laughed out so loud and fast that it made my head feel like it was going to pop, like a piece of tasteless over chewed gum. Satan stopped laughing at a Hell's pitch and tuned his laughing into somewhat normal, well for Satan.'

'Nobody wants to ever hear Satan's laughter. Wings being ripped off Angels, would sound like Angelic hymns from Heaven compared to what Satan laughed out so joyously.'

'Satan slapped me on my back like I was a friend that should be enjoying some laughter as well. So I obliged his evilness and laughed. Damn, Satan stopped laughing instantly looking at me like I was dead. Lucky thirteen my ass.'

"What the fuck you laughing at you ass brained human. You laughing at me?"

"No, I'm laughing with you."

"Well that is different my son. It warms my heart high up to Heaven to know, that you feel that it is funny to the fact that I have burned your mortal shell to ash."

"You are dead, what you are now is not some pathetic dream self, no, no, no. No, now you are a freed soul, with no body to go back to. In other words, you are in the perfect condition to be taken to Hell. I'm going to beat you personally for just my Hell of it all. Barry Goldrum, I love you. Like Hell I do but I will love beating your soul to death."

'I stood there in shock, wondering how I was going to get myself out of this.'

"In Hell there are many souls that I and my torture demons, torture to the point to where even their immortal souls cannot take it anymore. When I or they get to that point we stop, let them rest so we can torture them again and again to the point of their souls death for all eternity. Yes Barry Goldrum a soul can die. Your soul will die, I will see to that, yes I will."

'I stood there in shock, wondering how I was going to get myself out of this.'

"Now to prove to you that I am fair and just, that at one time I was the Greatest Angel ever created, this is the time I will allow you to beg for your soul. It will do you no good but none-the-less give me your best. If you do not beg your very best, well then I will have no choice but to punish you."

I was getting mad, I'd had just about enough of Satan the over powerful evil prick. "Punish me? You are going to kill my soul, what kind of punishment could be worse than that?"

Satan laughed, "You dumb idiot human, man are you funny. Like I said I use to be the grandest of all Angels so I have a very, very tiny speck of compassion left inside my being even after my great fall.

I was going to leave your manhood alone, you know your pecker. Just let it burn to ash along with the rest of your soul untouched. But if you do not beg, like begging is your life, well when I drag you to Hell the very first thing I will make happen to you is this."

'Satan stopped talking, he laughed out this little laugh, like he was trying to hold it back. He did this three more times before he was lying down on The DreamVerse laughing his master of Hell ass off. He tried to talk but his extreme laughter would not let his words take form. So I had to stand there and watch Satan laughing out loud like an asshole until he finally had it in him to stand back up.'

"Off it goes Barry Goldrum."

"Off what goes Satan?"

"Your pecker."

"My pecker?"

"Yes your pecker. I will have my nastiest, ugliest lady demon bite it off you and eat it. How does that sound to you Barry Goldrum?"

"You Evil bastard, you leave my pecker alone!" I screamed at Satan.

'I was pissed and in my mind was an attack chant of my pecker is my life. Satan stood still as I attacked him in anger and fear with every power up inside myself raging out of control. I hit Satan with everything I had, I kept hitting him 'til my arms went numb. Then I kicked him, while he just stood there and took it, like it was causing him little to no pain at all. I was out of breath, I gave Satan a few more punches then I collapsed.'

Satan looked down at me expressionless, he cleared his throat and said to me, "You are not very good at begging."

'I looked up at Satan, told him to fuck off, then I, yes I had my turn at laughing my ass off at Satan's expression. I was still laughing when the Messenger of God walked up to us and stood side by side with Satan. Satan was two feet taller than the Messenger of God which made him a giant figure of ten feet tall, horns and tail included.'

'The Messenger of God asked Satan if my soul was more evil than it was good. Satan laughed out loud knowing he would claim his prize in the end.'

"Not yet Messenger of God, but very soon, maybe, it's all up to him. Will Barry Goldrum stay close to the light, letting in darkness when he needs its brutal edge in battle? Will he turn his soul dark, go against the word of God? For this I will wait in Hell, watching its outcome to be."

Satan paused, "Barry Goldrum if you turn your soul dark, it will not be of my actions. No I will let you deal with that thick, evil inside you when you receive it for the second time. This has never happened before, some human just like you Barry Goldrum receiving all this evil. Furthermore you stinking human full of blood and puss that evil is mine, it is mine..."

"God created you to receive this evil to keep it away from me. It calls out to me like it loves me. This evil hates you, it wants to kill you. Do not look at me like this with eyes of aren't I dead already. No, you fool you are not dead, all I made you see was an illusion. My body, my body, pathetic."

'Nothing was funny anymore as I stood up on my feet and looked up at Satan.'

"I'm pathetic. No Satan you are Pathetic. You tell me that you will just kick back, like it's your choice and watch from Hell to see if I lose all my grace so to say. Yeah right Angel of Fire or how I like to say it, Angel of burning shit. You can't interfere you have been grounded, ha, ha, ha."

"God has put you on the bench. This evil that calls out to you I will bend to my will. When we meet again Satan, I will have the most evil soul that never lived inside me. All you have is millions of evil souls that lived a human life until they died and their evil souls went to Hell. You're not special, you're served the same old shit everyday."

'Satan had enough of my wicked tongue, he was going to strike me down when the Messenger of God grew larger in size than Satan, standing in front him blocking his path to the thing he wanted to rip apart.'

"Out of my way Messenger of God, his tongue I will rip out of his disrespectful mouth."

"No Satan, stand down or back to Hell, I will send you. You will go back to Hell without claiming your prize. You do still want your prize, do you not Satan? The chance, maybe the only chance you will ever have at tasting the evil that may never come your way. Inside Barry Goldrum are traces of that evil, no way even I can get all this tremendous evil out of a soul once it has settled in."

Satan hissed fire out of his mouth, "Warning Barry Goldrum, when I am back in Hell, I will think of the most horrible things I ever had done to a soul and make them look like patty cakes. You better go around and kiss all the Angel ass you can for their favor. If your soul comes my way, your soul will not die, I've changed my mind..."

"I'm going to let demons come up to you and shit on your face you damn human. No one has ever spoken to me like you just did, no matter how evil and powerful they think they are. You are something different all the way around. When I look at you I say to myself, I Satan make sense in the good verses evil tragedy. You do not make a bit of sense Barry Goldrum, you're good, you're evil. One of each in one body and soul..."

"You will fail, only I, Lucifer, Barry Goldrum have what it takes inside me to control this evil. Give up before you start, call out to me when you receive your ultimate evil and I will ease the burden on you. Do it fast, do it without haste Barry Goldrum and no torture will ever come your way. You will sit beside me as my mightiest General. Even over my most trusted Demon. No former human will ever have the place in Hell you can have Barry Goldrum."

"Only God."

"What was that you just said?"

"I said only God, Satan."

"Only God what human?"

"Only God can take out this evil once it's placed in me for a second time. You are not God, he is number one. No you are Satan the devil of Hell which makes you number two."

"You are a fool Barry Goldrum, your afterlife could have been almost pleasant. It is Hell after all."

"I get it Satan, I sit beside you so you can feel the evil power inside me. Day by day feeling its pure evil of the likes you have never tasted. Except for yourself of course. Well suffer dude, you will never have a taste of my evil."

"Never Barry Goldrum? Fool I will have my taste in a matter of moments."

"What are you talking about Satan? I have not this evil inside me yet."

"Traces you fool, traces that will be like bacon on a burger. When I rip out of you all the power ups you have taken in these past twelve Earth days."

"Bacon on a burger, well Satan your burger needs to be flipped because it is burning..."

'I was getting ready to continue on with my back and forth banter with Satan when the Messenger of God yelled out in anger.'

"Silence Barry Goldrum."

'I went silent and stared at the Messenger of God.'

"Barry Goldrum you did not come to my aid when you came into this DreamVerse and witnessed what Satan had done to me."

"Yes Messenger of God but that was a farce was it not?"

"None-the-less Barry Goldrum that does not matter. What matters is good over evil and you have failed. If you would have come to my aid and died in your effort to save me from Satan your soul would have went straight to Heaven. You would have been pure Barry Goldrum but look at you now..."

"I never question God words or the things that he does, like you. God knows why you are to be this champion of The DreamVerse Barry Goldrum but when I cast my eyes upon you I do not. I see just a selfish Human who only thought of himself."

Two on one coming at me, not fair, "So what, yes I looked out for myself, no one else will do this. I know I'm on my own when two over powerful immortals such as the both of you stand back without getting your hands dirty. All these humans that live in The DreamVerse were put here by God. They were left on their own under the control of a blood thirsty, pain loving, madman, monster filled with evil. What else could have happened..."

"All these souls were damned from the beginning.

Either of you with all your power could have stopped this easily. But no. Satan I understand, could careless about all the souls save one, Grover. You Messenger of God could have been there for them, you should have been there for them, led all these unfortunate souls to the light."

"Yes Barry Goldrum I could have done this many times over but you were the chosen one to do this by God not I. Do you understand now? What you see as a burden on you is doubt in your mind. Doubt belongs to the Devil and Hell, not God and Heaven. You Barry Goldrum better make fast heed of it in your mind before it becomes so thick that it reaches your soul."

"Yes Messenger of God I understand all to well but there is one thing you do not understand."

"What is that Barry Goldrum?"

"Human, I am only human."

"This is true Barry Goldrum and it solely lies on you to become more than human. God believes in you ,why can you not? Keep your answer Barry Goldrum, for I do not want to hear it. Satan are you ready for your prize?"

"Hell yes I am, Messenger of God."

'I stood there looking at both the Messenger of God and Satan wondering to myself what was going to happen to me. I did not have to wonder for very long. The Messenger of God with one quick and powerful punch knocked me down on my ass. Surprised I looked up at him while he shook his head at me and said, "Look at your future Barry Goldrum, Satan himself, we still have much to discuss. Okay Satan claim you prize."

'I watched as Satan bent to the ground over me looking like a beast that is going in for the death wound to its prey.

Satan grabbed me by my throat and said hold still human. With his other clawed hand he reached into my dream self and ripped out every power up I accumulated for the past twelve nights. The pain, the pain was unreal, Satan was not allowed to kill me, but he had the green light to make sure I knew what intense pain felt like down to the very bottom of my bleeding soul.'

"That's enough Satan take you claw out of Barry Goldrum. He has felt enough of your pain."

"No Messenger of God, the traces of Grover's soul are too tasty to stop tasting now, let me have more."

"I said that is enough Satan."

'Satan would not stop digging deeper into my dream self which I figured out right then was the same thing as my soul. All this time what I thought of as my dream self was actually my very soul stepping out of its mortal shell to roam around and gather strength.'

'I was blinking out of existence as I felt Satan's claw being ripped out of me.'

"Get the Hell away from him Satan!" The Messenger of God warned a smiling in ecstasy Satan.

'I watched as the Messenger of God opened up his cloak to expose his void of nothingness and absorbed Satan into it. The look of the Messenger of God's eyes changed from good to evil in a instant.'

"Look at me Barry Goldrum, see my burden that I have to carry. I do so because I must, because God wills me to, I would have this no other way. I feel pain, I just saved your soul from dying Barry Goldrum because God willed me to. If it was not for God's command that I save you, I would have let Satan keep on digging into you until you died."

206

I looked at the Messenger of God and said, "This is not you."

"Yes it is Barry Goldrum. This is me until I get this evil Devil out of my void of nothingness and back to Hell. If I said no to God, the Devil would eventually make his way out of my void of nothingness and I would then be under his command..."

"God's mightiest warrior serving in Hell with one will left in my mind, to take over Heaven. I will never fall Barry Goldrum, because I love God. What about you? Do you love God Barry Goldrum?"

All I could say was, "I don't know."

"Yes I know Barry Goldrum that is why there is a chance your soul may still fall to Hell instead of rising to Heaven after your death."

'The Messenger of God, straightens himself up and endures his pain.'

"Stay where you stand Barry Goldrum, I will be back for you. Perhaps to punish you, perhaps to heal you, perhaps both together at the same time."

'Weakened and alone, I stood there wondering what's next. I stretched my tired dream self.'

(My Soul I know, calling my soul, my dream self makes it feel a little bit less heavy on my mind so I give myself this facade. A little white lie that helps me to keep going on. Yeah right, like I have a choice, I'm God's pet.)

'I was in a lot of pain, I was not healing. Worse I began to notice as a flash of pain came to me like it had been holding itself back in reserve to bring itself to me right then. Pain that I felt all the way to my dream self's bones.

Bones that in mere moments started to feel like they were becoming hollow.'

'The blood of my dream self became too heavy for my brittle dream self's bones to endure. They snap and crumbled to dust within my dream self. My mind was racing as my dream self was collapsing to nothing but a bag full of blood. Everything I had gained was gone, all the power ups, all the dream food I ingested, gone.'

'It felt to me like my dream body was not meant to be able to exist within The DreamVerse anymore. Satan the soul hungry evil bastard ate my soul to empty. I was just a consciousness that was fading out of existence one thought at a time.'

'I remembered one night. I was on a date, she was hot, we were talking before our dinners arrived. Wow, how free and easy she was. She told me not to give much thought in wondering if we were going to have sex. Which she told me was yes. I was happy and relieved as I let the conversation of sex continue on.'

'She put her hand up to my lips and said no sex talk now that is for later when we are having sex. You wouldn't want me to talk about food to you while we are having sex would you? I said no. She said good and just like that my date started to talk about something else.'

'What it was, I do not remember for what came next was something I will never forget. Our dinners arrived. The waiter mixed up the dinners when placing them on the table before us. I looked down noticing that my dinner was not mine it was my date's. I looked up to tell her that we needed to switch our plates when this happened instead.'

"Hey waiter this is not my dinner."

I told her, "It is mine."

My date looked at me and asked me, "Are you me?"

I said, "No."

She told me, "Shut up or no sex for you."

'I looked at the waiter with a weird smile on my face like sorry man, I'm horny. He looked back at me like you poor bastard.'

Then my date screamed out loud, "Hey waiter dumb ass, look at me not my stud for the night."

He looked back at her pissed off, when she said, "I want this wrong dinner from out of in front of me and I want you to replace it with a new dinner that I ordered."

'He told her that he was sorry and switched our dinners.'

"What are you doing? This damn dinner is not new, it is used."

"He didn't touch it," the waiter responded.

"So what he looked at it, he breathed on it, did he not?"

'Life is funny, you meet someone new an hour or so ago. Everything is going fine then something like this happens. I'll get back to this date in a bit I have to get to this other first date first.'

'Once after having sex with another first date, when we were done she got mad at me because I did not thank her ten times in a row before I put back on my clothes. She told me to take my clothes back off or she would rip them off me. After I humored her, she told me that we had to make love again, exactly like we did the first time. Then she made sure to tell me that I better thank her ten times in a row after we're done this time before I put back on my clothes. Not nine times not eleven but ten.'

"Okay she was kinda crazy but I figured why not. Little did I know how serious she meant by exactly as the first time. I started all wrong and she yelled at me, calling me stupid. She had me start all over again but still I was wrong, for the first time I was not smiling.'

"Off me, off me, you damn dummy. You better listen to me you damn dummy and listen to me good. I have to go to the ladies room, when I get back we will start all over again. If you get it wrong this next time, I will hit you in your head with the heel of my shoe."

'She got off the bed walked over to where her clothes were laying along with her shoes. She brought her red shoe back over to me (I think it was the left one).'

"Look at the blood stains you damn dummy. I am so tired of you men that do not even know how to fuck correctly. Do you want your blood to stain my heel you damn dummy?"

'No I told her, while holding on to my pecker.'

"Good." Then she softened up and said, "You know Barry, I think, I'm falling in love with you." She went to the ladies room and I ran out of the hotel room very naked as fast as I could. The good old days.

'Where was I?'

(So what he looked at it, he breathed on it, did he not?)

Our waiter just looked at her when my date said, "Buzzz, time's up! One dinner on the floor, here we go."

'My date picked up her plate and slammed it on the floor.'

"What one's not good enough for you?" My date yelled out so all could hear with little ease.

'My date grabbed my plate that I did not want to give to her, which made her more mad. My date let go of my plate, she reached into her purse, pulled out her phone, she fiddled with it a bit and then smiled.'

"Here you go honey, look at these naked pictures of me."

'My date handed me her phone, I looked at the first naked picture of her on it and then I scrolled to the next picture as she threw my plate on the floor beside hers. I was up to naked picture number twelve when my date and the waiter started yelling at each other back and forth. I was not paying too much attention to them as I scrolled to the thirteenth picture on my date's phone.'

"What the fuck! What is this crazy shit?" I asked my date.

'She stopped yelling at our waiter and looked over at the picture I was showing her.'

"Well Barry you were not suppose to see that picture or the ones that come after it."

"You mean there are more."

"Yes many more, I like sex."

Our waiter also looked over at the picture I was showing my date and said just like I did, "What the fuck?"

My date said, "You men, I swear. What that man is wearing, Barry and waiter, is a sanitary suit, I had made for the men I have sex with to wear while we have sex. That way only their pecker is exposed while we have sex. I do not like germs but I love sex, so safe sex is the best kinda of sex."

I asked my date, "I am to put this thing on before we have sex?"

"Yes but it is not that easy Barry. First you must take a twenty minute very, very hot shower. Then you put on the sanitary suit. Barry after you put on the sanitary suit, I must then clean your pecker with a special cleaner. Now sometimes there is discomfort after I scrub a pecker extra clean. This is a must for me, just think of it as foreplay."

"Foreplay?" I yelled out in even more shock than when I laid eyes on her thirteenth picture.

'I looked up at our waiter who was looking down at me. I said move to him, he stepped out of the way and I got up, dropped my date's phone on the table and took off running to save the life of my pecker. I heard a rumor that my date and our waiter left together that night. Freaks!'

'Damn it's funny what you think of when you feel like you are getting ready to die. I was still laying down helpless when I felt a presence standing above my dream body. I painfully looked up and there was Death standing beside me sickle and all. (Well one of them anyway.)'

Out in the distance I heard the the Messenger of God say, "Stand down Death, this soul is not to be reaped as of yet, but stay close Death for you may still have this soul to reap..."

"Barry Goldrum you are about to die, your soul is fading away, are you still in pain?"

"What difference does it make?"

"Nothing to me Barry Goldrum, all I need is your answer."

"Answer? You haven't asked me a question, other than if I am in pain."

"Still have your sense of humor Barry Goldrum? That is very good."

"I am dying Messenger of God."

"Yes Barry Goldrum, this I know. What I need to know is if you want to live longer."

"Yes I want to live."

"Are you sure? You can die right now and Death can take your soul to Hell."

"No I want to live, Messenger of God."

"Fine you can live Barry Goldrum but there is a price."

"I figured as much Messenger of God. What is this price I must pay?"

"That can wait for a moment, first I better hurry and heal you a little bit first before you die."

'I watched as the Messenger of God took his large right hand and shoved it deep into his chest. Seconds later he pulled this small shiny piece out of himself. He bent down to me and placed this small shiny piece inside the middle of my chest. The pain I felt was like being shocked back to life. Bam, like a missile was fired inside me and this missile's target was my soul.'

'I was dying, I was in a lot of pain, then Bam! I was on my feet staggering around trying my best to learn how to use my body again. I was that close to death and that pissed me off. The Messenger of God watched me walk around like a new born calf until I got my footing.'

"Barry Goldrum, if only you would have come to my aid all this would not be necessary. Remember Barry Goldrum this choice is yours you can still say no, die and go to Hell."

"Why would I want that Messenger of God?"

"Your price, what I am getting ready to do to you will scar your soul forever Barry Goldrum."

"Do your worst Messenger of God, do your worst."

"I will Barry Goldrum, I will. In my void you will return. This time Barry Goldrum when I heal you, in my void will be traces of Satan left there from his return trip to Hell. While I heal you Barry Goldrum these left over traces of Satan will enter your soul and by doing so they will turn part of your soul evil."

"I am not a fool Messenger of God. This was planned was it not? How else would I later be able to take Grover's evil soul into my soul without it changing me to total evil."

"Yes Barry Goldrum however you had an out that God gave you that would have led you to Heaven. But by not helping me, you and you alone led yourself down this dark path. I wish you well Barry Goldrum."

"Messenger of God, I had an out. Did I make a mistake for not taking it? I think not. I am down this dark path because God wants me to be. What human, Messenger of God, would attack Satan right after coming up on him killing an Angel?"

"A braver one than you Barry Goldrum."

"Perhaps Messenger of God. Maybe a fool instead. Fools rush in where Angels fear to tread. Messenger of God you were dead as far as I knew. I am chosen by God to do my part in this DreamVerse. I am not to fail, I must carry on..."

"War for thirty days, today is only number thirteen, I am not finished. Heaven would have not been my afterlife. Satan would have killed my mortal soul making it become immortal so he could bring it home to his Hell..."

"Leave out the Holy lies when you tell me my destiny this

time Messenger of God, I dare you."

"Betray God's word for you mortal, I think not."

"Try being human for one moment."

"I could not do this, nor would I want to Barry Goldrum. Humans are mortal within their minds. This was put in their minds by God. For humans to become more than mortals during their before death existence, all humans on Earth would have believe that God did not exist at one time..."

"If this would happen then humans would awaken the part of their brains that was created exactly for this purpose so humanity's minds can achieve living enlightenment. This will never happen Barry Goldrum so we will never be equals even in Heaven."

"Belief in God is the only thing that will save our human souls?"

"Yes Barry Goldrum."

"Well I believe, so stop wasting my time. Make me become the mighty warrior that has evil soaked inside his soul. Fight fire with fire. I will be just evil enough to complete my charge."

"If you fail?"

"If I fail, well I am only human no big waste. So I get Hell. Fuck that. I will do what I have to Messenger of God. I will kill whoever God wants me to. But now I have a clear conscious. This is not my doing. I do not want to kill, God wants me to. I am clear and free as long as I follow my orders. Heaven, Messenger of God is what I want. Heaven is what I will obtain, no matter how many blood stains stain my human wings.

I will endure, I will become stronger, for God loves me even though I do not love him..."

"This game tonight has grown tiresome. Take me Messenger of God into your void of nothingness. Change me forever. Make me become an evil bastard that will call Heaven my afterlife home. You, Sam or even God will not be able to stop me from obtaining Heaven. When I die and my evil filled soul enters Heaven it will be God's fault that my soul is not filled with grace, not mine."

"Very well Barry Goldrum. God does love you. In time even with all the evil that will fill your soul, you will love God. Have faith Barry Goldrum that in the end you will feel love..."

"This love for God may be the only thing that can extract enough of the evil inside your soul so you can feel a little bit of peace in Heaven. This love will make you change your greedy want for Heaven into a feeling like you belong there instead of feeling like you pushed your way into Heaven, even though you know you do not belong there."

"Messenger of God, right now I do not care. Heaven or Hell, there is no choice. Tell you what Messenger of God, when I get to Heaven, I will not forget to flush and spray. Because my shit smells like shit which means it stinks. Your shit stinks Messenger of God, even though you do not think so. You know why this is?"

The Messenger of God looks at Barry Goldrum like he wants to smack his head off his shoulders. While Barry Goldrum tries to stay calm, for he fears he pushed the Messenger of God too far.

"No answer? I understand. Truth is truth. Shit is shit, it stinks even if it comes out of your Angel ass or God's."

"Barry Goldrum, I am going to kick your human ass. Right now human, let's go..."

"Just you and me one on one. What do say, are your human balls big enough to make you jump? Yeah human jump, so I can knock you down on your ass. Then you stupid human, I'm going to kick you and kick you all around The DreamVerse."

'The Messenger of God, starts to sing'

"I Hate You", "You're Going To Die", "I Hate You", "I Will Rip Your Soul Apart".

I simply replied, "Fuck you, bring it on."

"Fun time is over Barry Goldrum, I am now going to kick your human ass. Get ready to feel my pain, the pain that comes from the light of Heaven. Damn human, you're fucked."

'I just stood there waiting for the only shot that I would get. I was going to strike first with every bit of rage I had in myself. I blinked, Messenger of God was gone then the sorry bastard kick me in my ass really hard. Picked me off the ground, my dream body felt sick instantly almost what can be only compared to being kicked in the balls.'

I ran around holding on to my ass, screaming, "My ass, my ass you bastard, you kicked me in my ass."

Sorry bastard replied, "Come back over here and I'll kick you in you ass again. Suffer human, I will kick you even harder this time. This time I'm going to put my foot so far up your ass, I'll even kick off your head in the process. So right now come over here to me you stupid human so I can do this to you."

'My ass still hurt really bad and all I wanted to do was run around 'til it stopped hurting. But those last words made me stop running around and stand up straight.'

"Fuck this shit, Angel or not, no way will I ever bring myself to you, like I'm some weak prey that's too afraid to fight for my life. Fight me fair Angel, or are you a chicken shit Angel?"

"Fight you fair, I am an Angel you dumb ass. There is no fair when there is a comparison like a mighty, beautiful Angel like myself and a lousy, stinking human like you. Does a shark swim slower out of compassion for its prey? Does this same shark then bite down not so hard, so its prey can live longer? No and no, dumb ass human..."

"Pray for your soul you are now going to die. Do not blink your eyes this time Barry Goldrum or you will miss your death."

'I wondered to myself how much pain I was just about to feel, but to my surprise, the Messenger of God took three steps towards me and stopped walking. He looked at me like he was holding back a really funny joke.'

"You should see the look in your eyes Barry Goldrum, I'm going to die and it's not fair." The Messenger of God started to laugh but only for a minute, then he stopped real quick like and said, "Do you need time to cry Barry Goldrum?"

'This confused me, this Angel is whacked. The Messenger of God let out his laughter that he was holding in. Moment by moment I could see the ice break away from his being. The Messenger of God just kept on laughing and laughing at my expense.'

When he stopped laughing he wiped his eyes and said, "Damn Barry Goldrum you need to loosen up. It's not the end of the world you are facing. You're special, you were chosen to fight this war in The DreamVerse. Look at me Barry Goldrum. I am the Messenger of God, I bring bad news along with good news. Sometimes the news is so bad that death is the only answer.

I bring that death Barry Goldrum for so many since the existence of humanity. Yet life goes on another day. Understand this Barry Goldrum and get over yourself. Leave that pity you have for yourself in your mortal shell when you come to war in The DreamVerse..."

"Find your peace, live your life, follow God's orders and once in awhile have yourself a good laugh. Or too many years filled with too many tears will fill the rest of you short human life."

"So I'm not going to die?"

"Yes you will die Barry Goldrum but not today."

"So all this was what, you were just?"

"Yes Barry Goldrum, I was fucking with you. Now get ready to feel pain so bad that, that kick to your ass I gave you will feel like only a pinch."

'The Messenger of God spread open his blue cloak so wide making it the size of a skyscraper. My instinct was to run but I stood there without blinking while I was swallowed up. Darkness and silence greeted me once again. First I felt nothing, then like a warm mist was coming down on me I started to slowly feel better and better, until my soul was completely healed.'

'I was feeling high in the sky, I had a big smile on my face, I was feeling so very good then Wham! Satan's specks came at me like Hell's fire burning my soul with its intense evil. I was on fire, my soul was on fire. I took what I could stand until I passed out. When I woke back up I was laying down upon The DreamVerse, red as the Devil himself.'

"Damn, you look like a piece of crap that was dipped in Hell. Get up Barry Goldrum, have a great time, run around saying my soul has been burned Hell red.

You do that while I drink a beer and laugh at you. How does that sound to you Barry Goldrum?"

"Messenger of God it seems like I am at a loss for words once again so fuck you, asshole Angel. What the fuck did you do to me, I'm all red?"

"No shit human. You're as red as the Devil's red, fat, stinky ass. You know Barry Goldrum, I should get paid for this. No I should have to pay to have such fun like I'm having at your expense."

'Even my dick was scolded burning red, my poor balls. Damn right, I had enough of God's shit once again.'

"I will do what I am commanded to do Messenger of God. But no fucking way will I let my soul look like it just stepped out of Hell. I may be only human but even to God I deserve better than this crazy shit."

"Do you human? You should be thankful Barry Goldrum that I didn't leave you in my void of nothingness longer, so large and small things could be burnt clean off your body."

'I stood up, it felt good to get off of parts of my dream self, my soul, that were making contact with The DreamVerse. But damn the soles of my feet, standing up right was pain coming at me constantly. I moved around trying to figure out a way to get myself away from all the intense pain I was feeling.'

'While I was doing this the Messenger of God was drinking a beer, he burped real loud and said,'

"Excuse you. Damn Barry Goldrum you're making me feel sad."

He paused for a moment, dropped his beer down onto The DreamVerse, where it disappeared. He smiled at me and open up another beer.

220

The Messenger of God downed his beer and opened up another one, not even hinting at asking me if I wanted one, which I did.'

"Okay, okay Barry Goldrum, I'll heal you again, go ahead and jump back into my void of nothingness."

'I looked at him like he was a dumb ass.'

"I did not tell you to eye ball me human. I told your sorry human self to jump into my void of nothingness. What are you scared?"

'There was no way I was going anywhere near the Messenger of God's fucked up void.'

"Fuck you times a million, Messenger of God. No way will I ever go back into your void of nothingness. Heal me, kill me if you want but no way you fucked up Angel."

"You're calling me fucked up, you fucked up human? That's it I'm going to kick you up your ass again. Bend over human, show me your burnt red sorry looking ass. What? Do I have to do count to three and say go human?"

"Well Sam instead of kicking my ass why don't you kiss it instead. How does that sound to you Sam? Would you like to kiss my burnt, red, human ass. I think the smell would do you some good. Pucker up Angel."

"Kiss your own ass human, then kiss mine. And never call me Sam again."

"Well don't act like him."

'We look at each other for a few moments.'

"Would you like a nice, cold can of Heaven's beer Barry Goldrum?"

"Yes I would."

"Well too damn bad, get your own, you cannot have any of mine."

'The Messenger of God downed the rest of his third beer and this time he threw his empty can at me, right at my face.'

"Damn fucker!" I said reaching down to pick up the can that barely missed me. Before I could reach it, it disintegrated away.

"Ha, ha too damn slow human, here try this one".

The Messenger of God threw me a full can of beer.

"Drink hearty Barry Goldrum, you deserve it. I have to tell you, you are one tough human. No one ever in all the time that humanity has been around has ever felt the pain you just felt. Be proud, for I and more importantly God is proud of you."

'With tears in my eye, I drank my beer down in one gulp, damn was it good.'

"That's the way you drink Heaven's beer, here have another one."

'I caught my second beer, while I was opening it up the Messenger of God reached deep into his chest and pulled out another small shiny piece out of himself to heal me.'

"Open your mouth Barry Goldrum."

'The Messenger of God threw his small shiny piece of himself at me like it was a peanut. I opened my mouth and it landed perfectly inside it. I swallowed and chased it down with my second Heaven's beer.'

'I burped out loud like I had no manners at all, while the small shiny piece of the Messenger of God did its trick. I laughed out loud as my dream self was almost completely healed. I got it, pain and beer just like on Earth, but one thing that is for sure Heaven brews some mighty fine brew, nothing on Earth is even close to it. All I needed was a woman and a joint and for the party to start and not get over with 'til first sunlight.'

"You feel better, Barry Goldrum?"

"I feel great."

"Do you?"

"Yes I do."

"I don't know, you may be healed but are you missing anything?"

"Like what?"

"I don't know, like all your power ups and all the dream food you consumed before this war started."

'Damn he was right, I was so happy not to be in intense pain anymore that I did not realize how weak I truly was. It was all gone.'

"Do not fret Barry Goldrum, you have the rest of the night off from war. One time and one time only, tonight I will let you enter dreamer's dreams. Feast yourself Barry Goldrum. Build up your strength for tomorrow night, war for you will restart. Four more nights, three more lists with one hundred names on them."

"Three lists not four?"

"No tomorrow night you will fly free with traces of Satan inside your soul. You will still be weaker than before.

I will send word out to The DreamVerse that you are not the same beast. Attack you the Gemini Dream Legion will. Fight them off, so you can fly away to save the life of your weakened soul. Fight them to the death to restrengthen your soul, use what you have inside you now as a weapon. Use it or perhaps die..."

"The three days that follow, you will be given a new list. Which will lead you to your eighteenth night of war."

"What is so important about my eighteenth night of war, Messenger of God? But first give me another beer."

"Simple Barry Goldrum, it is the night that I will give back to you all of Grover's evil power, that will stay inside you forever."

"Well I can't wait for that."

'The Messenger of God and I held up our beer to each other in a salute, then we drank them down.'

"Enjoy the rest of your night off Barry Goldrum. See you tomorrow night."

"You're not going to be waiting for me at sunlight, Messenger of God?"

"No Barry Goldrum, I have something better in mind for myself for the rest of the night."

"What is that Messenger of God?"

"I'm going back to Heaven and I am going to drink some more beer then I am going to get myself laid. I could use that right now Barry Goldrum."

"So could I Messenger of God, so could I."

'The Messenger of God spread open up his golden wings

and flew away. I stood there for a few minutes then I went dream jumping for the rest of the night. I found some really evil dreamers that I gave almost death nightmares to. By the end of the night, I was a lot stronger and I was also very horny.'

'Entering dreamer's dreams with traces of Satan in my soul at the end of my thirteenth day of war was wild. I entered my first dreamer's dream like a starving beast. I made this evil man bleed and cry out for help.'

'What was once a feeling of justice for an evil soul inside me that I gave a nightmare to now felt more like satisfaction. A satisfaction that wanted death at the end of nightmare.'

'I stood there watching this evil man begging for his life and I just laughed at him. I took a few steps towards him to bring him what I wanted to give him... Death.'

'My mind cleared a tiny bit right before I had his dream self's neck in my clawed hand. To myself. This is what Satan wants. This is what Satan wants you to do. Bring this damned soul sooner to his Hell. I stopped with this thought in my mind and said out loud fuck you Satan.'

'The rest of the night I took unlucky evil dreamers to the brink of death. Feeding the bits of Satan inside my soul just enough to strengthen them but not allowing them the final pleasure of feasting on death.'

'The bits of Satan inside me were enough to make me understand what true evil feels like. It would have been so easy just to let myself go. Snap my fingers and my soul turns evil forever.'

'After I finished with my last evil dreamer for the night, I was hanging out in his dream when in my mind I was imagining what Satan was thinking to himself. How mad he was that I did not turn all the way evil.'

225

'I imagined him standing up from his throne and kicking the shit out of any Demon that was in his path of rage. This I felt was truly funny so I laughed out loud sounding more like a Demon than myself.'

'Behind me a man that was crying and praying to God asked me if I was Satan. I turned around to look at him with my eyes burning red and I said nothing to him. I left his dream with his question unanswered.'

'When I woke up Shelly was laying beside me looking so very hot and sexy. I saved her life three times that morning.'

'I got up, took a piss, brushed my teeth, got dressed and ate breakfast. Shelly went to work, while I hung out by myself the rest of the day. Then it was dinner time and off to bed, so I could go to war.'

'The next four nights were... My fourteenth night of war was filled with evil. My eighteenth night, well things got a whole lot more interesting for me after that.'

Chapter Four:

'My fourteenth night of war I rose out of my mortal shell into The DreamVerse, where the Messenger of God was waiting for me.'

"Good to see you on this night Barry Goldrum, here let me look into the eyes of your soul. Yes, yes Barry Goldrum, I can tell those tiny traces of Satan inside you have left their mark. How much did it take for you not to kill even one dreamer?"

"A lot."

"It was hard on your soul I can tell. I can also tell that you have changed, the brightness inside your soul has grown dimmer and darker. You have evil inside you Barry Goldrum but I am pleased that you did not let this evil take over."

"Me too."

"Soon very soon Barry Goldrum, this evil inside you will feel like a small lake compared to the ocean of evil, that fills your soul. Take heed this night Barry Goldrum for you may die. In your mind I want you to think this while fighting for the life of your soul. Will you choose death over turning totally evil? If you turn totally evil Barry Goldrum and survive this night, I will kill your soul and take it to Hell for Satan to own."

"But of course."

"I hope this does not happen Barry Goldrum, I want you to survive this war, I do not want to kill your soul. However, I will without hesitation. Good luck Barry Goldrum. Are you ready to fight for the life of your soul?"

"Yes I am Messenger of God, I will survive. I will be evil but I will not become totally evil."

"Good, I wish you my best."

'The Messenger of God stepped over to me so we were standing side by side. Then with the wave of his hand he took away the veil that was hiding the army of the Gemini Dream Legion in waiting to kill me.'

"I thought I would do you a favor Barry Goldrum. Now you do not have to go on the hunt for your prey. Your prey has come to you united to take out the big bad beast that hunts their resting ground. Go get them Barry Goldrum, they are yours for the killing."

"I guess this is God's way of showing tough love?"

"No Barry Goldrum, this is to see if you are to survive or die. But I do love you bunches."

"Kiss my ass Messenger of God, this is total shit."

"Good, then it matches your face Barry Goldrum."

'I looked over at the Messenger of God who had a shit eating grin on his face. I laughed and took a very deep breath trying my best to calm myself as I let it back out slowly.'

"Aren't you glad there's no list tonight? I'll save you a beer Barry Goldrum."

"Fuck that, I want a twelve pack."

"It's yours. Come on hurry up I'm getting bored."

"Well Messenger of God why don't you take the time you have and pull your head out of your sorry Angel ass."

"Nah, I'd need more time. You're going to be dead in under fifteen minutes."

"Won't even give me twenty? Thanks for the confidence."

"Not my place to build it for you Barry Goldrum. That's all on you."

'I took a couple of steps forward, I spread out my wings. Like always they were feathers at first. I put the thought in my mind to turn them into steel. They turned to steel but a very weak kind of steel. I flapped them, they sounded cheaply made. I flapped them harder and pieces of my steel wings started to flake off. I realized that my steel wings were only steel covered. They were fake, was I as fake as my wings?'

'I looked back over at the Messenger of God, he could not look me in my eyes. Yes I got it. I'm on my own, I live through the night or I die. If I have to use the evil inside my soul too strongly, I'll turn totally evil and I die and go to Hell. Then a question came to my mind, if I am killed by this massive amount of people will I get to go to Heaven after that? I believed no Heaven for me only more Hell. Damn the universe.'

'Thousands of people stared at me. I'm the monster staring back at them, wanting nothing to do with this. The chant for my death serenades The DreamVerse. I will never forget the pain I felt this night. I will never forget how it felt to almost die hundreds of times in one night's time. I flew at thousands of chanting Gemini Dream Legion people, like a bug heading straight towards a windshield.'

'I survived this night. I bled this night like I never have before. I survived this night with a handicapped soul. I should be proud but I'm not. For what I had to do to survive this night changed me forever. After this night I never laughed as purely.'

'When I woke up in the morning, I was almost evil. Shelly and I. We...'

'No, I'll save my morning of getting the evil out of myself for after I remember more bloody war.'

'Every time I remember this night I feel like raging out of control. Come on world, fuck you, try to kill me, kill me dead. Have to calm myself. Have to remember this is only a memory. Yeah right. This memory makes my soul bleed and cry. I fucking hate this. I want to get off this couch and go get laid.'

"Kill him, kill Barry Goldrum."

'Humor myself.'

'I, the mighty warrior of The DreamVerse all shiny and beautiful did not break a sweat. I pulled out my sword of frozen Heaven and with one swipe, I killed them all.'

"Kill him, kill Barry Goldrum."

'Let the truth be revealed.'

"Kill him, kill Barry Goldrum."

'My heart is beating out of my chest.'

"Kill him, kill Barry Goldrum."

'This is what I heard as thousands of the members of the Gemini Dream Legion came here this night to make their chant come to life all bloody and war raw.'

'First blood was mine. I struck as powerful as I could, with my clawed right hand, I hit this man. I made him bleed, I hurt him only, he did not die. I failed. Second blood was theirs, which came to me from four men at one time. I got knocked back almost on my ass. I flapped my cheap wings as these four men turned into a hundred or more, all standing behind the others, pushing their way forward to be the one that killed me dead and gone.'

'Their fingers grabbed at me and my wings. My wings which before would have cut their hands off clean to stubs. Now my cheap ass wings gave them paper cuts, that they did not feel due to the rage that was in their beings for my blood and life. I was being shredded to dust that turned into ash that disappeared when it made contact with The DreamVerse. I felt like a giant fly having its wings pulled off by thousands of hateful humans. I'm dirty, I get in their faces, I messed up their party, I must die.'

"Get off me, get off me!"

'I screamed out for my life. I looked down into the eyes of my killers, theirs eyes were dark and hallow as Demon's eyes. This gave me a surge of power. Not enough to save the day but enough to get me back on my feet where I did the best I could to fly away to safety.'

"Kill him, kill Barry Goldrum, kill him, kill Barry Goldrum, kill him, kill Barry Goldrum."

'Over and over again this mob of killers, chanted and yelled out in a bloody rage to me.'

'Strange thoughts come to your mind when you are trying your best to heal your wings up enough so they can be flight worthy. My thought was tacos, I wanted some delicious tasting tacos right then. In my mind I know, but I swear the belly of my dream self started to rumble out of control. I was at the point of just adding taco sauce to my taco and bringing it up to my mouth, when I was hit from behind hard enough to knock me down on my face.'

'They stomped on me and kicked me so many times on the back of my head, neck, back, hips, legs and feet. They only stopped long enough to turn me over.'

'The pain of having my teeth stomped to dust inside my mouth, well I can't explain it, it is something you have to go through to understand. My teeth grew back and were stomped to dust just like my spine that was severed and healed back up.'

'My eyes were popped out of their sockets. I went blind in one eye, I went blind in both eyes, then I could see once again. The worst was either having my throat stomped on or my balls stomped on. I was almost dead so many times that I lost count. Why would I not die all the way? My mortal soul was weak and drained dry. Something was saving the life of my mortal soul?'

'Satan, his traces of himself inside my soul was my answer. I had to shake away the notion that I could not use Satan's traces as power. I readied myself hoping I would not use them too much to make myself become totally evil.'

'I was just about to go for it when it felt like something entered my mind. I paused and from inside my mind came the voice of Satan.'

"Hello Barry Goldrum, how are you doing? Is this a bad time for a talk? Well then I'll make this short..."

"I'm in Hell, I cannot wait for your mortal soul to die which will kill your mortal body. With the death of your mortal body your soul will come back to life with no mortal shell to reenter. This immortal soul of yours will come to me, come to my Hell, where I am waiting..."

"I'm going to torture your immortal soul Barry Goldrum even more than I tortured Judas's soul. You should have heard Judas's soul Barry Goldrum. But I did it all for you Lord Satan. Like that meant a fucking thing to me."

"He was a greedy, stupid human, Satan."

232

"How stupid are you Barry Goldrum?

"Not at all."

"The only way your soul will live through this night is by using my evil that is inside your soul. Yes, the Messenger of God will kill you, this is true. However if you call out to me right now I will make those tiny specks of myself inside you charge up. Charged up with power, that will be a thousand times stronger than they are now."

'Here came the deal to save my soul.'

"All I want you to do after you receive my power up is kill everyone in The DreamVerse. Then after that I want you to kill the Messenger of God. Do this for me Barry Goldrum and your eternal stay in Hell will be so peaceful to you. You will feel like you are in Heaven instead of Hell. I promise, trust me Barry Goldrum, you will be a very rare soul in Hell, that feels nothing but peace and love..."

"When you receive lemons Barry Goldrum, make lemonade."

"Damn Satan, lemonade? How desperate are you? I'm weak on the outside, yes this is true. You Satan, you are weak on the inside. Nobody loves you Satan, you are all alone in your Hell. All your minions do for you out of fear not out of love. Now shut the fuck up, I have to save the life of my soul."

"You will lick Hell shit off my hoofs for those words Barry Goldrum."

"You have shit on your hoofs? Why the fuck don't you wash it off?"

"What the fuck did you just say to me?"

233

"I told you to wash the Hell shit off your hoofs, you nasty walking around in shit, satanic bastard..."

"By the way, it wouldn't hurt to wash your ass off as well Satan. You're probably a bad wiper. Then again I don't know you all that well, for all I know, you do not wipe your ass at all. And the shit that's caked between your ass cheeks is for quick energy snacking in between torturing the souls of the damned..."

"I feel for you Satan, must be so hard to be the Devil of Hell. Quick break here and there and you believe your life is your own."

"You shit faced human, you dare call me a shit eater. I am Satan, you stupid, fucking human. I am going to beat you on your head, until all the shit you call brains, squirts out of your ears. I'm going to, I'm going to..."

"What Satan are you at a loss for words? Don't matter for all you spew out of that ass mouth of yours is the same old shit..."

"If I die tonight and my soul goes to your Hell, I'm going to kick your ass so bad, you will give me the keys to your Hell... While you run away after like a scared, Ex-Angel lousy, shit smelling, bitch."

'I had a idea, I had a plan. There was nothing more that I could say to Satan to make him grow even crazier with intense, evil hatred for me. I waited in my mind, while my dream self was being ripped apart. It took everything inside myself to hold back the pain that I was feeling.'

'Satan roared out in anger and hate at me so loud it popped my ears causing me to lose my hearing for awhile. But the great thing was Satan did what I wanted him to do for me. Give me my edge so I could break free and not die this night.'

234

'This much hate coming at me from Satan, with traces of himself inside my soul. Bam, they came to life, I did not call for them, they came at me by Satan's command.'

'Satan the wisest, Satan the greatest trickster, got played like a fool by me, a mere human. I was correct and it felt so fucking good because I knew right then I would survive.'

'The one thing Satan was not to do on his own, was to bring to full life his traces of himself inside my soul. Big no, no. I did not call for my intense power up, it was given to me which made it belong to me. I hoped to Heaven that was the case and I was right. Satan's traces came to life to kill me from the inside of my soul all the way to the outside of it. But nope, they came at me and I snagged them up as quickly as I could with all of the power I had left inside my soul.'

'I felt God smile inside my soul as Satan screamed even louder. I flinched my evil power up making my weak steel wings that were almost ripped off me turn into the strongest steel wings I had ever created.'

'So sharp were my new wings that I, like a buzz saw, flapped them faster and faster causing chunks of the Gemini Dream Legion to spread out like a splattered looking portrait, titled Blood and Death. Faster and faster I flapped my wings 'til I began to smoke, then like a speeding demon I took off flying.'

'I flew a thousand miles away from where I was in ten seconds. I stopped to check myself out. Everything I had was bigger and stronger including my dick. Damn did I feel so fucking great, evil but great.'

'I turned back around to look at the direction I had just flown from, I blinked my eyes a few times and thousands of miles away turned into just a few feet away from me. From where I stood still, I could see all the carnage I created.

Hundreds and hundreds of the Gemini Dream Legion, bleeding, crying, dying and already dead.'

'I flapped my wings feeling no pity for any of them. In a very short thirteen seconds I was back standing still, staring at them, 'til I felt like attacking them.'

"Please Barry Goldrum no more we are sorry, we love you. Please do not kill any more of us."

'I am only human, tears came to my eyes but fuck it, I had a job to do so I flapped my wings and attacked.'

'Thrown in my path came a can of Heaven's beer out of nowhere. I stopped flying and caught it. I looked around and there was the Messenger of God, drinking a beer with one hand and holding on to case of beer with the other. War was over for the night, it was time to get drunk, then wake up and get laid.'

'Wow my hot Shelly, she always knew what I wanted, like she could read my mind. I woke up.'

"Hush sweet Barry, you had such a hard night. I want you to do nothing but pull down your shorts and lay still. I will make you feel like a man, I will take away your pain. Thanks for saving my life. Get ready for me to make you explode all that extra evil out of you."

'I could not believe what I was feeling. Shelly was great but damn this morning she was the best ever. A gift? A miracle? All I know is that it was so intense, I was in Heaven then Shelly changed. It was so crazy..."

'If I moved around too much Shelly would stop, reach up and slap me across my face and tell me to be a man. I would then hold still and Shelly would restart. Shelly must have slapped me across my face ten times at least. Every time I was like crazy bitch, Shelly laughed and restarted.'

'I couldn't help myself, I forgave her until she slapped me across the face the next time. The real fucked up thing about it all, was every time Shelly smacked me across my face, she smacked me even harder.'

'Imagine getting turned on and turned off every minute or so, it will drive you crazy. I moved one time too many and Shelly had enough of me.'

"Damn it Barry, I have a job to do and you're making it take too damn long."

'Shelly rose up and punched me in my face three times.'

"Take that you bastard. Now hold still, if you move again I will smash a lamp over your head."

'I was stunned and bleeding and before I could say anything, Shelly was giving me more of her special favor. I looked down at Shelly, she looked back at me and growled. I did not dare move. I closed my eyes and focused like I never did before, for fear that Shelly might bite my pecker off.'

'Moment by moment, I felt better while Shelly turned into more of an evil, demon-like lady. When I was finishing, I had the displeasure of feeling Shelly take her nails and sink them into my chest and rip them downwards to the bottom of my belly.'

'I like it soft, I like it hard. Sex is a lot of fun. I never before nor have I ever again felt that incredible combination of pleasure and pain.'

'I guess I had too much Devil in me that needed to be released. Poor Shelly after we were finished she jumped off the bed and ran around the bedroom like a mad woman that didn't know what to do. Good thing, Shelly was thinking and, well, didn't swallow.'

'Shelly looked at me and my boner and said, "You're done!"

I said, "Well, I could use a little bit more of your loving."

"Oh really? Well why don't you fuck yourself for once. We are done this morning you understand me."

"Yes ma'am."

"Good then, now jump your horny, stinking ass in the shower, I'm going back to bed to wake up."

'When Shelly and I met up a few minutes later, she was still very grouchy. Saying to me, I don't know, I just woke up pissed off at the whole damn world this morning. I told her I would make breakfast, she just grunted out loud. When we were eating our breakfast together, I still had a boner, while Shelly ate her breakfast like a cave woman.'

'When we were through eating we talked a little bit about the weather and other non-important things. Everything was calm, I was drinking my coffee when Shelly said.'

"I don't know why but the palm of my right hand hurts."

I shook my head not wanting to replay anything back to her.'

Shelly then said to me, ""You know Barry, my mouth is sore as well. It feels like I went to sleep and I kept my mouth opened up as wide as it could be."

'I looked at Shelly, with coffee in my mouth that I could not swallow. I did my best but it came spewing out of my nose and mouth. After that I laughed so hard that I fell off my chair and landed on the floor. I laughed and laughed, harder and harder, my eyes were tearing up, my brain was pounding so hard that it felt like it was going to bust out of my skull.'

'I stopped laughing and Shelly asked me with a look of bewilderment on her face, what the Hell is so funny Barry? I started all over again. I could not help myself.'

'A little bit later Shelly left for work. I was in a great mood and I was still very horny. I walked outside into the morning sunlight, two houses down there was this hot looking lady standing in the middle of her front yard staring at me. I waved to her, she waved back. I walked over to her to say hello, while adjusting myself so my erection would be the first thing she noticed about me.'

'It was so funny, she was smiling all friendly to me while I was walking towards her. When I stepped into her front yard her eyes left my eyes as she looked down me until she stopped to notice something very special about me.'

"What the Hell? Are you for real? Is that for real?"

"Yes baby and it can be all yours if you **say yes**."

'This fine lady stranger looked at me all pissed off. She was just about to let me have her rage when I made my pecker wave hello to her. She shut her lips and shook her head.'

"Where have you been all my life you damn, hung, stranger you?"

'I had her top off and her pants half way down before we made it to her front door. Brandy was her name and Brandy gave me everything she had every morning I came a knocking after I told Shelly goodbye for the day.'

'Brandy could not believe it when I told her that Shelly and I were just friends that lived together. Brandy was a very warm lady, that invited a few of her best friends over to join us during our morning ritual. I never had this much sex in my life.'

'I never could go like this before and I was never as thick and full as before if you know what I'm saying, ha, ha. Satan the Devil in Hell must be one extra horny, large bastard. I hate Satan but for this gift I owe him one, maybe two.'

'I don't remember the number of the morning but I do know it was after my eighteenth night of war. When I was very, very evil having Grover's evil power up inside me. His dark soul combined with my soul that already has been affected by traces from Satan.'

'There was Brandy and five of her friends, including two new friends. Six ladies in all looking at me wanting to be first. I laughed out loud looking at six naked ladies I was getting ready to enjoy for hours, as they watched me pour six shots.'

"Line up ladies and grab a glass, I'll just drink from the bottle. Don't be shy for it's time to party. I have to say, I like all your tits and asses, so let's have a toast to them to get things started."

'I laughed out loud again as I started to feel a buzz coming to me. I walked back over to my six ladies and I poured them all another shot. I told them to wait a minute before they downed their shots. With my pecker hanging out of my pants, I walked over and grabbed up a kitchen chair. I took the kitchen chair into the living room and placed it directly in the center of it.'

'I sat down on the kitchen chair and it was too hard on my ass for the amount of hours I was going to be sitting on it. So I said, cushion and a new red headed friend grabbed the cushion out of Brandy's hand while saying let go bitch.'

'Sexy red head started to walk over to me with the cushion for my ass when she stopped walking, looked at me and downed her shot.'

"I'm first"

'Sexy red head threw the pillow at me.'

"Get conformable."

"Fuck this!"

'Brandy pushes sexy red head out of the way.'

"I'm first, this is my house, this is my stud, wait your turn, bitch!"

'Brandy took four steps and sexy red head pushed her hard down to the floor. By this time I had already positioned the cushion and was waiting to see who was going to be the first of six ladies to come over and sit down on top of me. Sexy red head was small but she was feisty as she pushed two more ladies out of her way to be first.'

'Sexy red head was so proud of herself as she looked me in my eyes. She definitely ran her home, getting what she always wanted. I enjoyed her as she smiled and purred then to show her who's in control, I stopped her and made her wait until I took three swigs from my bottle. When we were through, sexy red head was shaking out of control.'

'Like an uncaring bastard I told her, her turn was over with and she was fun. Her eyes, I'll never forget the look in her eyes. It was like a cloud was lifted from her eyes as she paused to get off of me.'

"You're evil, Barry Goldrum you are evil."

"Yes I am, sexy red head."

"You don't even know my name?"

"Did you tell it to me?"

"No, I did not but..."

"But what sexy? Are you having regrets?"

"Saying, I do to my husband. What am I going to do now Barry, I can't go back to having normal sex?"

"That my sexy red head is why I like being free and evil. I do not care, now kindly remove your sexy self off of me. There are five more ladies waiting and wanting to be made to feel like you are now."

'Power, sexual power I had and still have, I can turn on even the hardest souled lady making her fall in lust with me at first touch. One after the other I enjoyed five more ladies, Brandy went last. One by one I gave them their turn loving every minute of it.'

'When I finished with one lady, she slowly removed herself off of me and laid on the floor next to the one that came before her. All trying their best to gather themselves up so they could get dressed and get going back to their normal now even more boring lives.'

'That was a great morning and afternoon. I had many more of them until my thirty days of war was over with. War is Hell but at least the sex was great.'

Chapter Five:

'My fifteenth night of war I walked into The DreamVerse feeling evil and ready for war. I walked up to the Messenger of God, who was drinking more Heaven's beer.'

"Damn Barry Goldrum, I think every one in Heaven besides God and the Voice of God watched you this past morning and afternoon. What one woman not enough for you?"

"Yes, but Tina is dead and now I am evil so what the fuck can I do about it but splurge."

'The Messenger of God downed his beer and burped out loud and threw me a beer.'

"Yes you are evil Barry Goldrum but compared to the evil you will become in three more nights, you are like evil light."

"Evil light? Bet Satan would beg to differ."

"Well fuck that evil Angel of Hell."

'We both laughed for a little bit and had a few more beers before I was handed my list.'

"What the fuck is this?"

"What Barry Goldrum?"

"There's two hundred names on this list."

"So what? You're evil remember. Just double time it, use those traces of Satan inside you. Now that Satan turned them all up and boiling for you, two hundred names should not be a problem for you, Barry Goldrum."

"Yeah but..."

"But my Angel ass, Barry Goldrum, go kill like the evil bastard human you are."

"What's wrong Messenger of God? Did you wake up today with your halo stuck up your ass?"

"Barry Goldrum, I am not in the mood to hear your shit today, just go kill and get it over with so I can get the Hell out of this damn DreamVerse."

"Okay Messenger of God, what's your problem?"

"You Barry Goldrum, you are my problem."

"Me, what's wrong with me?"

"What's wrong with you? I'll tell you what's wrong with you, you have Satan inside your soul. I don't know if you know this or not but I hate Satan. Satan is a prick, Heaven is so much better off without him there."

"I imagine but maybe you should thank him."

"Why would I ever thank Satan, Barry Goldrum?"

"Because if he was not the one chosen to be the fallen Angel, somebody else would have had to take his place in Hell, maybe even you."

"No way Barry Goldrum, I'm too pure and good to ever be the ruler of Hell."

"I know, I'm just saying better him than you."

"Yes that is for sure Barry Goldrum. Now finish your beer and get to erasing those names on that list. And Barry, do not fuck with me, erase all two hundred names and not one less, do you understand me?"

"Yeah I understand you. Fuck it, give me another beer first, I'm still thirsty."

'Two hundred names, no big deal. Hard, but so true. Before this happened my mortal shell had to take a piss from all the Heaven's beer I drank. It was doing the pee, pee dance while lying down, so I had to go back into it and let my waking self take my piss.'

'This is weird and wild. This was the first time my mortal shell came into view before my eyes when it needed something from me. I walked forward, toward the vision of my mortal shell and turned into mist. I entered back into my mortal shell like it was the normal thing to do.'

'Very wild this first time, now it's nothing special just another of my powers. The comparison to before this happened was no mist I turned into, I was solid, transparent almost like but still solid enough to feel it when I re-entered my mortal shell. I also had to fly back where my mortal shell was lying down to re-enter it. Figures the first time is when I have to take a piss, oh well, at least it wasn't a shit.'

'After I took my piss, I went back to bed, falling back to sleep in almost an instant. My dream self was out and about in The DreamVerse, ready to re-take my list of two hundred names back from the clawed talon hand of the Messenger of God.'

'I stopped myself, wondering to myself if this new way could be also a two way instead of one. So in my mind I pictured my mortal shell and from thought to reality the vision of my mortal shell was before my eyes. I walked back to it like before, as I was turning back into mist I looked over at the Messenger of God as he was yawning.'

'Success was mine, I was back inside my mortal shell. No need to wake myself up so I stepped back out of my mortal shell, solid as the original way. Weird and wild just as much as The DreamVerse and God.'

'I had my easy, fast and safe exit from The DreamVerse, which I have used a few times. Even when I just want to escape from boredom. My discovery of my new power behind me, I walked back over to the Messenger of God.'

"Give me back my list that was created by a fascist."

"God is not a fascist, God is God. He is like nothing else in the universe, call him a fascist again and I will knock you down on your ass and then I will kick you in your stupid human head."

"I'm just trying to make you laugh, Messenger of God. You big, damn, ass head you."

"Make me laugh? Why would you calling God a fascist make me laugh?"

"I do not know, why would it?"

"What?"

"I mean, how am I suppose to know that ass head?"

"Okay Barry Goldrum, you made me laugh, on the inside where it counts the most. Now take this list and go fly the fuck away from me as fast as your stinking human ass can fly away from me."

"Nope, give me another beer first."

'I drank my beer down and dropped the can down beside my feet watching it turn to ash then disappear. I burped out loud for about six seconds then I flinched making my wings appear. I smiled and spat as I turned my feathery wings into the hardest, sharpest steel they could become.'

246

'Slowly I flew up to the Messenger of God and took his beer out of his hand and threw it on the ground. He looked at me like he could not believe that I had the balls to do that. The Messenger of God took a couple of steps back and shook his head. He looked me right in my eyes as he spread his wings that dwarfed mine. Face to face we stared at each other, while flapping our wings just enough to keep us airborne.'

"You asked for this Barry Goldrum, you could have flown off all nice and peaceful, but no you had to piss me off. You are going to pay dearly for your actions."

"Nice and peaceful? What have you been smoking, Messenger of God? There is no nice and peaceful in anything I have to do."

"Tough Barry Goldrum, we all have our job to do."

"Yeah so, why don't you do something about it."

"Like what?"

"Take the night off. Before you answer me Messenger of God, think about this. Take the night off and join me. Let's together, you and I, go kick the shit out of The DreamVerse."

"Tempting Barry Goldrum, but I cannot."

"What's the matter Messenger of God, you chicken shit?"

"Lead the way Barry Goldrum, I'll show you how to kill a human into dust in three Earth seconds."

"Big shit, I can do it in one Earth second."

"And you can kiss my Angel ass faster than that..."

"Come on you slow ass human, I'll show you speed of flight that will make your frail human eyes pop out of their sockets."

"Fly Angel, fly!"

'What a night, it's been a long time since I had a dude's night out. This of course the most bloody mayhem of them all. But Hell with it, have to take what you can get. It was cool having someone there with me as I cruised The DreamVerse. The Messenger and I flew so fast by a group of the Gemini Dream Legion that we caused them to fall down and be swept away in our current.'

'I am fast, the Messenger of God is the speed of light. We were flying, racing, talking having a great time as both of us pushed ourselves faster and faster or so I thought. The Messenger of God looked over at me smiling so very big as I was getting ready to push myself to my final point of speed and said to me, "Bored now."

'He became light, a brilliant, wondrous looking blue light that disappeared before my eyes. I slowed down to a halt, as I was catching my breath in the far distance in front of me I spotted the Messenger of God. Faster than I can drink a beer the Messenger of God raced back to me. When he stopped about five feet in front of me, his force of power shoved me back about five feet. I looked at an Angel I had no chance of defeating and wondered when I was going to have to fight him.'

"Powerful are you Barry Goldrum, nothing compared to me. I have to tell you this. After you get control over Grover's evil soul inside your own soul, I will be coming after you. I stopped this time without making contact with you and pushed you away. When I come after you for real, I will not stop. No Barry Goldrum, I'm going to hurt you. Because you are evil..."

"And what other chance will I have to battle a human evil, hybrid. I will not kill you Barry Goldrum, for God does not want me to. But he told me one on one that it is perfectly fine to make you scream and bleed."

"That so? Yeah you are the favorite but I fight down and dirty, like going after one of your pretty Angel eyes. Just rip it right out of its socket."

"I like you Barry Goldrum but I also hate you, you better hope when I come after you, God is in the waiting to pull me off you, just in case I do not feel like stopping the kicking of your ass. We wasted enough time, time for you to get to your list of two hundred names."

'I thought about being a smart ass but instead I just flew off, thinking to myself, fuck him. That night, my fifteenth night of war, I was in a bloody, blood, kind of mood. The first name's location on my list came to me. As I flew to him, another first time came to me. Out of nowhere the location of the eighth name on my list came to me, then the twenty third and so on.'

'At final tally forty seven names location came to me and the great thing, they were all very close together. I barely had to stop flying when I attacked and erased them. Ten minutes was all it took until I was standing still, blood soaked from head to toe. Screams of die monster die, came to me as I looked at people that were not on my list and sighed.'

'At the end of this night, not thinking about it I flew back to my mortal shell instead of making it appear to me. Next to my stop was a a six pack of beer and a sign that read gone fishing, see you tomorrow night.'

'The next night my sixteenth night of war, I entered The DreamVerse not knowing what to expect. As usual the Messenger of God was waiting on me and drinking beer.

249

'I walked up to him and he threw me a beer.'

"Two more nights Barry Goldrum."

"Yes I know Messenger of God."

"Here is your list, no need to look twice, yes there is four hundred names on this list tonight. Are you going to complain about it?"

"No, what's the point?"

"Very good, it's very good for you to understand that you have no choice."

"You going to be an asshole again tonight Messenger of God?"

"No, what's the point?"

'I drank my beer and three more, grabbed my list and took off flying to erase four hundred more names from The DreamVerse. Just like the night before many names came to me at once. It took me only three hours to finish my list. When I was on my last name on the list the Messenger of God came flying up to me to watch his ending.

"Damn Barry Goldrum, are you pissed at the universe tonight? I cannot believe you are done already."

'I said nothing as I wiped the blood away from my hands.'

"Have it your way Barry Goldrum, don't talk to me. Here is another list, this time there is five hundred names on it. Go do your worst."

'It took me two hours and thirty three minutes to eliminate five hundred more names from The DreamVerse.'

'I flew back to my mortal shell feeling twice as strong as I did when I entered The DreamVerse about six hours before. The Messenger of God was waiting on me with a beer in hand.'

"If you have another list for me tonight Messenger Of God you can stick it up your sorry Angel ass."

"No more lists tonight Barry Goldrum, you are through for the night. You have almost two hours left before you are to wake up, would you like to re-enter your mortal shell and dream normal for these two hours or would you like to drink some more beer with me?"

"Both, first I am going to drink this beer and two more then I am going to dream a nice and peaceful dream, without any of the shit in my life in it."

"Good for you Barry Goldrum, you have earned it."

'When I re-entered my mortal shell, I slipped back into it all nice and comfortably and dreamed about a great big open field with its grass all nice and cut short.'

'I laid down in this field on a blanket I created. I shut my eyes and a few moments later it felt like someone was laying next to me. When I opened up my eyes, what I saw made me so very happy. It was Tina, she was laying down beside me, looking as beautiful as she did when she was still alive. We looked at each other for a few moments before we said a single word.

"Barry, I come from Heaven into your dreams to tell you that Heaven is so very beautiful. I want you after you die to be in Heaven with me. But so sadly Barry I have to say to you.. That when I look down from Heaven at you, my eyes, my Heavenly eyes do not like what they see. I fear that your soul has turned dark..."

"Too dark already to take in anymore evil, let alone all the evil that is in Grover's soul inside your soul. Tell the Messenger of God, no. Tell him that killing is wrong, even if it's evil ones that you are killing. Do this for me Barry, my sweet Barry, that I miss so much. If you do this, I swear my Heavenly soul that you will find your soul inside of Heaven instead of Hell."

"My dear Tina, if I say no, everyone, all of the Gemini Dream Legion will die and go to Hell. Worse than that, I will go to Hell. I cannot say no. Saying no is saying no to God, which is a not so smart of a thing to do my sweet. No my sweet, I will do what God commands of me then after I am through and I die, my soul receives Heaven."

"But there my sweet Barry lies the Problem?"

"What problem?"

"The thought of what your soul will look like and feel like, gives my soul nothing but fear."

"Fear me not Tina, I am on the side of the Angels, not of the Demons."

"I don't know Barry, maybe we are looking at this whole thing the wrong way."

"What do you mean?"

"Well Barry... Maybe you're just evil and your soul belongs in Hell?"

"I cannot believe that."

"I know, but think about it Barry, God wants you to kill people? In my opinion, that makes you have only one use for God and that is killing..."

"Barry, God would not have a good soul do what you have done for him. No Barry, God would choose a soul destined for Hell for all that Hellish killing."

"Tina stop, all this is too much for my mind to take. I'm so stressed out, I need a few hours off from all this heavy to just feel some peace and quiet inside myself."

"You are being selfish Barry Goldrum, what about me? Your soul will fall to Hell because you will not listen to me. (Silence.) I got it Barry, I know just what we should do, to insure our souls an afterlife together."

"What is that my love?"

"Barry you have to disobey God and take the deal Satan offered to you. That way it will be your choice and when you go to Hell, Satan will look at you as a friend, instead of just another soul to torture. Believe me Barry, Satan hates you right now, take his deal and he will forgive you."

"Just like that Tina?"

"Yes Barry, Satan can be kind if he wants to be or if there is a cause for him to be."

"Okay Tina. What about you?"

"What about me?"

'Well Tina I go to Hell and you are in Heaven, how are we suppose to have an afterlife together?"

"For you my sweet Barry, the one I love more than Heaven itself, I will sneak out of Heaven to live an afterlife together in Hell with you my love."

"Okay you are not Tina, who are you? Let me guess, you're a Demon Lady from Hell?"

"Barry I guess I am wrong, I told Satan that you were too stupid and weak inside for your dead hag of a wife to say no to me, as I appeared looking like her to you. Hell Barry, I figured by now I would have you licking all the Hell bile off my hoofs. Pity, I was having so much fun, I love you Barry. Yeah right you human piece of crap, the only love I would ever have for you, would be the pleasure of eating your soul."

"Okay, so you're not just a Demon Lady from Hell, you are one of Satan's sluts. Well Satan's slut, no sale here. So why don't you get the fuck out of my dream and go back to Hell where a slut just like you deserves to be?"

'Demon lady from Hell got very pissed off looking and then she grabbed a hold of my pecker with one of her clawed hands and squeezed down hard on it.'

"Call me a slut again Barry Goldrum, I dare you. Please, please call me a slut and I will rip your pecker off... Then Barry Goldrum, I will slap you across your face with your very own pecker, while it lies bleeding in my hand."

"Let go of my pecker, you damn Demon!"

"Beg me human, beg me real good, to save the life of your worthless human pecker."

"You bent, evil, Demon slut let go of my pecker or I will..."

"You will do what human? Do not answer me, for I know that your answer is nothing. There is nothing you can do to me Barry Goldrum, I on the other hand, I can rip off your pecker and take it back to Hell with me, to use as stock for my soup..."

"What nothing to say?"

"I, I, I...."

"Shut up, you're babbling and it's pissing me off. What are you going to do next Barry Goldrum, cry for the life of your pecker? Yes, cry like a pathetic human to me."

"Eat my shit, slut Demon from Hell!"

"That's it, I'm going to pull your pecker off your body for that distasteful comment at my expense."

"To Hell with you Demon slut!" I yelled out to a Demon that was no longer paying attention to me.

"Shut your mouth you stupid damn human, God is talking to me..."

"Please, please, I didn't mean any harm. I was just playing with this human. I would not have ripped off his pecker. Please, please forgive me, it's not my fault, it's Satan fault. I would never dare to do something like this, unless Satan himself told me to do so. I am so sorry God, please forgive me. No, please do not kill me. Satan will take my dust and throw it into the fires of Hell."

'No please, was the last thing this Demon lady from Hell said before she melted away to painful ash right before my dreaming eyes. What an evil trip that dream turned out to be. When I woke up, I was turned off. Poor Shelly it took her the better part of ten minutes of trying to turn me on before I was fully ready to go.'

'My seventeenth night of war, I was handed a list by the Messenger of God, that had one thousand names on it. I took my time, it took me all of five hours to finish my list. I drank beer with the Messenger of God for an hour and then I went back into my mortal shell to sleep for the extra two hours I had left. When I woke up I laid on top of Shelly and made love to her for an hour. It was so wonderful and loving.'

Chapter Six:

'My eighteenth night of war...'

"No time to waste tonight Barry Goldrum. The beer we usually drink, is over there in waiting for the winner of our fight. I'm going to do something for you Barry Goldrum to make our fight as fair as I can make it for you. I will not use my void as a weapon against you."

"Don't bother, Messenger of God, I wipe my ass with fair. Give me Grover's power now. When I wield my double shot of evil, I don't think I'll be the one who's looking for fair in our fight."

"Full of confidence Barry Goldrum, for something you haven't fully received as of yet?"

"All the up's and downs, all the twist and turns, I've been through as of late... I don't know what is going to happen and I don't fucking care. You want your fight, you got it. I'll bleed Messenger of God, which I have no doubt. However tonight for the first time in Heaven, a mere human like myself gets to have power given to them, that an Angel like you wants to check out for yourself, for you just have to know how powerful my new power level truly is."

"Yes Barry Goldrum, what you speak is the truth. You are the most powerful human that ever lived as of right now. Very soon you will wield power only Angels and Demons have wielded before."

"This upsets you, Messenger of God?"

"It pisses me off. For the first time I ask why."

"Why what?"

"Why you? You're not a bad human, but believe me when

I tell you that you are not a good human either."

"Don't hold back now Messenger of God, get it all out."

"Yes I will. If there has to be a mere human, that is to wield such power, you should have never been considered. You're flawed in so many ways, Barry Goldrum. Sex alone should disqualify you."

"Sex? Because I'm a Man?"

"No dumb ass, it's because you have a lot of sex now and before in your life."

"Sex is a no, no to you? Well get over it, I like sex, almost every human does. I just happen to be very great at it. Stop by sometimes and watch me, I'll teach you something Angel, that will make your wings blush."

"Human, don't make me laugh. Sex on Earth is so timid compared to having sex in Heaven."

"Really? Tell me about it."

"No! I'm here to kick your human ass, not turn you on."

"Like you could. Enough of this wasteful shit, give it to me, then try to kick my ass."

"I will do just that human."

"Bring it Angel, for all I hear is a bunch of thunder, but I don't feel a drop of rain coming from your storm."

"That was quite witty, Barry Goldrum and you deserve to bleed a little bit more for your lame ass whit."

'The Messenger of God said nothing more as he opened up his void, about six feet wide and pulled out Grover's power up from within him and placed it inside me. When it was all contained deep inside me, the Messenger of God, stepped back and watched my eyes turn red.'

"Yes, I can feel it Messenger of God. The power inside me is rising higher and higher. My God, what power I wield now. Fear me Angel, fear that I might tear off your wings."

'The Messenger of God, stood still and silent waiting for me to fully transform. There was no fear In his eyes.'

"Power, power, I am power now... What is happening? The pain, the pain! Help me Messenger of God, take this evil power back!"

"I cannot do this for you Barry Goldrum. You will have to endure or die. The death of your soul will be brutal, find the good inside you to help ease the pain of your transformation."

"I can't, it's too powerful."

"I told you that you were not worthy, Barry Goldrum."

"Go to Hell, Messenger of God."

"No Barry Goldrum, Hell is for you in a matter of moments."

"Was this God's plan all along?"

"Yes, this is it Barry Goldrum, survive or die. I hope you die. Still, I would love to kick your ass."

"Kiss it instead before it's too late Messenger of God."

"You always have to be yourself Barry Goldrum, even when it comes to your ending. Such a pity."

"Do not pity me Messenger of God, I almost made it."

"No Barry Goldrum, you have failed, just like I knew you would. It was inevitable, you are just a too flawed and weak of a human to wield this power. Do me a favor, hurry up and die, I'm starting to get bored."

"Kiss Satan's ass, Messenger of God!"

"No Barry Goldrum, that displeasure, will be all yours."

'On my knees, the pain I felt inside myself, was like the traces of Satan and Grover's power up, were tearing the other apart in their own war to the finish, where the winner takes it all. I felt like death was moments away and inside my mind, I realized that I willingly played the fool for God's morbid play of puppeteer and puppet.'

"It was God's belief Barry Goldrum, that you would have the fortitude to use Grover's power to conquer the traces of Satan's to your will. How does it feel human to know that God believed in you but you did not?"

'The pain inside me was still enormous, I was weak and felt like giving up but the Messenger of God pissed me off, made me feel like my balls were the size of peas.'

I took a deep breath and screamed, "Fuck it!"

'On my feet, I wobbled back and forth but I stayed standing. In victory, I raised my hand for the outside of myself as the inside of myself still felt like it was dying fast.'

"Bravo Barry Goldrum. This is truly amazing... Wait a minute, what is this I see in your eyes? Nothing but false bravado. Pathetic, I might as well put you out of your misery."

"No Messenger of God, that will be my pleasure."

"Who dares? It had to be you. Satan, what the Hell are you doing here? If you wait a minute, Barry Goldrum will be dead and you can take what's left of his warped soul back to Hell with you."

"You always persist that you can tell me what to do Messenger of God?"

"But of course, Satan, it's my duty."

"Well from now on Messenger of God, I relieve you of this duty. Now step out of my way, I will retrieve my traces from this worthless soul."

"Like Barry Goldrum, would say... Fuck off Satan."

"That's very funny, God's number one ass kissing Angel. You always get the shit work."

"Yes Satan, you resemble shit... By the way, I heard from somewhere you also like to eat it."

"Angel, bastard of Heaven, I will tear your golden wings off you and beat you to death with them!"

'Satan attacked the Messenger of God so fast and furious, that it was a blur to my eyes. The Messenger of God, down fast on his back, with Satan on top of him.'

'I tried to speak, I tried to tell, the Messenger of God to use his void of nothingness, but not one word came forth. I took a step forward and slipped back two steps backwards in the process. I was helpless and useless, just like the Messenger of God told me I was.'

In my mind, "Help me, help me Barry Goldrum, Satan's killing me. I've turned off my void of nothingness and I do not have the strength to turn it back on, from the pain that I'm feeling. Please help me before it's too late."

'Mentally I respond back, don't know how I just did it.'

"Messenger of God, I'm dying. I blame you, I blame God. In my end, I will not be like the two of you, I will help the light prevail over the the dark. I will help you Messenger of God, I will use the last bit of my strength inside me to pull Satan off you. Giving you the time, you need to turn your void of nothingness back on. You better make it quick, for I do not know how long I will be able to hold him at bay."

'Painfully I walked over and grabbed Satan by his left horn and pulled him. Not amused Satan, smacked me away. I stumbled back, pissed that Satan just back handed me.'

"Fuck off Barry Goldrum, give me a minute, I'll be glad to kill you then."

"Hey Satan, when God takes a piss in Heaven, does his piss fall on top of your head? Do you put your head down, or do you point it up, with your mouth wide open?"

'Satan stopped beating on the Messenger of God, he then let go of his grip on him, making the Messenger of God drop to the bottom of the DreamVerse, like a sack of broken bones.'

"You fucked up human! First you call me a shit eater, now you call me a piss drinker."

"Yeah Satan, but at the least, it was God's piss, I said you drank."

"Like that matters. I do not eat shit, I do not drink piss... Say this with me Barry Goldrum, before I rip your head off your shoulders."

"Okay Satan, you eat shit and you drink piss. How was that? Did I get it right?"

'Satan did not answer back. He stepped closer to me and put his massive, clawed right fist straight through my chest, pulling my heart out my soul.'

'My soul nor does anybody else's soul, have a heart, my soul does not breath in reality. It's a facade, created by dreamers that allows them to survive in their dreams. Or if worse comes to worst, it becomes the instrument that causes their mortal shell to die in reality.'

'I looked at my still beating heart, that now resided in Satan's hand. I looked past them and see the Messenger of God on his feet, healing and opening up his void of nothingness, extra wide to engulf Satan's being.'

"Look at you Barry Goldrum, you're dying. Over there your mortal shell breathes it's last breath. Very soon it will be dead and I will take what is in front of me to Hell. You are so very stupid, why would you help someone that wanted you dead just as much as I did?"

My last words as my mortal heart stopped beating were, "Because Satan, you fucking suck. Go back to Hell, where you belong."

"Big words, that mean nothing dying human... What the fuck... let go of me Messenger of God!"

'The last thing the eyes of my soul saw was Satan being engulfed in the Messenger of God's void of nothingness until he was gone. I blinked a few times, then I died.'

'I do not know how much time went by while I was dead. I was nothing. I was gone, then a spark in the darkness of where I was came to light. I was back when I heard the voice of the Messenger of God say to me...'

"Barry Goldrum, you have proven yourself worthy to God, you have proven yourself worthy of the power you wield.

It is time for your mortal shell and your soul to rise from death to life. Come back Barry Goldrum and accept your new role in the universe of God."

'Heaven, it felt like Heaven had touched me. I was blessed as I rose from death to life. Count to ten, the smile dropped from my face as the intense pain returned to me, ten fold. I fell to my knees and cried from the pain I was receiving. It was too much, I felt like my soul was getting ready to die once again.'

"Barry Goldrum, push your limits, you can control your power. Have faith in yourself. Take my hand, rise to your feet and accept your pain. It is yours to endure for the rest of your mortal life."

"I can't."

"Yes you can, take my hand."

'I grabbed the Messenger of God's hand and he lifted me up to my feet.'

"Are you invincible, Barry Goldrum?"

"No, I am human."

"Then ask for my help, ask God for help. Heaven will help you, if you have faith."

"Help me God, help me Messenger of God."

'The Messenger of God, removed piece after piece of himself and placed them inside me until I was healed. It took so many of his pieces of his good to balance the evil that was inside me. When I was fully healed, I felt amazing.'

"Now get control of the evil inside you Barry Goldrum."

'Like it was hardly an effort, I did as I was commanded to do. It was easy, too easy, I thought but I let that thought pass me by as I felt like I had the strength of ten thousand souls inside me. Bonus, they were all superhuman in strength.'

"How they hanging, Barry Goldrum?"

"Large and in the center. What are my orders, who must die by my hands now?"

"That is up to you Barry Goldrum."

"What do you mean?"

"The DreamVerse, it is yours to command as you see fit. Rule it by force, pain and punishment, or rule it with kindness and compassion. It is all up to you. The fate of the DreamVerse solely lies within your hands and mind."

"What about the war?"

"It still goes on for the next twelve days. However you have the power to end it and bring peace to the DreamVerse."

"That is what I want. So I have to come back the next twelve days to the DreamVerse, no matter what?"

"Yes. Remember this Barry Goldrum. God will have no more of his good children killed in their dreams by The Gemini Dream Legion. The time for this is over with."

"I understand. What about the bad children of God?"

"What about them?"

"Are they to be spared as well?"

"God has no use for them in his Heaven."

"Which means?"

"What may happen, let happen. Maybe you should judge the bad in various ways. Make the punishment match their sin or sins."

"That's good advice Messenger of God."

"I'm always here to help, Barry Goldrum."

"Are we suppose to hug now?"

"No, now we drink beer, Barry Goldrum."

"You know I was only kidding about hugging?"

"Sure, Barry Goldrum. Where are you going?"

"You grab the beer, I'm going to create independent homes for my people. No charge, free for all."

"Is that wise?"

"I know, the fighting over homes will not take long to occur. I will have to call for peace. Tomorrow, I will call for everyone that still lives to one massive meeting."

"Why not do it today?"

"Today, they come upon their free homes and feel inside them a change. They will feel the beginning of what freedom feels like."

"Tomorrow, Barry Goldrum?"

"Tomorrow I will end the war. Tomorrow the DreamVerse, changes forever."

"Good luck, Barry Goldrum, I'll see you tomorrow night."

'When I woke up Shelly was waiting for me. She was so calm as she rubbed my body with her soft, small hands. I tried to speak to her but she hushed me with a low hush. On top in control, Shelly looked down at me and sexily said twelve more days.'

'Shelly and I were silent while making love however at breakfast, Shelly was full of words and emotions. After she went to work, I stopped over at Brandy's house for a few more hours of loving. Brandy opened up her door wearing a green teddie.'

'Two of her friends that I've never met were on her couch kissing and touching. I watched them and they invited me to join them. I sat on Brandy's couch as she and two of her friends, kissed and licked me from head to toe. I got really turned on being their mid-morning to noon male treat.'

'That night I entered the DreamVerse as ruler of it. What I wanted to create came to my mind and it was created with ease. What I created to be dissolved later was benches upon benches everywhere, for The Gemini Dream Legion to sit, while listening to my proclamation of no more war and no more causing the deaths of human's in their dreams.'

'I paused and told my people that I thought that calling themselves The Gemini Dream Legion was stupid. Mixed emotions over this as it was decided upon to change our name to simply 'Dream Beings'.'

"My fellow Dream Beings, God, Heaven, Satan and Hell exist. I have fought off death to become your new leader. In truth, I am not one of you, that is why I have been chosen. Your former selves have killed so many humans in the past that all of you are tainted by evil.

266

God is giving me one chance and in return he is giving you one chance..."

"War was brought to the DreamVerse by God, through me. That is over with for now. No more war, I will not kill any more unless I have to. I have to be hard, I will be fair. Curb your need to kill or be eliminated. Peace will blossom in this DreamVerse or it will be discontinued. This is by the order of God."

"Many of you believe that none of you died, before I came into this DreamVerse. This is false, Grover killed many of you through the years for power. He fed off you like a parasite. I will not, you are free to do as you will. If you do not kill, you will live an eternity in peace."

"Together we can do this. We better, for we have no choice but to do so. If you decide to have a civil war, God will not allow it and all of you will die and fall to Hell."

"I have met Satan, he's a real asshole and he hates everything and everyone, including himself. In his Hell, Satan has had his damned souls dig a special pit for everyone of you to burn in. I think he will fill this pit with every nasty thing he can think of including shit."

"Great news comes along with the bad... No more will you have to live huddled together in one fortress. As you can see I have created houses for a lot of you. This is only the first neighborhood that I have created, there will be many more. There will be a home for everyone, no one goes without a home to live in. I want nothing from you for this. This is not a gift, this is your home and that is it."

"Everyone of you have tasted and fed off dream food from the nightmares of human beings. It is all you have ever tasted. I am here to tell you there is another kind of dream food for you to feed on and live better off of.

I know that all of you have been in human dreams that were not nightmares. This kind of dream food you do not like for it is tasteless and stale to your palates."

"This is not your fault, it's the design of it all. None of you was taught by Grover or by The Elders about this other kind of dream food. This other kind of dream food can only be obtained by helping humans in their dreams. It will take some time getting use to doing this but once you taste and feel what this new kind of dream food is all about, you will want nothing else.."

"I will teach some how to obtain this new dream food and in kind they will teach the rest of you."

"I am not a tyrant, yes I have killed many of you, including Grover and all The Elders. I do not want to kill any more of us. I was ordered to by God, if he tells me to do this once again, I will. I feel this will not happen if we get along and kill no more."

"I am to be your leader of this DreamVerse until the day comes when my mortal life dies. The number of years may be long or they may be short, I do not know. So I will need the best of you to step forward and become local leaders. The best of the best will take my place as leader of the DreamVerse when I die."

"Let's spend what is left of the rest of the night for me, creating new homes for as many of you as time allows. This is only our first new day together, there will be many more. Let's start this first day off the best we can, please no fighting over homes."

'This is how I spent my first night as leader of the DreamVerse. I only had to kill around twenty Dream Beings. Not my fault, they decided to kill, I was left with no choice, I had to set an example.'

'The next day through meeting and greeting my new family, the day before, I picked out one hundred Dream Beings to be my assassins for evil human dreamers. These one hundred and the rest I recruited after them are the only ones that are allowed to kill humans, through nightmares. By the time the war that was no longer a war ended I had two hundred and two nightmare assassins.'

'The next ten days were pretty much the same every day. I did some counseling and negotiating. I did some separating, that both sides approved of. Every day but the sixth day to go. A war started when I was awake, ten thousand died on both sides before I entered the DreamVerse. I stopped the war within minutes and banished the rest of the survivors of the war, both sides to Grover's old fortress for one year.'

'Day thirty, the last day of the war, I was leaving the DreamVerse and there stood the Messenger of God to send me off.'

"This is it Barry Goldrum, the war is over. When you wake up Shelly will not be in waiting for you. Her duty is over with, she is free. You and she are allowed one more day and night together as friends or lovers before you are to leave the next morning to go see Michael Mellow. Also God wants you take a couple nights away from the DreamVerse, return after Michael Mellow accepts."

"How will I get to him? And how will I find him?"

"How you get to him has been covered. How you find him? You'll just know. Goodbye Barry Goldrum."

"Goodbye Messenger of God?"

'That was that. I woke up and spent the morning and afternoon with Brandy and that evening to early morning I spent with Shelly. If I only could have had them at the same time.'

269

After The War

Chapter One:

'The great big morning after I took off without saying goodbye. While Shelly slept nice and deep with one of her arms stretched out to touch someone that is not there anymore. I felt great, I felt bad, my war was over. To me my wife only died two months ago instead of eight. I walked out of the front door with two bags, one in each hand and no ride. I looked down the street and there was a man standing by a dark blue 1973 Dodge Dart. I looked at this man admiring his car when he noticed me and started to walk over to me.

"Hello, good morning Mister Goldrum. Over there that classic kick ass beast of a car is all yours, here are the keys."

This stranger handed me the keys to my new car. I said, "And?"

"And what Mister Goldrum?"

"Well, where is the catch?"

"No catch Mister Goldrum, okay maybe one you have to pay for your own gas."

"That's it?"

"Yes."

"Who sent you?"

"Let's just say I owed a favor to someone who owed a favor to someone else so in the end all I had to do to get this favor over with was to give you my fucking car. So enjoy it and don't wreck it, it took me years to get it in the fantastic shape that it is now."

'I asked him if I could drop him off somewhere. He told me no, that he had to walk away from his car as a show of acceptance for his punishment of his sins.'

I looked this man in his eyes and said, "God here, God there, God everywhere."

'He said nothing more as he turned away from me to walk away while I could barely hear him praying quietly to himself. I watched this man walk away 'til he was almost out of sight, I then ran over to the car before it could disappear. I stopped just a few inches away from my new car then I reached out so very slowly and touched her. Cold, hard, steel, she was for real, I had my ride and then some.'

'I got in and started her up, damn did she have such a loud purr that brought a tear to my eye that I wiped away quickly after I found an envelope with $10,000 in the glove box. Food, lounging and beer all three were taken care of for a month or three. I drove south for two hundred and seventeen miles until I decided it was time to get dinner.'

'I pulled my bad ass car next to endless amounts of trucks and got out. On the way to this small town I stopped and bought myself a great looking jacket and a pair of sunglasses, a couple of Cd's, beef jerky, water and some scratch offs. I won almost to the penny of what everything cost besides my jacket which I did not buy at a gas station.'

'Everyone that was out in the parking lot looked and watched my car and myself do our thing. Damn even the sheriff rolled on by my car real slow as I was ordering my steak. I wanted a beer I was going to order myself one until I spotted the nosey sheriff, looking for the driver of my car.'

'Waitress was half good looking, wanting me to flirt with her as I ordered my steak medium with my fried potatoes crispy and my salad green with a splash of sweet fat free french dressing and the tomatoes on the side. She was about to walk away when I told her that I was interested in ordering my dessert now as well.'

'Her frown turned upside down as she shook with intimidation of my not from around here looks. Pecan pie was my choice, it was homemade and damn was it delicious. My waitress was so eager she came back to my table so often she was almost like company. So on the way out, I let her make me smile while I drove around her small town until she was finished. That was later after everything became cool.'

'Before I could get to my dinner, I had the privilege of having a conversation with this town's very own sheriff. Who was I? Where did I come from? And most importantly was I staying was the topic. Sheriff was a normal prick that was freaking ugly to boot.'

'Within one trip back to my table, I knew the sheriff had a hard on for my waitress who had no desire to ever let him have any of what she had to offer. That was when my idea of letting her make me smile came to my mind. I held back the urge to laugh in this hating sheriff's face. I thought to myself of how I would not fuck his first choice because she was not good enough. But I'll let her use that mouth he wants to kiss so bad to make me smile.'

'Later that night I picked a small hotel to crash in about fifty miles away from my dinner with a smile at the end. Place was cheap and run down but all I needed was a bed and a shower. I tossed and turned for awhile, I was happy the war was over, I won thirteen days ago. I was also glad to have my freedom. I liked Shelly a lot, our one time plus thirty had to be it for both of us to go on with our lives.'

'I tried and I could not fall asleep. Sleep was not coming. I wanted a beer so I took a drive to a local bar. Had to remember in flesh and bones I was normal, well above normal, I had the strength of two men.'

'The bar was loud, it was full of losers and some hot ladies. One hot lady in particular was sitting all by herself. This lady is use to having men drool over her, yet she still sits by herself. I take a closer look on top of her table and all I see is her glass.'

'Like Queen, hot lady of the bar, she waves me over to get a better look at me. I let her speak first.'

"Yes, you will do nicely. Come sit down beside me and buy me another drink while I touch what's going to please me later."

'I sat down, not saying one word, while never taking my eyes off her.'

"The silent type, I like that. I talk a lot. If you don't, I don't have to worry about you interrupting me. Stranger, I see this as a plus. Just don't be so silent of a Stranger that you don't over comment about my body."

"Why don't you stand up, then turn around and let me see if your ass is as pretty as your face."

"Stranger, I like your style. It just happens to be that my ass is one of my best features. Later you will see my best feature as long as you want, or as long as you can hold out."

"I have to know. Why isn't one of these losers licking one of your shoes by now?"

"I like you very much Stranger, call me Lady. Why is that not happening? Because they know better. I'm what they all want and never leave with."

"That's for hung, great looking Strangers like me to do."

"Yes it is and in your case, very soon at that."

"It would be my pleasure, Lady."

'Two drinks later, Lady was all over me as I felt like King of the bar. I followed her to her house. There I stayed until morning. Lady was great, she knew how to please a man and she made a great breakfast as well. I looked over at Lady and I saw Shelly and I knew what I had to do. I had to go drop off my key, grab my stuff and hit the road to meet Michael Mellow and convince him to be my dream twin.'

'Later that evening I pulled into a driveway that called out to my mind like a beacon. I knocked on the door and a nice older lady opened the door and told me to come in, that Michael was waiting on me.'

I was lead to Michael's room, "Michael, Barry is here to see you."

"Have him come in mother."

'Michael's mother opened the door where he laid in his bed paralyzed from his neck down. I walked in slowly not knowing what to say.'

"It's you, Barry Goldrum, it's you. It feels like it took forever for you to finally get here."

"You've been expecting me?"

"But of course and I'm ready."

"You agree to be my dream twin? You know what this means?"

"Yes, I have to die."

"Here I thought I had the impossible task of talking someone into dying and becoming my dream twin."

"Look at me Barry, I'm already dead from neck down."

"Do you know how you are to die?"

"Yes, you are to take my life in my dream, making me die in real life."

"Me? I don't think so."

"Sam told me to tell you this, this is from him and not me."

"I understand."

"Barry, you lousy human, who do you think would be the one to take Michael Mellow's life?"

"That piece of..."

"I'm not through yet, there is more."

"Go ahead and finish, I can't wait to hear this."

"You thought you would enter his dream and what? Bore him to death. Or it would be all magical, where he would slip away comfortably in the night? You truly are a dumb ass. I wish I could see your face right now as you realize that after this you will have human blood on your hands and not just, what are they called now?..."

"Oh yeah, Dream Beings' blood on your hands. Sucks to be you. I think you're damned. Just kidding good luck and be seeing you real soon."

"That sounds like the Ass of God. Heaven might suck sometimes with him in it. Okay, let's fall asleep so I can kill you."

"Good luck, I'll try to die fast so that way you won't get that much blood on your hands."

"Michael, thanks and all, but you're not making this any easier on me."

"Sorry, this is the first time I agreed to let someone kill me in my dreams."

"I imagine. This is not something one does everyday."

'A quick laugh later and both of us try to fall asleep.'

"Damn I can't fall asleep. Barry don't you have some sand or something to sprinkle in my eyes?"

"I'm not the sandman, Michael. Wait a minute, I forgot something. I'm not allowed to enter the DreamVerse until after you accepted."

"That's not a problem, I already have."

"That might be the point Michael. We're dealing with Heaven here. Accepted might refer to after you're already my dream twin. If this is the case, I don't know what I'm to do without entering the DreamVerse. I'm powerless on this side of it."

"No you're not. You have the power to unplug my machine."

"No way, fuck that."

"I have one more thing that Sam wanted me to tell you, if you said no to what you truly have to do."

"I hate this, let me hear it."

"Barry Goldrum, God commands this from you."

'With a tear in each of my eyes, one for myself, one for Michael, I walked over and unplugged Michael's machine. Three minutes later Michael and I are hand and hand when he dies. His soul, I seen only in a flash, entered my body and all of a sudden there was Michael hanging outside my body. We look at the other like this is really fucking weird and then Michael disappeared from sight.'

'Ten minutes later Micheal returned and told me that he flew around in the DreamVerse with wings of steel. He was so happy. He was free, he never felt more alive in his life than after his death.'

'I turned back on Michael's machine and called out to his mother that something happened to him. Michael hung unseen outside my body watching his mother cry tears of loss for him. Through my voice, I let Michael's mother hear her son's last words to her.'

"Mom I am free now. I'm right next door to Heaven and very soon I will enter Heaven where I will be waiting for you. We will walk together in fields of green grass."

'Michael's mother stopped crying and smiled at me then she fell over dead on the floor.'

"My mom, what did you do?"

"I didn't do anything. It was your idea to talk to her. I think, I'm in trouble here. I can hear Sam now, what one human life isn't enough for you, Barry Goldrum?"

"Relax Barry, my mom is fine, she is flying to Heaven. She tells me now that she'll be waiting for me there."

'From that day, until now three years later, Michael and I have done what we have been commanded to do. I think it's time to get off this couch and go to bed.'

Chapter Two:

May thirtieth 2050, seven years later.

"How many more miles, Barry?"

"Three or four, Michael."

"This is the last one for the night? Tell me yes Barry, I want to get back to the DreamVerse and get laid. It's getting late and you're going to go to bed pretty soon and I want to make sure I have enough time to finish before you enter and I have to stop. Believe me Barry, I wouldn't be very happy if I don't get to finish."

"Yes Michael, this is the last one for the night. Besides all you need is five minutes or so I've been told."

"No Barry, I think you're thinking about yourself."

"Shit I last an hour, if I last a minute."

"So Barry, what's the evil about these brothers?"

"Same old shit Michael. They kill people. Together they have killed over fifty people. Tonight that all ends, with their deaths."

"I can still go into their dreams and nightmare them to death. It would be my pleasure."

"I know Michael. The punishment these two deserve is to be that one kills the other. Let's end this fast and sweet, make their souls fall to Hell in under an hour."

"That is fine with me Barry, step on the gas and let's get this over with."

"We're here, you know what to do?"

"Yes I do Barry."

Barry gets out of his car with Michael in tow and watches as Michael creates hundreds of zombies in the brother Green's front yard. Barry knocks on the door loud and steps around to the side of the house to be out of sight.

Brother Green one and brother Green two come running out of their house with guns in hands. They see the zombies all over their yard and scream.

Michael with precision brings the zombies around to the Brother's Green location until they are pointing their gun at the other brother and fire the killing shot.

"They are dead in record time I think Barry."

"It seems to be, let's get out of here."

Later at home Barry gives Michael two hours to get laid before he falls asleep. Upon entering the DreamVerse, the Messenger of God is waiting for Barry.

"Long time no see, Barry Goldrum."

"It has been a long time Messenger of God, it is great to see you."

"Barry you have been working too hard as of late. God feels you need a break away from the DreamVerse. After tonight you are to take the next two days off. Think of this as a birthday present."

"That's right my birthday is in two days, I almost forgot."

"That is understandable Barry Goldrum. Here let's drink a beer, like we did in the good old days of long ago. Can you believe it's almost been ten years since you've been the ruler of the DreamVerse?"

"I know, time flies by fast, when you kill sinners in their sleep or make them die by their own hands."

"Yes, fun, fun, fun. I have to tell you Barry Goldrum, I'm quite impressed. You've done a great job with the DreamVerse."

"Thanks, give me another beer."

"Happy to, here you go."

Barry and the Messenger of God drink a few more beers together before they say their goodbyes.

"Wait a minute Messenger of God. Did you come here for any other reason?"

"Nope just to say hi and to take a couple of days off."

"That's a little light."

"There is no heavy Barry Goldrum, everything is going as planned. Just the way God wants it to be."

"Good, tell him I said hi."

"Will do. See you soon Barry Goldrum."

"See you Messenger of God."

"There is one more thing, Barry Goldrum."

"What is it?"

"On your birthday, at this time, at this location, you need to be here." The Messenger of God touches Barry's forehead with his fingertips, "You get it all?"

"Got it, see you then."

June first, 2050. Barry parks his car and is walking to where the Messenger of God told him to be. Barry's had a good birthday so far, he just got done having a steak and a beer. Last night after twelve o'clock Barry escorted two sexy ladies to a hotel room. These three lovers had one sexy time and Barry kept on loving until he passed out.

Barry smiles, remembering last night, "Give it to me!" Barry turns around and sees a man, with a shaking hand, holding onto a gun that seems too heavy for him, "I said give it to me man, give me your wallet, or I'll shoot you!"

"Alright, calm down... Here take it."

"That's more like it but I still have to shoot you."

"Don't do it."

"But I want to Barry Goldrum."

"Sam? Is that you, you twisted, ass faced Angel?"

"Yes it is, you small balled, human, bastard... Here take this." Sam pulls the trigger of his gun and water hits Barry in his face, "How's that feel Barry Goldrum? I got the water out of a local toilet."

Sam runs off, "Come back here, you fucked up Angel!" Barry chases after Sam but loses him when he turns around a corner. Barry out loud, "I'll get you back Sam, one day I'll take a piss on your stupid looking, Angel face."

Barry shakes it off and begins walking to where he is suppose to be in a few minutes. Barry is calmer as he passes by strangers on the sidewalk, some who are fine ladies, he'd like to know for an hour or two.

Barry to himself, 'Fuck the Voice of God, I'm not going to let him ruin my birthday.'

From behind Barry comes a loud screeching sound, Barry turns around and sees a car sliding out of control. Barry looks closer as a fourteen inch piece of sharp flat steel, comes flying out from under the car towards Barry's direction. The piece of steel keeps flying as the car it was underneath crashes into a school bus and catches on fire. In a few minutes this car will blow up and kill the driver in the process.

Rewind back a few heartbeats and screams ago. Barry closes his eyes as his head is cut clean off his shoulders. Barry's head flies ten feet away before it comes to a halt, when it strikes a lady across her face, breaking her nose. This lady had a cup of hot coffee in her hands, when Barry's head struck her face she threw it away from her straight into a man's face that was standing three feet away from her.

This man screamed and ran into another man named Dirk knocking him down into the street where he was ran over and killed by a police car. The pressure of the police car stopping right on top of Dirk's shoulders made Dirk's head pop off and fly into the street. Dirk's head hit the street and rolled until it almost made it to the other side of it before it stopped rolling. When Dirk's head was picked up its eyes were still open. Dirk's soul is looking at its former head laying in the road and then it looks up at the sky and leaps upwards into a bright clear light that feels warm.

What a scene of death, all the people that just watched this happen in their varied ways from start to finish all had their own reaction to this horror. Screaming and yelling from some, while others were silent as the presence of death froze their souls icy cold.

The Messenger of God cries for the death of a friend in Barry Goldrum, as he watches Barry's soul walk over to him, with a smile on it's face. "Are you ready to go home, Barry Goldrum?"

"Yes I am Messenger of God."

"Any regrets?"

"Yes, many. But there's nothing I can do about them now."

"Step inside, Barry Goldrum." The Messenger of God opens his void of nothingness and Barry steps inside it, to fly to Heaven.

"It's over Messenger of God, I'm free now. No more DreamVerse, no more war, no more killing strangers. I can't believe I finally get to rest and reflect on my past life... And best of all, I saved for last."

"What is that Barry Goldrum?'

"Not what, it's who, Messenger of God. Tina, I get to see Tina once again. I can't wait to hold her in my arms."

Satan watches as the Messenger of God takes Barry Goldrum's soul to Heaven. The driver's (Kayden Hart) soul is suspended in a field of light, protecting it until the Messenger of God gets back from Heaven and takes it there as well.

Satan hisses and bursts into flames. Those that see Satan turn into flames, will be seeing him again very soon, like when they die and their souls fall to Hell.

Rest In Peace: Barry Goldrum
Born June First 2010
Died June First 2050

Rest In Peace: Kayden Hart
Born June First 2025
Died June First 2050

"We're here Barry Goldrum, Heaven is waiting for you."

"Let me out, I want to see it."

"Not so fast Barry Goldrum, you have to go in front of God and be judged."

"Why? I thought.."

"It's just a formality."

Barry Goldrum steps out of the Messenger of God's void of nothingness and looks around. Barry's smile fades as he looks into the eyes of his friend.

"Messenger, what's going on?"

The Messenger of God, cannot look at Barry, his friend a mere human, "Come on Messenger, what's going on?"

The Messenger of God says nothing as he leads Barry to a giant pair of doors, "Go inside Barry Goldrum."

"That's it Messenger, not even a hint?"

"Go inside these doors like you belong here in Heaven, Barry Goldrum. Whatever comes your way, you have the strength inside your soul to face it."

"Bad news?"

"Have no fear, God is in there waiting on you."

"That's what makes me worry. Any good news?"

"Yes, we will see each other someday very soon, Barry Goldrum."

"In Heaven?"

The Messenger of God turns around and walks away, "Take it easy Barry Goldrum, try not to let Sam piss you off, he is the Voice of God after all."

"No promises there, but I'll try. What's God like?"

"Powerful and wise."

Barry looks for handles to open up the doors with and sees none, 'No handles again? I guess handles are an Earth only thing.'

Barry pushes the doors open to God's judgement hall. In the back of it he sees Sam and Michael standing together.

"Go inside these doors like you belong here in Heaven, Barry Goldrum." Barry remembers these words spoken by his friend, the Messenger of God. Barry walks on until he stands face to face to face with Sam and Michael, he sizes up his maybe competition and feels confident.

Three beings stare at each other, none of them blinking or saying a word. Stillness is disturbed by the presence of something huge making its presence known.

God sits upon his throne and waves one of his hands and three beings are separated from each other. God looks at his Voice, who stands up straighter and begins to speak his words for him.

"Barry Goldrum, I am very proud of you. You served me very well until your death that brings you here to me. I will tell you your judgment now..."

"Barry Goldrum, you served me very well in the past and you will continue to do so now. Your task is not over, even your death will not end your task for me. I command this to be and so shall it be."

"Heaven, will always be denied to you Barry Goldrum. This is not a punishment, this is a reward. The DreamVerse, you will be the ruler of for all times to come."

"Yes my Lord."

"I am fair, I will give you a few minutes to say hello and goodbye to Tina, after I tell you all you need to hear."

"Yes my Lord. Thank you my Lord."

"The man that took your life, the man that was driving the car, you will look out after from time to time as he fights his own war for me. This man's name is Kayden Hart and his war will reside within Purgatory..."

"You Barry Goldrum, will go back and forth between the DreamVerse and Purgatory. Make sure Kayden Hart makes it out alive his first day of war. He's strong but his mind is a mess, why this is does not matter."

"Yes my Lord."

"After this war goes on for a bit, I want you to gather up four or five thousand Purgatorians and take them to the DreamVerse for safe keeping. You will bring them back to Purgatory at the end of this war."

"Yes my Lord."

"Kayden Hart's war will last for many years, you will make contact with him when I tell you to and only when I tell you to. Any help you have to give him at first has to go unknown to him."

"Yes my Lord."

"Barry Goldrum, you are my first mortal to wield the power that I give you to wield, Kayden Hart is my second.

In time Kayden Hart will gain power that will be stronger than yours. If he can control it and use it to end his war I give to him to win for me, then your task for Kayden Hart for me, will be over with. If Kayden Hart does not have it in him, even with the help from my Messenger to control this power, you will kill him and win the war of Purgatory."

"Yes my Lord."

"How will you have the power to kill Kayden Hart, I know you want to know, Barry Goldrum?"

"Yes my Lord."

"I will combine your soul, Barry Goldrum and the soul of Michael Mellow once again to form the powerhouse, that will be powerful enough to kill Kayden Hart."

"Yes my Lord."

"I am done with you for now, enjoy your short time with Tina. Then go back to the DreamVerse until I call for you."

"Yes my Lord. May I ask one favor, my Lord?"

"Ask Barry Goldrum, maybe I'll grant it."

"Will you let Tina's soul live with me in my DreamVerse?"

"You ask a lot, yet you ask for so little, Barry Goldrum..."

"Yes my Lord."

"My command is as follows..."

"If Tina agrees to this, I say yes. If Tina tells you no, you will respect her decision and never ask her again."

"Yes my Lord. Thank you my Lord."

"You are welcome, Barry Goldrum, now go find out your answer, I wish you the best of luck."

"Thank you my Lord. Lord?"

"Yes, Barry Goldrum?"

"Where is Tina?"

God Laughs, "You are funny inside your soul Barry Goldrum. This is Heaven, I am God, there are no mysteries here. Barry Goldrum just walk and you will come upon her in time."

"Thank you my Lord."

Barry turns around and starts walking, 'Damn, I was ripped off. Never do I get Heaven, what the fuck? I killed all those people for God and he gives me the DreamVerse? I guess, I'll have to turn DreamVerse into my own Heaven. As long as Tina says yes, I could careless if my Heaven is a back yard with no grass.'

'Wow God. I just met God. What power the being that is God is. There is something that came to me when he told me of my exile and task... No, I won't think about it, just in case he can read my mind.'

(What Barry won't think about, but needs to be told, is that to Barry, God seemed like more than one being. To Barry it seemed like he was listening to two different beings combined into one larger being. Two different sides of the same coin. Twelve and a half, times two, makes one brand new, shiny quarter.)

Barry keeps on walking, as what use to lie behind him turns into darkness. Barry walks ten minutes before there is something in the distance. It's too large to be Tina, but Barry takes off running towards it anyway.

Twenty three miles of running pays off as Barry stares at the outside of a cabin in the woods. Barry quickly runs up and knocks on the door and a man that Barry cannot believe to be true opens it up.

"Can I help you Barry?"

"What the fuck? You're me."

"And I am you, yes I know."

"What do you want?"

"It's what you want. No, it's what I want."

"What is that?"

"Tina, I want Tina. Sadly she did not want me, she loves Heaven more than me. Tina will do the same thing to you, which was I, just a few minutes ago. Save yourself the heartbreak, save me the heartbreak ask someone else to be your wife of the DreamVerse."

"You are not me. If you were, you wouldn't ask me to do this for you or I. Who are you?"

"I have to work harder, when I portray a stupid human."

"Sam, you silly, smelly Angel, what the fuck are you doing here? I owe you payback don't I? You just had to kick me before I died didn't you."

"That is a great way to put it Barry. Yes, I wanted to give you one last more for the road. You really deserved it."

"Where's Tina?"

"How am I suppose to know that. I guess she took one look at you and said damn he's ugly. I'll just stay in

289

Heaven with my Sammy."

"You and Tina? You're pathetic Sam. Tina would laugh in your face."

"No she wouldn't."

"She did, didn't she? That's my lady, the lady I love the most, in all the universe."

"Okay Barry, you want the truth?"

"Give it to me if you can."

"Okay smart ass, here is the truth. You suck."

"Fuck off Sam, I'm leaving to go find Tina."

"Wait, I just couldn't help myself, okay here is the real truth... The reason Tina is not here Barry is solely because of you."

"Me? What did I do?"

"What didn't you do Barry Goldrum?"

"Meaning what?"

"Let's see, you killed a lot of helpless people and fucked a lot of women as well. Tina didn't want to believe it until I showed her Heavenly footage of it."

"You lousy bastard."

"No that is you Barry Goldrum. I told you one day I would make you pay for your arrogance. I am the Voice of God and you treated me with no respect at all."

"You didn't deserve any. You're a fucked up angel."

"You're fucked up and fucked over human, scum. Now go fuck off somewhere."

"Glad to. It would beat staying here with you. The further I can I get away from you the better."

"Then you're going to hate hearing this."

"Now what?"

"I, Barry Goldrum. That's right, I am now once again your handler for God. Instead of the Messenger coming to you from now on, it will me, relaying God's commands for you."

"Perfect, let's become best friends. You can kiss my ass, while I kick you in yours."

"Like you could, human."

"Shittt, Angel, I'll kick you twice, bend over and I'll show you just how I'll do it."

"Bend over and kick your own ass human. I've got better things to do, like telling you what to do."

"You mean telling me what God what's me to do, you sack less Angel?"

"Enough, I tell you what human..."

"Then tell me, Angel."

The Voice of God stays silent, while Barry knows what's going on, he's being talked to by God.

"Yes my Lord, I was just having a little bit of fun at Barry Goldrum's expense, it's so fun and easy... Yes I'm done having my fun, I'll be back in a few minutes. Yes I'll tell him, my Lord."

Sam looks at Barry like Barry just got him in trouble, "Well tell me."

"Tell you what human?"

"Tell me what God wanted you to tell me."

"You only have ten more minutes left to talk with Tina. I'm sorry, it looks like I took almost all of your time with Tina all up. Oops, silly me."

"One day, Sam."

"You might as well threaten yourself Barry, for threatening me will do you no good. I'm an Angel, stupid human, I'll kick your ass, like really bad."

"We'll see, until then Sam, fuck off."

Sam slams the door in Barry's face, a moment later, Tina reopens back up the door and runs into Barry's waiting and stretched out for her arms.

"I've missed you so much Barry, you've finally came home to Heaven. We can be together forever now."

"I'm in Heaven, My Love but I can't stay."

"Why not? What's going on? You're not going to Hell are you Barry?"

"No Tina, no Hell for me. I have to live in the DreamVerse for my afterlife."

"The DreamVerse? I never heard of it before."

"The DreamVerse, has to do with what I was going through when I was still alive. You remember my dreams? Well they led me to the DreamVerse."

"I don't understand what you're talking about Barry, you're confusing me."

"I'm sorry Tina, I'll explain everything more clearly later, I promise. But now I need your answer."

"My answer to what, Barry?"

"Will you leave Heaven and go to the DreamVerse with me, to be my wife forever?"

"Leave Heaven? Why can't you stay in Heaven?

"God will not allow it, My Love."

"Why? What did you do Barry? You weren't rude to God were you? I know for myself that sometimes you can be a little bit more than just rude..."

"Tina my love, I was not rude to God. I'll explain everything later. I need to have your answer. We do not have much time Tina, maybe only about five minutes before I have to leave Heaven. I am only allowed to ask you once, if you say no, we will never see each other again."

"That's not fair! I love you Barry, I miss you, I want to be with you forever. Heaven Barry, I'm in Heaven, it is so wonderful."

"I understand. I love you Tina, I hope you have a great afterlife in Heaven."

"Don't you dare turn away from me Barry Goldrum. My answer is yes, Yes I will live my afterlife with you in the DreamVerse. Besides who needs Heaven, when I have you forever, the love of my life and afterlife?"

"I love you Tina, I thought I lost you forever."

"Not us Barry. We said until death do us part, now we get to say in afterlife forever."

"You were always the smart one, Tina."

"Don't you forget it Barry."

"I won't. Let's go to the DreamVerse and spend as much time together before I have to go to war again."

"War? What do you mean by war again, Barry?"

"In time My Love, you will know all."

"Will I like it?"

"I don't know Tina, let's just hope for the best, shall we?"

"You better not make me regret leaving Heaven, Barry."

"I won't dear. Remember what you just said, who..."

"Needs Heaven, when I have you Barry Goldrum."

"Shall we, Tina Goldrum?"

"Take me to our new home, Barry."

Barry picks up Tina in his arms and flies her to the DreamVerse where they will live together in happiness forever. War be damned, it will not tear the love of these two eternal lovers apart.

Thus ends the story of the DreamVerse. Will this adventure of Barry and Tina continue on? Only fate can answer that for now. Kayden Hart's tale of his own war will come to be known in two separate novels, the first, at this time will be scheduled for release in May 2019.

Peace and be true to yourself.

Keith Starblue

www.ingramcontent.com/pod-product-compliance
Lightning Source LLC
Chambersburg PA
CBHW051414170626
46809CB00006B/2160